The Men of Ness

The Men of Ness
by
Eric Linklater

Illustrated by
Bryce Wilson

THE ORKNEY PRESS
1983

Publication subsidised by the Scottish Arts Council.

Published by The Orkney Press Ltd., 72 Victoria Street,
Stromness, Orkney.

ISBN 0 907618 03 0

Printed in Orkney by The Kirkwall Press,
Victoria Street, Kirkwall.

CONTENTS

ILLUSTRATIONS

INTRODUCTION

The Men of Ness, published in the early 1930's shortly after Eric's best-selling novel *Juan in America*, did not please his publisher Jonathan Cape, who expected a sequence of *Juan* books adapted to every country under the sun.

It was never Eric's way to write the same book twice, and here instead is a stark tale of Norsemen a-viking from Orkney around the coast of Scotland to England, told in the spare language of the Icelandic sagas.

Scholars and other devotees of the sagas are enthralled by the literature and the philosophy of the Norsemen which, after all, is part and parcel of the early history of the British Isles. The sagas influenced not only Eric's sense of history but also his use of language — almost as much as did his classical education. Indeed his life was guided by the qualities which the Norsemen most admired — stern justice and the fatalism which ruled in those heroic days.

He started reading the Icelandic sagas at the age of twelve and has said: "I've always derived great pleasure from these both as literature and as cracking good stories. In Orkney and Shetland we are very conscious of the fact that a great part of our descent is Norse and that is important. We know who we are."

The Men of Ness is indeed a cracking good story. Interwoven are historical accounts lifted directly from the *Orkneyinga Saga*, such as the death of Earl Sigurd. His territory, which extended over the whole of Shetland as well as Orkney, had been given him by his brother Earl Rognvald who in turn had received the earldom from King Harald Fairhair. Earl Sigurd quarrelled with Melbricta Tusk (in this book the quarrel is on account of cattle-stealing from Skallagrim in country north of Inverness). It was agreed between the two opponents that each should meet the other in combat with forty men — a kind of duel or tournament. But Earl Sigurd deceives Melbricta by mounting two men on each horse and, with double the number, overwhelms Melbricta and slays him. With the head of his adversary attached to his saddle, Sigurd rides along the north shore of the Dornoch Firth and as he rides the tusk or tooth protruding from his victim's mouth bangs against Sigurd's shin. The slight wound thus inflicted becomes infected and within a few days Sigurd is dead. Poetic or Norse justice.

But for the most part the tale of The Men of Ness — Ragnar, Thorlief Coalbiter and his sons Skallagrim and Kol; and of Thorlief's wife Signy who drives these sons to revenge the death of their step-father Bui slain by Ivar the Boneless — all these are pure Linklater invention. And of all these inhabitants of Ness in Rousay the truly original one is Gauk. He is the anti-hero of this remarkable saga. Gauk is everything the Norse hero is not. Hen-pecked and artful, he yet possesses essential qualities for survival — endurance and wit.

"Gauk was the son of Kisping, the son of Bran, who was Ringan's son. They were not men of mark, but they were known for this, that they had all been born in Orkney, and so also had Ringan's father, whose name is now forgotten." Thus establishing that Gauk is the indigenous Orcadian, living in Orkney long before the Norse invasion — perhaps right back to Pictish times and beyond. He survives to this day in Orkney.

In his illuminating study of the saga, The Ultimate Viking, Eric says: "As literary documents the sagas have the virtue of presenting moments of conflict with remarkable clarity. This they do, with apparent simplicity, by drawing the opposing lines of conflict as diagonals that lead to the middle of the picture, where — well-lighted, unencumbered by detail, and, as it were, frozen in time — the blow falls with a startling impact." This is the formula Eric uses for The Men of Ness.

It is appropriate, I think, to quote again from The Ultimate Viking in order to explain the apparent ruthlessness of the Norsemen's behavior. "The pugnacity of their temper must have been supported by a physical constitution of the utmost hardihood — a tiger's complement of swift, self-healing muscle — and their physical strength was not inhibited by their minds' occupation with thoughts of pain. Our awareness of pain has increased *pari passu* with scientific discovery of the means to alleviate pain, and in the heroic age of the north, when analgetics were unknown, the *grands blessés* of a battle could make stoical comment on the loss of a leg or an arm that are quite incompatible with our sensitivities."

The Men of Ness was not popular in this country. To quote again, this time from *The Conquest of England* (Eric's account of the Norman Conquest commissioned to coincide with the 900th anniversary in 1966): "It has long been a critical habit to esteem the Mediterranean as the source of all that is, or has been, good in the civilisation of western Europe, and no one with a particle of judgment would deny or disparage the inestimable gifts of Palestine; the arts and philosophy that a truculent and ingenious Hellas bequeathed; the ordered authority and evangelical expansion of Rome; the medical and mathematic additions to knowledge that an Arab imperialism brought from the southern shores of the inland sea. But all the virtue in the world, and the moral, aesthetic, or administrative products of virtue, are worthless, because inoperative, without a physical ability, a strength of mind and body, to give them action and by example proclaim their value." And this strength was injected into Britain and as far as the Mediterranean from the North, by the Vikings in the first instance.

Although unacclaimed in this country, *The Men of Ness* was an instant success in the Scandinavian countries. Our home in Orkney was the focus for academic visitors, and links with Norway were firmly welded. Bergen is closer to Orkney than is London, and even in those days "small is beautiful" was an axiom which inspired talk of a "Back to Norway" movement.

Frans G. Bengtsson, the Swedish poet, translated into Swedish most of Eric's books, which certainly benefited from Frans G's inspired translations. He was known to his friends as "Frans G." (pronounced Fransgay), and he in turn made use of Eric's idea to write his own *The Longships* which brought the acclaim denied *The Men of Ness*.

I hope that a new generation will recognise the merits of this remarkable novel which is re-published in Orkney where it has always been esteemed. Now it is time that it should take its rightful place in the mainstream of English literature.

MARJORIE LINKLATER
Kirkwall,
Orkney.
September 1983.

NOTE

A *howe* is an earth mound raised over a burial place. Many of the howes in Orkney come from a time before the Norse, and have stone burial chambers beneath the outer covering of earth. The one called Orka-howe by the Norse is still known by its other name, Maeshowe. A *roost* is a strong tide-race in a narrow channel and *scat* is a land tax. A *scarf* is a cormorant or shag, and a *skua* a fierce, piratical gull that lives by swooping on other birds and forcing them to disgorge the food they have taken.

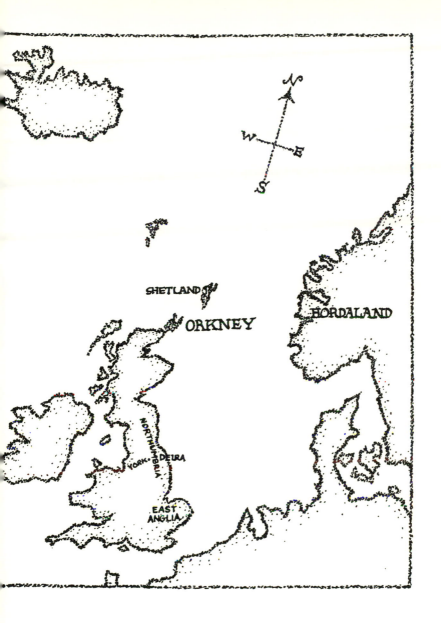

SHETLAND

ORKNEY

HORDALAND

NORTHUMBRIA

YORK·DEIRA

EAST
ANGLIA

N
W   E
S

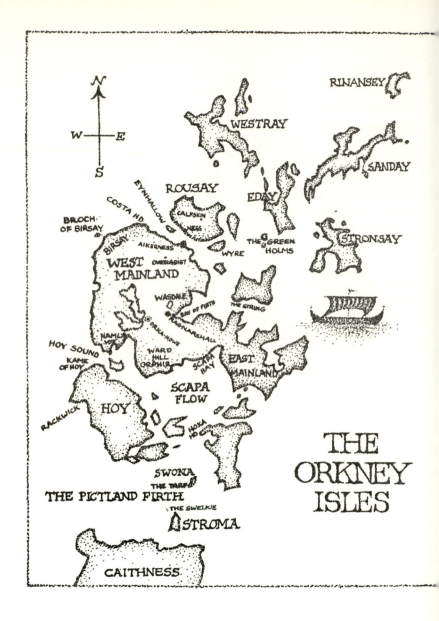

THE
ORKNEY
ISLES

RAGNAR HAIRYBREEKS was the most famous of all vikings. He was the son of King Sigurd Ring, after whose death he ruled in Denmark. But he was driven from his kingdom and then he harried far and wide, in Frisia and against the Franks, in England and much in Ireland. There came a season when he sailed up the river Seine as far as Paris. He had more than a hundred ships and a large host of men.

It was late in the year when he sat down to besiege Paris, but the weather was hot and his men drank much new wine. There was no lack of anything, of corn or meat or wine, for the year had been a good one, and every day the vikings slaughtered sheep and cattle and cooked them under the walls of Paris, so that the smell of cooking might anger those who were behind the walls and had small store of food.

But presently a kind of sickness fell on the Danish camp and men's bowels were loosened all hours of the day and night. Though they drank abundantly and ate well to keep their strength the sickness did not abate, and Ragnar began to think he would have to raise the siege.

There was a man called Nicolas, a prisoner whom Ragnar had taken. He was a Christian. He said to Ragnar, 'Let your men no longer worship Thor and Odin, but let them worship Christ and pray to him, and they will be healed of their sickness.'

Ragnar thought there might be something in that. He had a son called Thorlief who was in the booth when Nicolas was speaking. Thorlief was a big man, very strong and comely, but no manslayer. He was called Thorlief Coalbiter because he sat by the fire and would not go outdoors. He was a good lawyer, and though he spoke in a mild voice there was often great wisdom in his words. Now he said, 'Let the men eat no meat nor

drink new wine. That will give them time to say their
prayers.' Ragnar thought there was some sense in this
advice also, though he doubted if the Danes would be
pleased by it.

But they did what he bade them and worshipped
Christ in the way that Nicolas instructed, nor ate meat
and drank no more new wine. And presently they grew
better of their sickness. Then they gave thanks to this
new god, the white Christ, and made a great attack on
Paris and destroyed it completely, killing very many
and taking all manner of booty.

Then the fleet rowed down the river and the vikings
looked for winter quarters. Some found them in south
England and many went to Ireland. But Ragnar and his
four sons who were with him sailed north to Orkney
with ten ships that were his. Ragnar had built a good
house in the mainland of Orkney, on the side of a hill
behind Firth Bay. So they landed there, and put rollers
down, and hauled up their ships and tented them for
the winter.

Ragnar's sons who were with him were these:
Halfdan, Ubbi, Ivar the Boneless, and Thorlief Coalbiter. They were the most famous of men and were all
great manslayers except Thorlief. Ragnar had other
sons, Biorn Ironside and Sigurd Worm-in-the-eye, who
harried in all countries even as far as Italy. But they do
not come into this story.

Now at this time Orkney was full of vikings. There
was no law there, and he who was strongest was
commonly held to have the best chance in any dispute
that arose. Few people troubled Ragnar and his sons,
and they dwelt there three years and sowed corn each
year. But in summer they made cruises to the South
Isles and Ireland, and took what wealth they found.

II

There was a man called Bui who lived at Ness in Rousay. He had taken much land there and was the wealthiest man in that part of Orkney. His wife's name was Signy. She was a very handsome woman, cheerful, hard-tempered, and rather greedy. Her hair was so long it came down on both sides of her bosom and she turned the ends of it under her girdle.

When their first spring-sowing was done Ivar the Boneless took a skiff and six men to row round the Mainland of Orkney. In no great while they came to a firth where there was a roost so fierce and wild that they thought it best to go no farther that way. On their starboard side was the island of Rousay, and between that and the mainland a little grassy island called Eynhallow. But beyond Eynhallow was the roost, and though there was no wind waves rose that were big enough to swamp a longship, and the sea ran as fiercely as in a winter storm.

Ivar told his men to land on Rousay, near to Bui's house at Ness. Bui had just come ashore and was hauling up his boat. He had been fishing, and the bottom of his boat was full of codfish and haddock. Ivar greeted him and said he must be a good fisherman.

'Men say that I am good enough at other matters also,' said Bui hardily.

Then Ivar asked if Bui would give him some of his fish, and Bui said yes, for he had plenty. So Ivar told his men to carry some of Bui's fish down to their own boat. They carried them two at a time, choosing the biggest and sticking their fingers in the gills.

Presently Bui said, 'Have they not taken plenty?' But Ivar did not answer and his men carried away more of the fish. And again Bui said, 'Is what they have already taken not enough for you?'

Ivar did not answer, but said to one of his men,

'Why do you carry haddock when there are still cod,
and the cod are bigger?' So the man put down the
haddock and took up two codfish.

Then Bui grew angry and swung the small hand-axe
he carried, and ran at Ivar. But Ivar avoided him. Ivar
had a great axe broad in the blade and bound about the
haft with iron. He raised it aloft and again avoided Bui,
for he was very nimble. Then Ivar hewed at Bui and his
axe fell between shoulder and neck and cut down to the
midriff, so that Bui was dead immediately.

Then Ivar said, 'He was in truth a good fisherman,
but maybe not so good in other matters as he thought.'

Now Signy, Bui's wife, had seen her husband landing
and when he did not come home she went down to the
beach to find what was amiss. There she saw Ivar and
his men, and her husband dead of a great wound that
near split him in·two. For a time she was silent, and
then she began to rail against Ivar in a loud voice and
with very bitter words.

Ivar listened and said, 'I am not Bui your husband.'

Then Signy grew red in the face and said more
quietly, 'But a little while are hands fain of fighting,
and I shall live to hear of your death.'

'They live long who are slain with words alone,' said
Ivar, and bade his men push out the skiff. And so they
rowed home.

III

Signy was nowise minded to let matters rest there, and thought it right that Ivar should pay atonement for her husband's death. But she had no kinsmen in Orkney who might plead her case, and there was no man in Rousay who would take up a quarrel with Ivar Ragnar's son. So in the end Signy said she would speak in her own behalf.

She dressed herself and took Ottar her son, who was a child three years old, and bade her housecarles make ready a boat. Then they rowed round to Firth Bay and she walked up the hill to Ragnar's house.

Now Ragnar had gone a-viking, and Halfdan and Ubbi with him. But Ivar and Thorlief stayed at home, Ivar to look after the house and guard it, and Thorlief because he said he had gone often enough to sea and now he would rather be left on land. These brothers were sitting on a bench before the porch when Signy came. Thorlief greeted her well, but Ivar grinned and said nothing. He was a dark-haired man, very pale of face, and his teeth jutted out.

Signy said what her errand was, and asked for atonement for Bui her husband.

Ivar grinned at her and answered, 'There is no law here in Orkney, nor any Thing where men may take their suits, nor for all I know any lawyer except Thorlief my brother.'

Thorlief asked if she had any kinsmen, and Signy said no, except only Ottar her son.

'He will need to grow before he comes looking for weregild,' said Ivar.

But Thorlief said, 'Men will speak better of you if you pay the atonement she asks.'

They talked for some time and the end of it was that Ivar took off a gold arm-ring he wore and held it to Ottar. 'Will you take that as weregild for Bui your

father?' he asked. The child would not answer but
grabbed at the ring.

'Gold is better than grief,' said Ivar, and looked hard
at Signy.

She said he had paid a handsome atonement. She had
on a cloak of fine blue cloth and under it a scarlet
kirtle. Her hair was braided .and the ends of the braids
were turned up under a silver girdle. Ivar said, 'It will
be lonely at Ness now, and you have no kinsmen to go
to. You would do better staying here. There are good
beds, broad enough, and we have not wives to fill
them.'

But Signy said scornfully, 'No bed that you came to
would be broad enough for me,' She took Ottar and
left them. The child was unwilling to give up the gold
ring, but Signy took it and put it on her own arm.

When she came to the shore she found that only one
of the housecarles was waiting beside the boat, and he
was wounded in the leg. One side of the boat had been
cut down to the keel with an axe. The housecarle said
some men, whom he thought were Ivar's thralls, had
come down and driven away his fellows and hewed
open the boat. Signy said nothing. She began to think
that Ivar would have his way and that did not content
her.

She climbed the hill again to Ragnarshall. Thorlief
had gone indoors but Ivar still sat on the bench outside.
He did not seem surprised to see her, and when she
complained of the thralls who had cut open her boat he
grinned and said, 'What is bound to be will always
happen. Stay here with me. When my father comes
back, and my brothers Halfdan and Ubbi, there will be
plenty of fine cloaks and kirtles and silver brooches to
give away, and you look like a woman who does not
think scornfully of good clothes and jewels. There is no
lack of anything in this house and I will be a better
man for you than Bui.'

'Till someone kills you as you killed him,' said Signy,
'and as that is not likely to be long perhaps I can put
up with you.' She saw the house was well made and
that she would want for nothing while she stayed there.
She also thought that if she went back to Ness some
other man might force his way in to her who was
neither so wealthy nor so powerful as Ivar. But she was
not pleased by what had happened.

So Ivar sent a grieve, a good man, to the farm at Ness
and Signy stayed at Ragnarshall. There was not much
love lost between them but she looked after household
matters fairly well. She was rather greedy, but very free-
handed with what did not belong to her. Thorlief sat
by the fire, or on a bench outside when the weather
was warm, and Signy would talk to him more often
than to anyone else.

IV

Ragnar brought home a vast quantity of booty from
his voyage that year, and when Yule came men stayed
all day in the drinking-hall and their horns were seldom
empty. Many games were played and often the play
grew rough. The men took to bragging of famous deeds
they had done.

There was a man called Narfi of whom no one knew
much except that he was a great boaster and so strong

that he might easily have done some of the things he bragged about. One day he said that he had broken into two howes at different times and found much of value in them. 'It takes a bold man to do that,' he said, 'for often there is a howe-dweller who does not care to be disturbed, and such people are worse to deal with than berserks.'

Ivar had been listening and was tired of Narfi's boasting. He answered, 'I do not see that robbing a grave or opening a howe can be thought worthy of praise. It is often dangerous to rob a living man, but the dead are not much good at throwing spears or swinging a sword. It is foolish to be frightened of ghosts.'

Many fell silent at that. Narfi said, 'This can be put to the test if there is any howe near at hand.'

He was told there was a great and famous howe not more than four miles from Ragnarshall. It lay inland beside a lake and was called Orka-howe. There were said to be three kings buried there but no one had ever tried to open it, because most people thought it safer to leave such places undisturbed. It was moreover rather difficult to come to, for it stood in swampy ground and there was a very wide and deep ditch all round it.

Narfi said to Ivar, 'If howe-breaking is so easy and ghosts are nothing to be afraid of, why do you not open Orka-howe and take the treasure that will have been buried with the three kings?'

Ivar grinned and answered, 'There is marsh all round Orka-howe and I do not like to get my legs wet.'

But Narfi said, 'There has been hard frost for a week now. Both marsh and ditch will be frozen and you can walk there dryshod.'

Then Ivar said, 'These last few years my brothers and I have taken plenty of treasure. We take it out of ships and from towns that stand on top of the earth. We do not need to dig into the earth like dogs looking for an old bone. We leave howe-breaking to you, Narfi.'

That was thought to be a good answer and there was much laughter against Narfi. But Narfi grew angry and said, 'Would you not dig like a dog if you knew what dog had buried the treasure, and knew too that it could not hurt you? It seems to me, Ivar, that you are more frightened of ghosts than you care to let people think.'

Ivar jumped up and there would have been a fight immediately but Thorlief caught him by the elbow and said, 'You mocked him first. He is answering you, Ivar.'

Then Ivar said he was frightened neither of ghosts nor howe-dwellers nor anyone else alive or dead, and if they wanted him to break open Orka-howe he would do it. But many said that was ill advised, and told him to pay no heed to Narfi who was always making trouble.

Ragnar had not listened much to this argument, for he had drunk heavily all day and was rather sleepy. How he wakened and asked what all the talk was about. When he was told he said it would be both foolish and wicked to do that. No one knew what might happen when a howe was opened, he said. Ragnar was a man who was very careful in such things. He would talk often of Odin, with whom he felt on good terms, and did not speak too hardily against trolls and such creatures.

Narfi thought this advice of Ragnar's came in good time for Ivar, and he said, 'Only the half-grown lapwing will sit under the old bird's tail.'

Then Ivar grew angrier than before and said on the morrow he would break open the howe no matter who tried to stop him. Ragnar paid no heed to this for he had gone to sleep again. Men sat and drank a little longer, then the benches were pulled out from the wall and the beds were laid down. There were some who thought a bad night's work had been done that night.

V

In winter the night is long in Orkney and the sun
does not return till morning is half done, so that men
used not to rise very early unless there was need to. But
now Ivar got up a long time before daylight came, and
dressed himself, and took his axe from the peg where it
hung inside his shut-bed, and walked noisily about the
hall. Signy said he had not slept well, but tossed angrily
all night in the shut-bed.

When it was daylight Ivar asked Narfi if he would
come with him to open the howe. Narfi said, 'I will
come to watch you, Ivar, but not to help. I have
opened howes before. Now it is your turn.'

'I have done greater deeds without you at my back,'
said Ivar, and bade five or six housecarles make ready to
come with him, and told thralls to bring spades and a
crow-bar and rope. Then he asked Halfdan and Thorlief
if they were minded to come. Ubbi had gone to keep
Yule elsewhere. Halfdan said he would go gladly and if
Ivar got into trouble in the howe he would be the
better pleased, and help him, because he had never yet
fought with trolls or howe-dwellers and would like to
see how they compared with his wonted enemies. But
Thorlief said, 'Enough trouble comes without going to
seek it. I shall stay were I am.' And he stretched out his
legs to the fire.

Ragnar was angry and said he would have nothing to
do with so impious a deed. But when Ivar and those
with him were gone a little way he told a thrall to
bring his horse, and he mounted and rode after them.

The ground was all frozen and the snow was hard.
Fresh snow had fallen during the night, but not much,
and it was easy to ride. By-and-by they came to Orka-
howe. It was round like a bowl, higher than the height
of six men, a hundred paces about the bottom of it, and
covered with snow. A very deep ditch went round it,

that was thirteen paces broad. But the water in it was now thick ice. Beyond the howe there was a great lake.

Ivar got off his horse and climbed the howe, and the housecarles carried up spades. Halfdan and Narfi followed them, but Ragnar sat on his horse on the other side of the ditch. Now when they began to dig the snow was so hard and the earth beneath it frozen so deeply that their spades would not go through. So Ivar took his axe and said, 'It has broken byrnies, it can break the howe's helmet too.' And he hewed with his axe. Halfdan and the housecarles took axes also and hewed manfully, but Narfi stood and watched them. Presently they reached softer earth and could use their spades. Then they came to built stones and struck at them with the crow-bar and pulled them out. But some of the stones fell inward into the howe, and from the sound they made it was empty and very deep.

When they had made a hole big enough for men to go through Ivar tied a rope beneath his arms and took a torch in one hand and his axe in the other and bade the housecarles lower him into the howe. Those on top heard his axe strike once or twice on hard stone, and in a little while they could see that his torch had blown out. Then Halfdan said, 'Bare is his back that has no brother,' and took a rope and let the housecarles lower him also. There was more noise in the howe when he had gone in.

Now the housecarles took fright and were minded to run from the howe, but Narfi threatened them with his sword so that they thought it no more dangerous to stay where they were. Ragnar got off his horse and came towards them.

Halfdan shouted to them from inside the howe. They threw down the rope and began to pull him out. But there seemed a weight like the weight of ten men on the rope, and they called to Ragnar to come and help them. When Ragnar came they pulled Halfdan out of the howe. He was red-faced and sweating. Narfi asked where was the treasure.

'They were kings in a poor country,' said Halfdan, and showed three iron swords with no ornaments on them. He said that each of the kings lay in a side-chamber of his own with a heavy stone shutting the door of it. Narfi asked if there had been any fighting in the howe.

Halfdan said, 'With nothing that axe would bite on,' and wiped the sweat off his forehead.

Then they threw down the rope to Ivar, and when they pulled it seemed that twenty men's weight was on the rope. Ivar was white in the face. His eyes were staring and he seemed more ill-favoured than ever. His lips were drawn back and his teeth showed, not pleasantly, in a grin. Narfi asked what treasure he had got and Ivar showed a few rings and brooches of no great worth.

'That is small reward for hard work,' said Narfi, and told what goodly ornaments there had been in howes when he was used to break them.

'It may be we shall pay dearly enough for what we have taken,' said Ragnar. There was little talk as they rode home and no one spoke any words to Ivar. Nor was there much ale drunk that night, but men went early to bed and thought the day had been unlucky.

In the middle of the night there was a great clatter at the main door, and the door was rent from its posts and broken and thrown down. Men leapt from their beds. Benches were hurled about in the hall, and tables overturned. The light that burned in the hall was knocked down and no one could see who was playing these cantrips. Ivar woke in his shut-bed. There was loud banging on the wall of the bed so that it shook and Ivar's shield that was hanging there fell down. The door was bolted and Ivar did not go out. There was confusion all through the house for a long time. When

the noise stopped lights were kindled and men saw that
nearly all the benches were broken and weapons had
been taken from the wall and thrown about. The three
swords that Halfdan had brought from the howe were
no longer where he had set them. But Ivar had taken
the rings and brooches with him into the shut-bed.

Ragnar said, 'We have not yet heard everything
which those kings have to tell us.'

The next night the same thing happened again. The
door was broken, benches were thrown about, and now
two men were killed. They were housecarles, strong
and well thought-of. Thorlief said it was a pity that
men should be killed for the sake of a few rings that
were indeed worth very little. But Ivar said he was in
no mind to give up what he had got with difficulty.

Now Signy would stay no more in Ivar's bed but
went to sleep in the women's bower. And on the third
night the kings come out of their howe again, and
break the door of Ragnarshall, and throw swords and
axes from the wall. And now they beat on the wall of
Ivar's shut-bed so that his shield falls down. Ivar draws
back the bolt, opens the door, and hews at them with
his axe. But the axe will not bite, and now Ivar is
caught up and cast on the floor, and the kings trample
on him, and find their rings and brooches and so leave
the hall. For no one can stop them.

Thorlief said, 'It is well he is named Ivar the
Boneless, else would he be Ivar Broken-bones now.' Ivar
did not take that in good part. Narfi said, 'It is strange
that a man so famous as you could not defend himself
against howe-dwellers.' Ivar reached and hit him such a
clout that Narfi fell and lay as one lifeless. No one saw
any cause to be sorry for him.

Ragnar said, 'Now perhaps we can sleep at nights,'
and in truth the howe-men troubled them no more.

A thaw came, the snow melted, and all the low land
was like a marsh. Then it froze again and when the

ditch round Orka-howe bore ice thick enough to walk
on Narfi and certain others went to see what had
happened there. It was said they were more curious
than wise, but nothing befell them. They came back
and told that all the roof was fallen in because of the
thaw, and a pile of earth and stones filled up the howe.
Some thought that this kept the kings from walking,
but others held they were quiet because they had won
back their swords and the rings that Ivar took.

But all men had this thought, that Ivar now had the
look of an unlucky man and that few of his affairs were
likely to prosper.

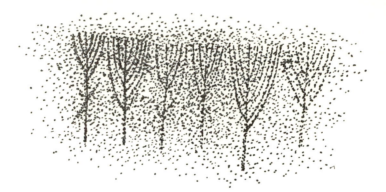

VI

The time came when Ragnar said, 'We have sat long
enough here in Orkney.' He was a man eager of fame
and seldom content to be any long while at peace.
Because Sigurd Ring had been a king in Denmark
Ragnar was not of the mind to be a lesser man than his
father. There were always many who were willing to
follow him, for he was skilful both in land-fighting and
sea-fighting and he had moreover good fortune. So now
he made ready to fare southwards and see what could

be got in the way of fame and riches. Many of the
vikings in Orkney said they would go with him and
harry in England or against the Franks or wherever he
thought best. Ragnar had twelve ships of his own and
the Orkney vikings twenty-four. There were also many
Danish ships in England and in Irish waters that would
follow him and harry under his leadership.

Ragnar's ships were taken out of their sheds and new-
painted above the water-line. Rigging was seen to and
oar-straps made. Sails were spread out and bent to the
yards. The sails of Ragnar's ships were striped red and
white and looked very handsome. The ship in which he
sailed and those his sons would sail in had each a
dragon's head at the bow, painted and lined with gold.

There was great stir and busyness in Ragnarshall.
Cattle and sheep were killed, meat was carried down to
the ships, and meal and stockfish. Men came from all
parts of the Mainland and the other islands of Orkney
and wished to sail with so promising a fleet. Ragnar
took his pick of sailors and fighting-men. Halfdan, Ivar,
and Ubbi had each command over so many ships and
chose their own men.

Now Ragnar said to Thorlief Coalbiter, 'There is still
a good ship here and no one to be captain in her.'

Thorlief answered, 'I have had all the seafaring I
want, for I am nowise greedy of fame.'

Ragnar said, 'Men will think it strange that you alone
of my sons shirk danger and take no pleasure in
fighting.'

But Thorlief answered, 'There is a very good farm
here by Firth Bay and there is Signy's farm in Rousay.
It is true that you have killed many of our sheep and
cattle, but because of that there will be the less to feed
over winter, and still there be enough to breed
from next year. Ten cows will carry as many calves and
a hundred sheep may drop a hundred and half a
hundred lambs. It is, I think, as easy to get rich on land

as by sea, and though there is little fame in farming
there is more comfort than you will get by fighting.
And so I shall stay here in Orkney. Moreover since all
the brawlers, berserks, holmgangmen and other unruly
fellows, will be aboard your ships there will be no one
left here who is likely to cause trouble. And that will
suit me very well.'

Ragnar was ill-pleased with this but he showed little
outward anger and said, 'Two men will often count
different numbers in the same flock, and it may be
there is some worth in a quiet life that I have not seen.
Do as you will, though what you do does not seem
good to me, nor will it seem good to many others.'

But Ivar jeered openly and said, 'It seems that a thrall
was sometime begotten in my father's bed.'

Signy heard that and said, 'Worse than thralls were
got there.'

Ivar had been hard to live with since luck went
against him at the opening of the howe. He had been
moody and ill-tempered, seldom speaking except to jibe
at other men or upset their words, yet unwilling to be
alone. He would walk about the hall with an axe over
his shoulder, scowling this way and that, but men
would pretend not to see him. Had he been a lesser
man many a quarrel would have been fastened on him.
But few gainsaid him except Signy. She had a hardy
temper and it had come to this, that she hated Ivar. She
said his eyes shone like a wolf's eyes at night, and his
hair was wolf-grey.

Ivar asked what her meaning was when she said that
worse than thralls were begotten by Ragnar.

Signy said, 'Not a thrall, but a troll.'

Some thought that like enough, for Ivar seemed not
less ugly than a troll.

Ivar said, 'When I have gone there will perhaps be
someone more to your liking to creep into your bed.'

Signy said that might well be true.

'Thorlief Coalbiter knows all the warmest places in the house,' said Ivar.

Signy and Thorlief were often talking together and it was said that he had tried to beguile her. But she was not the kind of woman to be beguiled against her will.

Now Ubbi said that if Thorlief stayed at home in Orkney and had the land and beasts at Ragnarshall and Signy's farm in Rousay also, then he would need to pay a just share of that value to each of the brothers. But Thorlief answered, 'You have slain the fattest cattle and all the year's lambs. You have taken what meal you could find, stockfish and ale. Do you pay back my share of that first, then I may think of paying shares of what is left.'

Ubbi said that Thorlief could come with them if he liked and take his fill of meat and ale, but they could not carry fields with them in a ship.

Ivar held Signy by the hand, but in no friendly way. She had on her arm that gold ring which Ivar had given as weregild for the slaying of Bui her husband. He pulled it off, using her rudely, and said, 'If you go to a new wedding it is not I who shall give you a dowry.' Signy said he was evidently a thief as well as a troll, and Ivar struck her on the head so heavily that she fell.

'That was ill-done,' Signy said, 'for now I am deaf in one ear, and I would need both if I am to hear the full tale of the ill deeds you will do and the worse luck that will befall you.'

Then that happened which was thought strange indeed, for Thorlief picked up an axe and swung it high to hew at Ivar. But Halfdan caught him by the arm and stayed him. Then the hall was in an uproar.

Ragnar came between those who were struggling and parted them roughly. He was taller by nearly a head than any of his sons and stronger than two men. He said, 'Has the old boar been quiet so long that now the piglings start to grunt?' He had the loudest voice of all men. He could shout so that his words would be heard though a gale were blowing and the ships were a long arrow-flight apart. Now when they heard him men fell silent.

Ragnar had grown very red in the face. He was the tallest of men there. He wore a rough jerkin of brown frieze and breeches of the same stuff, very hairy, and on his head was a black iron helmet with gold wings. He had on a blue cloak. He said, 'You have all lived too long in peace, grown fat, and slept warm at nights, and now you are good for nothing but bickering in ale-halls and matching your tongues against the clack of women. It is time you heard ravens croak again and shields clash. As for Thorlief, let him keep what we have left and get what riches he can out of so much dirt and his two-score of beasts. We shall find wealth in many places, nor need to wait until a cow calves to put our hands on it.'

Now they go down to the ships. The gang-planks are out and they go aboard. And now there are few men in Orkney but old men and youngsters, sick men and those who have little mind to viking ways.

There was a strong wind and Ragnar bade them hoist their sails. They sailed out of Firth Bay. Many other ships were waiting for them in other bays, in the lee of islands and nesses, and the whole fleet went southward through the String on a fair tide.

Bay of Firth

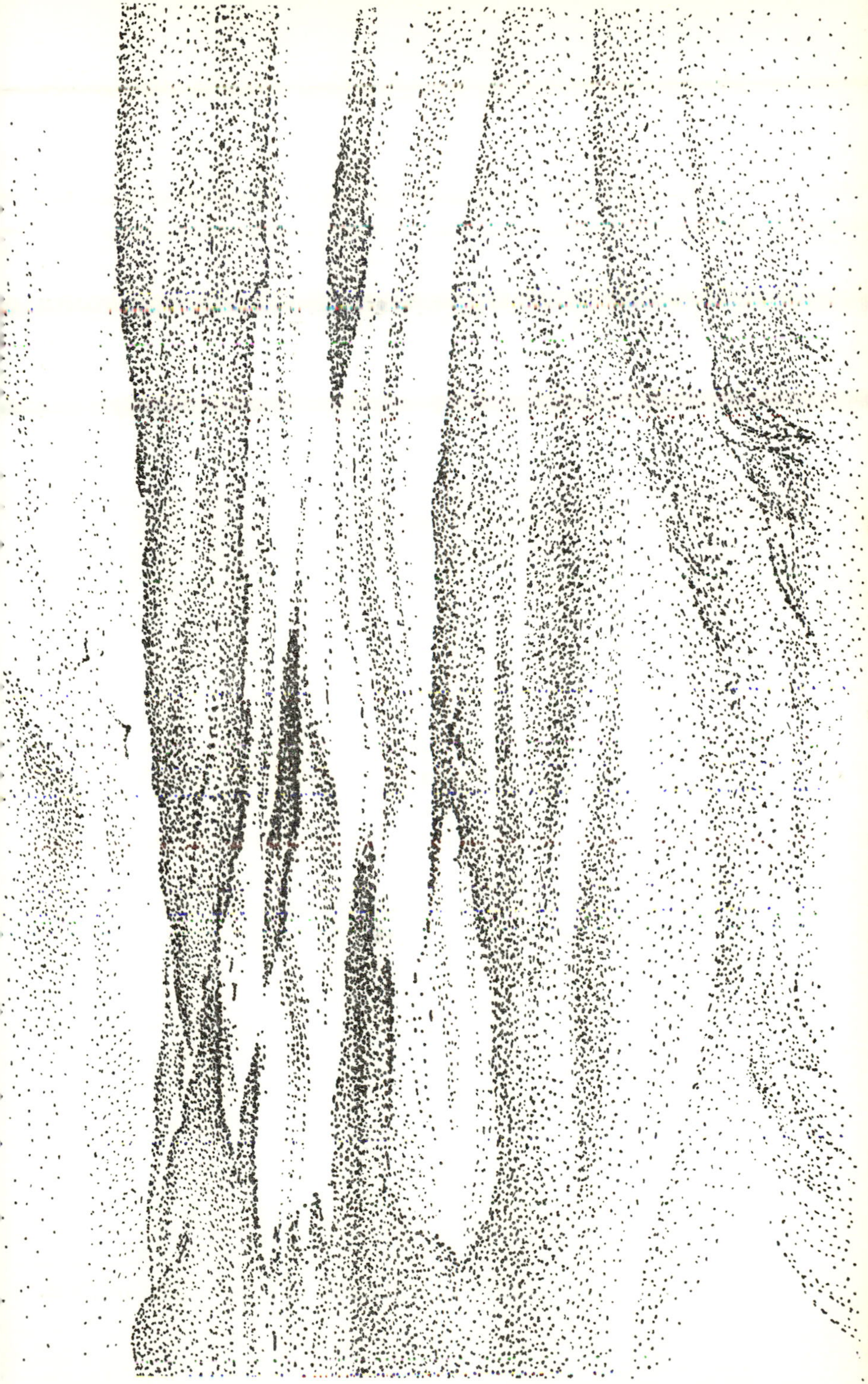

VII

Thorlief and Signy were alone in Ragnarshall except
for some housecarles and women and those thralls who
had been left behind. Ottar, Bui's son, was there also.
He was six years old, a comely boy, strong-built and
bold, and well able to look after himself.

Thorlief said, 'Now, Signy, you have no husband,
lawful or otherwise.'

Signy answered, 'So it seems. And it may be that
men will not run the risk of asking for me, since it is
known that I have a hard temper and am ill to please.'

'Nevertheless that is in my mind,' said Thorlief.

Signy said, 'There is none here to make a wedding
feast.' But Thorlief said they might do without that, for
there went more to marriage than feasting. There were
no men of any great worth or importance then in the
Mainland, but of those who lived nearest Thorlief called
six to come and be witnesses so that all should be
according to law. Signy was a widow and had no need
of anyone to give her in marriage. But the bride ale was
drunk and bread broken, and Thorlief took Signy to
bed while it was still daylight and the witnesses were
there.

So Thorlief had Signy to wife and they got on well
together. Thorlief was more active than before and yet
he did not exert himself too much. He sat often with
his feet to the fire and let men come to him for advice
on all matters touching the farm. He said, 'A good rede
is worth twenty ready hands.'

They stayed a year in Ragnarshall. Then Signy said
she would like better to live at Ness in Rousay. A man
called Mord was grieve there and looked after the farm
well. She said that Mord could be grieve at Ragnarshall
instead of at Ness, and Thorlief was willing that this
should be so. Then they took boats and flitted their
goods to Rousay, and Mord went to live at Ragnarshall.

Thorlief prospered greatly and grew rich. No man in Orkney had more cattle and he had money out at interest with his neighbours. Signy made a good housewife, and there was peace there in Orkney for some years. All the vikings were gathered in England.

VIII

Ragnar sailed southwards. Vikings came from all parts to meet him, from Halogaland and the Wick, from eastwards in the Baltic, from Denmark and the Frisian coast. They came from their harrying of the Franks and from Ireland. There gathered more than three hundred ships, seaworthy and well manned, and Ragnar was over all that fleet.

They sailed into Thames mouth. Ragnar landed his men and stormed London and held it for ransom. Then the vikings got horses and rode to Canterbury and sacked it. They marched north and put to flight Beorhtwulf, king of Mercia, and went south again over Thames and harried there. Then they fought with King Aethelwulf and the West Saxons and got the worse of it.

The vikings stayed that winter in Thanet, and had plenty of booty and lived in comfort. In the next year they sailed south round England into the Irish Sea and took Dublin and sacked it. Then many thought they had got plunder enough, and went their own ways. But Ragnar went back to Thanet and fought another battle there, and had the better of it.

Then he gathered more ships and harried far and wide. That happened most years. He and those with him got much wealth by plunder and in bribes the English gave them so that they might be left in peace. The time came, and that was the fifth year after he sailed from Orkney, that Ragnar wintered in Sheppey and again had with him a fleet of more than three hundred ships. He was now of this mind, that he would be a king in England, and build a king's hall and live in state, and go a-viking no more. But the ships he had gathered came from many different parts, and though they would all follow him in battle or for plunder the men were by no means content to live quietly on land, and have Ragnar as their king on land, and sow corn as he told them.

There was a man called Thord the Swart, a Halogalander. He said, 'It seems to me, Ragnar, that there are farmers enough as it is, and kings enough. We seldom go hungry though we do not sow our own corn, and though it is many years since I reaped barley I have never been thirsty during that time without soon finding enough ale to fill my mouth and often my belly too. I have no king, yet I wear a gold ring on my arm. I have no wife, but I had one not so long ago, and I shall get another when my hair needs combing and yet have no need to keep her till she scrapes me bald. And though it is true we may die the sooner by living as we do, I for one would rather go to Odin as I am than scratch at his door with an old man's nails and whimper to him in a sick man's voice. I think that if you want to live ashore, Ragnar, it must be that your strength is going and age is coming on you.'

That put Ragnar in such wrath that he struck at Thord and cut off his right arm at the shoulder.

Thord looked at his arm, where it lay on the ground, and said, 'You dealt some good blows, and yet I do not think you had come to your full strength.' Then he fell beside his arm and so died.

The men of the fleet that Ragnar had gathered marched inland and fought a battle with the English and had the better of them. Then they scattered and went their own ways, and Ragnar could not hold them together. After that Ragnar sailed north to the Wash, and landed and built a house there. He stayed there for some years and did nothing notable. But his sons harried so far away as Spain and Italy, and fought also in North Africa.

Ragnar made a voyage to Ireland but his heart was no longer in viking ways, and he longed to have a king's hall in some good country, and sit easily with ale before him, and have men do him honour. He grew old, and his strength became less. And still he was a strong man and great in fame, and no one cared much to thwart him.

He tried again to gather a fleet and a force of men. And now it was not hard to win what he wanted. Many leaders had been killed and there was no more plunder to be got anywhere from lands that lay near the sea. The vikings had laid all waste. So Ragnar got a hundred ships and many good men, and these said they would follow him and do as he ordered. But no one of his sons was with him. Ragnar was minded to march into Northumbria and fight with King Aella and be king instead of Aella. It was in south England that Ragnar gathered his fleet.

They set sail and had fair weather all the way, and landed in Northumbria on the coast not far from York. Ragnar had the ships hauled up, and took everything out of them that was of value, and set fire to them. When they were burnt he said, 'Now we must needs go forward.'

King Aella had with him more men than Ragnar had, but he was not eager to fight yet awhile. He offered to pay Ragnar danegeld, and while they were chaffering over this he sent here and there for help, so that by-and-by he had a force that was more than twice as big as Ragnar's. Then he said he would pay no danegeld, but would rather fight.

The battle lasted all day and the vikings had the

worse of it and many were killed. Ragnar was made captive. Aella's men pressed on him with their shields so that there were shields on all sides, and his arm grew too weak to break them. He was hemmed round by the shield-wall.

Then they took him to York to King Aella, and the king mocked him. But Ragnar made no answer. The king said he should be thrown into a snake-pit that was there. They took off his garments of thick hairy frieze, for it was thought the snakes could not bite through those, and Ragnar stood before them in linen shirt and breeches. Then they carried him to the snake-pit and threw him in.

At first the snakes would not bite, but a man took a long pole and stirred them about, and so they grew angry. Ragnar felt their fangs in his legs, and in his arms when he stooped to grip them. He thought of his sons and said, 'If my piglets knew how the old boar was suffering now they would grunt indeed.' There was a fallen tree-branch in the pit. Ragnar picked it up and struck at the snakes with it as though it had been a sword, and sang the song that is called his death-song:

'Hew, sword, hew!
Few my years were when first I wielded
You at morning on the murrey shield-moon,
And spears flew shrilly like brant flying
Black through biting arrow-hail—
Helmet-splitting was harder than sleeping
Snugly with a soft young sweetheart.

'Hew! Hew, sword, hew!
Flew fierce eagle, the she-wolf winded
My long-ships sailing to Scotland's sea-lochs;
Flinched not the valiant from fight, nor flinch

Wise men from Fate. Fell biting I feel
Of venomous adders. — Vain is all fear!
Odin is shouting for ale in Valhall.

'*Hew, hew, sword,*
Ward of my heart where the worm is housing!
Scowling with wrath my sons will wreak
    vengeance.
Death has no dread. The voice of the Valkyrs
Gathers new guests to the ale-hall of Odin.
Death comes. The board is dressed for the
    banquet.
Life's done now. Laughing, laughing I die!'

He had been bitten by many snakes. When King
Aella saw him fall he bade men take him out of the pit,
and he was already dead. Venom had gone all through
his blood and his body was swollen. No viking was
ever more famous than Ragnar Hairybreeks, and now
he is out of the story.

IX

News went to his sons that Ragnar had been
murdered by King Aella. A long while passed before
some heard it and then they were too far away to do
much. Halfdan was east in the Baltic with Sigurd
Worm-in-the-eye, and Biorn was in Spain. But Ivar and
Ubbi were in England and the news came to them

quickly. It was then too late in the year to make war
on King Aella. But the next year they tried to gather a
force, and that was not easy because men were
unwilling to take up a quarrel for Ivar, since he was
thought to be unlucky. So a year passed and nothing
was done.

Then Aella fell foul of a man called Osbeorht who
claimed his kingship in Northumbria, and there was
war between them and fighting in Deira. When the
Danes heard that they thought Ivar's luck had turned,
and they were ready enough to go with him.

Ivar and Ubbi sailed with a large fleet and landed in
East Anglia. They sent men out to find horses. Some
they bought and some they stole, and some they had to
fight for. When they had enough they took their
weapons and mounted and rode northwards round
about the Fens. They rode swiftly and came into Deira
and took York without hindrance. Aella had marched
out for a battle against Osbeorht and the town was
empty.

Then Aella made peace with Osbeorht and they
joined their forces and turned together against Ivar and
Ubbi. The vikings came out from York to meet them.

Aella's battle was in two arrays and somewhat
loosely marshalled. Ubbi attacked from in front but
Ivar, wheeling swiftly, fell on a flank and drove one
half the English upon the other. Osbeorht was struck
through with a spear and none could say who threw it.
Ivar thrust his way to where Aella stood and hewed at
him with an axe. Aella put up his shield, and that was
hardly strong enough, for the axe split it and fell on
Aella's forehead, and the king was dead of that stroke
immediately. Then the English fled all in confusion.

Ivar said he would cut a blood eagle on the king's
body so that men might see his vengeance clearly. Aella
was stripped naked and Ivar cut asunder the ribs from
his backbone. Then through those openings he pulled

out the lungs and spread them on the king's back. Aella's body was carried into York and shown in the street, and all men saw what had been done in return for Ragnar's death in the snake-pit.

In those years there was no peace in England but from end to end of it war and murder. Rich men were held for ransom, and poor men starved. Where tall minsters had stood and rich abbeys been there were now ruins and stones blackened in the fires that had burnt them. Much land was left untilled and many a hide of it was bartered for a little food. It was a common saying that men had little to eat and horses nowhere to drink, for in every horsepond blood had been spilt or a dead man thrown, and a horse would whicker and turn from the smell of it. Then the Danes parcelled out land among themselves, and called townships by their own names, and sowed their own corn. And some became traders and merchants and the English dealt with them and worked for them.

There was a man named Ecgberht whom the Danes made king in Northumbria after Aella was killed. But Ecgberht was king only by sufferance of the Danes and did what they told him.

Presently Ivar and Ubbi marched into East Anglia, and now Halfdan was with them also. The king there was Edmund. He had been fostered by Offa, king of the East Angles, and there was nowhere a better man. He was just and merciful, he was wise beyond the wont of kings but neither proud in speech nor aloof in manner. He followed Christ, and all the English held him in great love and honour. He was brave in battle too, and the Danes thought him a good foeman.

King Edmund brought his army together at Hoxne and there a battle was fought. The East Angles were more numerous than the Danes but neither so well-armed nor so used with war, and the Danes won a great victory. Many of the English were slain, and the king was made captive. Those who took him were Ivar's men, and he was brought to Ivar. Halfdan and Ubbi said he should be held for ransom or kept as a hostage, and bade Ivar treat him well. But Ivar thought differently.

He with his captains and some of his men had quarters in a farm, and took Edmund with him. It grew late in the year, and Ivar said it was time to make the autumn sacrifice to Odin, as he had given them a good harvest. This was thought strange, for Ivar used to have no dealings with the gods. But he said again they should make a sacrifice to Odin and offer blood-offerings in his temple. Then men said there was no temple to Odin, nor any other of the Norse gods, nearer than such a one. And they named one that was distant three days' march. Then Ivar said that was a pitty and great shame to Odin that he should have no temple to near at hand. Then he said, 'There is a barn here, long enough and tall enough. Let us call that Odin's temple.' And he bade them make a stall in the barn for Odin and stalls for Thor and Frey and other gods if they cared. After that he asked, 'Is there ale enough for us to feast with Odin?' And he was told there was plenty of ale. Ivar said that was a good thing, and told them to drive cattle and horses into the yard before the barn and slaughter them, and have blood-bowls to hold the blood of the sacrifice. All this was done as he ordered.

Then Ivar and those who were with him went into the barn, and King Edmund was brought in to them. Ivar made his high seat in the middle of a bench at one side of the room, and his chief men sat with him. On the lesser bench, at the other side, there was a high seat for the king. There were many men there and on the outer parts of the benches they sat closely. Fires burned on the floor, and there were cooking-pots hung on the fires, and the flesh of the sacrifice stewed in them. But the blood-bowls stood on the table.

Then Ivar took a sprinkler made of twigs and dipped it in the blood-bowls and sprinkled the stalls of the gods and the timbers of the barn, inside and out. He sprinkled his men with the blood and drew the twigs across King Edmund's face, and told him that was done in Odin's name. Then he said they must drink Odin's cup for the victory and lordship of the Danes. He filled a great bull's horn with ale and passed it through the fire, and said King Edmund should be the first to drink of it.

But the king said, 'I follow Christ, not Odin.'

Ivar said, 'I think Odin has the better of it in these days,' and the ale was held to the king's mouth. But the king thrust the horn aside and spilled it. Ivar grinned and drank ale himself, and all the Danes passed their cups through the fire and drank Odin's ale.

Now the flesh in the cooking-pots was ready and Ivar said they should eat. He signed the pots and the meat was taken out. A portion was brought to the king, and this was horse-flesh.

Edmund said, 'I am a Christian and I eat no meat that is unclean.'

Ivar grinned and said, 'Many Christians go hungry in these days.'

The Danes ate heartily and drank much ale. Then Ivar said they should drink the cup of memory to those of their kinsmen who had been noble and were dead. He brought a full horn to King Edmund and bade him drink to all those who drank with Odin in Valhall.

But the king said, 'I worship Christ, and will pledge no heathen men nor honour heathen gods.'

Then Ivar made out he was wrathful and said to his men, what should they make of such a one who spoke scornfully of Odin and would do no reverence to their dead. He said it was shameful that Odin should be so treated, and filled his men with anger, even those who themselves paid no heed to the gods. Many of the

Danes were already drunk. They got up from the benches and took weapons and would have murdered Edmund at once. But Ivar drove them back and said all must take a fair share in killing him. He bade them lead the king to the door of the barn and set him against it, and take their bows and shoot at him.

Edmund stood against the door and signed himself with the Cross but did not move otherwise. The Danes began to shoot at him, but were so drunk they could not aim well. Many of their shafts missed the mark and many gave Edmund flesh-wounds but did not kill him. The door was stuck full of arrows before the king was dead.

Then Ivar said, 'Take out the dead man.' But he was pinned to the door by arrows and they could not move him. They then broke the door from its posts, and carried it out with the king on it and threw it on the ground.

After that they sat down to drink again. In a little while a man fell off his bench, dead-drunk, and fell into the fire. His mates pulled him out and drew with him much of the fire off the stones, and then some had their clothes burning. Presently a bench took light, and flames spread to the timbers of the barn, and the whole building was on fire. Many of the Danes perished there who were too drunk to run, but Ivar and some others escaped.

Ivar got the greatest shame for putting Edmund to death, and of all the Danes in England there was no man whom men so hated. The English held him to be a murderer and a dastard, and many of his own comrades thought ill of what he had done and blamed him much for killing, in such a way, so good a king. Few of his affairs prospered after that, and now it was said that Ivar's ill-luck was clearly to be seen.

The king of the West Saxons died and his brother became king after him. His name was Alfred, and he fought much with the Danes. Ivar and Ubbi took their army out of East Anglia and joined those of their countrymen who were in Wessex. They fought nine pitched battles against Alfred, and in whatever part of the field Ivar was, there the Danes had the worse of it. This happened then, that few cared to fight beside Ivar's banner, and none but the most desperate and the most worthless men would follow him.

X

Now the story turns to Orkney, where Thorlief kept house at Ness.

Signy had borne no children to Ivar, but she and Thorlief had three sons and two daughters. The names of their sons were Grim, Kol, and Einar, and Thorgerd and Hallgerda were their daughters. But little is to be told about the latter.

While Thorlief's sons were still young there was peace in Orkney, for all the vikings and stirring men were making war in England, as has been said. And for Thorlief it was a good thing that little warfare troubled the islands, since he was a man who was not much inclined for fighting. But in peaceful matters he did well, and that without working too much himself. Signy was a bustling woman, always striving, eager for gain, and hard. No woman looked after household business better than she did. Often she would say to Thorlief when he sat in the chimney-corner or lay long abed, 'Is there no work to be done? Must I bake and brew, sew your shirts and wash them, card wool and spin it and milk kine in the morning while you snore on your pillow or yawn over the fire?'

And Thorlief would answer, 'Busy wits are worth more than busy bodies. The men are cutting this year's

hay, but I am considering next year's harvest.' Then he
would tell a woman-servant to bring more wood for the
fire, and say, 'A man cannot think well if his feet are
cold.'

This happened, that things went well if they were
done as Thorlief said they should be done, and he so
ordered matters that his thralls were always busy. He
was a good leech when cattle fell sick, and no man
could tell him a lie. He treated his thralls well and had
plenty of them, because there was no other man in
Orkney so rich as he was. There came a trading-ship to
Rousay one year, well-built and large, but all aboard
was in evil plight. The master of the ship was wounded
in the leg, and his goods had been taken. He had fallen
in with vikings who had robbed him and killed many
of the crew.

The master's name was Gilli and he came out of the
South Isles. He was a tall man, strong and bold in his
bearing, but very pleasant of speech. He was much cast
down, because he had spent all his wealth on the goods
that were in the ship, except some money that he kept
in a box. And the vikings had taken that also. Nor had
he now enough men to work the ship.

Thorlief said he could stay for some while at Ness,
and found quarters for his crew. Gilli took that
invitation gratefully and stayed all winter with Thorlief
and got on well with him. He was a merry man, good
at talking and quick in his answers, and time went
briskly where he was. Thorlief was held to have gained
in honour by having Gilli as his guest and giving him
and his crew so much hospitality.

But when spring came Gilli fell silent and was often
moody. Thorlief asked what ailed him. Gilli said he
should now be fitting his ship for another voyage, but
he had only half a crew and no money to get goods for
trading. Then Thorlief said he would buy a half-share in
the ship and also put down so much money to spend

on trading goods. Gilli was to be master of the ship, but half the profits of his voyaging should be given to Thorlief. Gilli said that offer suited him very well, and Thorlief paid him what money they agreed was fair. Nor was it hard to find men who sould sail with Gilli, for he and Thorlief were both held in much esteem. So the ship was made ready and hauled out of the shed.

Ottar, Bui's son, was now twelve years old, strong and tall beyond his age. He was rather quiet in his manner and did not say much. But he was hard of temper like his mother and could hold his own against men far older. When Gilli was prepared for sea Signy said, 'It is time that Ottar saw something of lands greater than Orkney, for he cannot learn here all the things it is needful to know before he bear himself properly in company with other men. Let him go on this voyage with Gilli and see what is to be seen. It is well, moreover, that he should grow used with faring far afield if he is ever to take up the feud with Ivar Ragnar's son for the slaying of Bui his father.'

Thorlief said he was willing enough that Ottar should go with Gilli. 'That rests with themselves, and if they would have it so and can get on with each other I will not say no. But as to the quarrel with Ivar, that is done with long since and it were best to forget it.'

Signy said, 'Forget it if you will, yet it seems to me that I shall keep it in mind for some time to come. But now there is little need to talk of it if you do not wish to hear such things, for it is no long-ship that Gilli has.'

So Gilli set sail and Ottar went with him, and was well pleased to go. Their lading was of no great worth, yet they had meal and stockfish, homespun cloth and dressed sheepskins, and they found a market for their goods in Dublin. Then Gilli said it would be foolish to go back to Orkney before they had got more profit on their voyage than that, and with the money they had taken, and that also which Thorlief had given them, he bought more goods in Dublin. He bought twelve Irish slaves, both men and women, and did not pay a dear price for them though the men looked strong enough for every kind of work and the women were young and comely. They went north round Scotland and got a good wind through the Pictland Firth, and so did not stop in Orkney but sailed on to Norway, and had fair weather all the way. They came into the Wick and landed where Gilli knew there was a market-town. They sold the Irish lading at a good price and got sixteen marks in silver for the slaves. They stayed that winter in the Wick, and the next year made other voyages about Norway and south to Denmark, and got rich profit on all of them. Then they sailed west to Orkney and came to Rousay in good trim.

Thorlief got much wealth from his share in those voyages. He had bought a farm in the north part of Rousay, and now Gilli went to live there and stayed ashore for two or three years. He and Thorlief were fast friends.

XI

Hoskuld was the name of a man who lived in that part of the Mainland over against Rousay. His farm was called Aikerness, and it was in sight of Ness. Hoskuld was the tallest of men, very broad in the shoulders, and fat as a fat ox. He was black haired, bald in front, and red in the face. He had a loud voice and was commonly held to be a great warrior and something of a manslayer. He had a good farm at Aikerness.

There was a time when a certain berserk rode into the country. He had come off a ship that was lying in Scapa Bay, and rode about the Mainland filling everyone with terror. Hoskuld said he would like to see this berserk, for it was long since he had fought with anyone of his own strength. 'And if he comes to Aikerness,' said Hoskuld, 'I do not think he will go hence again, for I will make short work of him, howl and jabber as he may.'

Now the berserk heard tell of this boasting, and one evening when Hoskuld and his men were cutting meadow-hay he rode on to their field. The thralls fell silent and moved rather away from the path he was coming. But some housecarles took up their swords and Hoskuld went to the side of the field where he had left his axe, the blade of which was an ell across.

The berserk said, 'Who is that man with the great axe?'

They told him it was Hoskuld of Aikerness.

Then the berserk said, 'He is the man I have come to see.' He got off his horse and looked keenly at the bonder. He was no less tall than Hoskuld, and the ugliest of men. He carried in one hand a huge axe, iron-bound on the haft, and in the other a long shield. He wore a good helmet and had a sword on his belt. Now he began to roar and bite on the rim of his shield. He howled and beat on his shield with the axe blade. He was battle-mad, and ran headlong at Hoskuld.

Now when Hoskuld saw him coming his spirits fell, and he turned and ran. The berserk howled with rage and chased him over the fields, and on to the moor beyond. But Hoskuld was so frightened he ran like a colt and could not be caught. Then the berserk turned back and went into the bonder's house. He was sweating all over and rather pale, but no one cared to withstand him. He drank what ale he could find, and turned things upside down, and left a great muddle behind him. Then he took his horse and rode off.

Now Hoskuld got much shame for his running away. Everyone laughed at him and thought he was not a man of such prowess as he made himself out to be.

Some time after that Hoskuld took a boat and was rowed across to Ness. He went to see Thorlief to ask him his advice about some money he had at loan. Thorlief greeted him well. They sat together in the house and Signy brought them ale.

Grim and his brother Kol were playing on the floor and making a great noise, but neither Thorlief nor Hoskuld paid much attention to them. Grim and Kol were still young, but sturdy boys and often hard to deal with. Grim was the older. Presently Thorlief and Hoskuld fell silent, having said what they had to say, and then they heard what the children were playing at.

They had wooden swords and shields and were chasing each other about the hall. Kol had a very clear voice, rather high-toned, and easy to hear. He said to Grim, 'Now it is my turn to be the berserk. You will be Hoskuld, and when you are frightened of me I will run after you' Kol bit the rim of his shield and howled as loudly as he could, and shook his sword. Then Grim pretended to be all fear, and made his arms and face quiver, and ran from him, and Kol chased him over the benches.

Hoskuld got very angry at this. He caught the

children and clouted their ears and rated them. He went out of the house without saying a word either to Thorlief or to Signy, but took his boat and went back to Aikerness.

Thorlief was not very well contented with the way things had gone, and said the children had shown little enough sense in jesting on such a matter when Hoskuld was there to hear them. But Signy defended them and said she would never stop them saying what they pleased, no matter who was there. 'They have a good spirit, and that is what men-children should have,' she said.

Two winters passed, and then Grim and Kol were in a boat fishing in the firth between Rousay and the Mainland. They lay off Aikerness, and were fishing for sillocks. They saw Hoskuld with a number of men and some women hauling at a cutter he had, to take it out of its winter shed and bring it to the sea.

Kol said, 'Let us go ashore and help them.'

Grim said that Hoskuld was no friend of theirs, and why should they heave and strain for his sake? But Kol took the oars and rowed ashore. Hoskuld seemed nowise glad to see them, but they said they had come to give him help in hauling down his boat.

He said, 'Take hold of this rope, then, and heave with the rest of us.'

There were men on each side of the cutter, pulling her down, and a rope was made fast to the bow. The women lay along the rope and hauled with a good will on it, and Hoskuld was at the end of it nearest the sea. He was well dressed and wore a blue kirtle and grey breeches of a good stuff, for he was a man who liked always to be smartly clad. Kol and Grim laid hold of the rope in front of the women and hauled with the rest.

Presently the cutter was far down on the sand and Hoskuld stood at the edge of the water. He said they must heave once and once again, and gripped the rope strongly. Then Kol took a small axe from his belt and cut the rope close to the bow, and Hoskuld fell on his back in the sea, and all the women came on top of him. They shrieked and screamed, and Hoskuld was wood-wroth.

Kol and Grim ran off, and Hoskuld after them. They made for their boat, but Hoskuld was nearer to it. Then Grim took his axe, and it was a small one, and threw it at Hoskuld and cut the bonder's leg. Now the other men chased them east along the sand, but Kol threw his axe at the foremost and wounded him in the face. Then Kol and Grim waded into the sea and swam over to Ness. And that was more than three miles.

Not long after that Hoskuld went over to Ness to see Thorlief, and he was still lame. Thorlief greeted him well. Hoskuld was in a somewhat ill humour and said that Thorlief must pay him atonement for the hurt that Grim had given him, and also for his freedman whom Kol had wounded. The man's face had been cut so that he showed all the teeth on one side.

Signy was there and spoke sharply: 'It seems strange to me, Hoskuld, that a man like you, wealthy and a man of prowess by what you have sometimes told, should take up a quarrel with children.'

'A young dog's teeth are sharp,' said Hoskuld.

Signy said, 'Men's flesh must be growing soft.'

Then Thorlief bade his wife be quiet, for Hoskuld was in the right of it, and he should have the atonement he asked. 'How shall men come to me for counsel,' he said, 'if I cannot judge rightly in a matter that touches my own household? Hoskuld has a fair case, and I say he shall be paid half the price of manslaughter for the wound that he has taken, that is six ounces of silver, and half a freedman's price for the freedman whom Kol wounded, and that is three ounces. But Hoskuld shall not bear enmity against Kol and

Grim, nor do them any hurt after this money is paid. That is my judgment, and I give it against myself because it seems clear that I should do so, and because it is not my will to have neighbours who think of me with unfriendship.'

Hoskuld was content with that judgment and took the money gladly.

But Grim was sulky when he saw how much was paid. He said, 'Hoskuld has got my axe. Must he not give it back now the atonement is made?'

Then Signy laughed loudly and said Grim should have another axe, bigger and more befitting a man, 'For I see that you can use your weapons like a man indeed.'

XII

Grim and Kol grew to be very strong and brisk in all they did. Grim was dark-haired, rather sullen in his looks, and pale-skinned. He could shoot well with the bow and throw a spear with either hand. He was so quick of eye that he could catch a spear thrown at him. He was very broad, and when he was fourteen years old he was like a man full-grown.

Kol was tall and most comely. His hair was long and fair and his eyes were a very bright blue. He had this trick, that when he laughed he threw back his head and shot up his eyebrows, and his eyes seemed to glitter. He laughed loudly with a high ringing sound, and it was said that he looked like a cock crowing in the morning. He was called Kol Cock-crow.

He was two years younger than Grim, but his equal in all feats of strength and as deft in handling weapons. They would often wrestle together, and it was never easy to say which had the better of it.

Nor was anyone their master in swimming. One day

they were swimming in the sea below Ness, and other
men with them. There was a thrall, bigger and stronger
than most, who swam well and was showing off his
skill. Grim swam to him and gripped him and forced
him under the water. He held him down for a long
time. Then they came up and now the thrall took hold
of Grim, and dived with him very deeply. They stayed
down till men began to wonder. They came up and
rested for a while. But Grim took the thrall by the
middle and dived and stayed under water till the thrall
was near drowned. But still he was not minded to give
up, and Grim would take him down again. Then Kol
swam to Grim and took him round the neck and dived,
and held him under water a longer time than any had
been down before. When they came up Grim was fit for
no more, so they swam to land.

Grim was rather ill-pleased, and asked Kol why he
had interfered.

But Kol said, 'If you want to drown thralls drown
other men's, not our own.'

That answer seemed to Grim a good one, for he took
after his mother in this, that he thought highly of
wealth and took good care of his possessions. But when
he was angry he cared for nothing.

Thorlief held every year a cheaping-fair on some land
near Ness. This was a piece of land, broad and grassy,
that grew narrower and stood out to sea in a rocky
point. Men came to the market from all the West
Mainland and the northern isles, and brought cattle and
horses and made-goods. There was often much drinking
there as well as cheaping, and games, and horse-fighting.

Hoskuld of Aikerness had a stallion that had never
been beaten. It was black in colour, very big and fierce.
He took it to the cheaping-fair and challenged all men
to fight. But no one cared to match his horse against so
good an animal as Hoskuld's.

Kol had a young stallion, red-roan in colour, that had

not been tried. Kol said it could fight well, but he was not much believed. Now he was minded to take up Hoskuld's challenge, but all said that would be the greatest foolishness and bring him no honour, for Hoskuld's horse was the biggest there and so well used to fighting that a younger beast would have no chance against it.

One man only said that Kol would do well to match his stallion against Hoskuld's, and his name was Gauk. Gauk was a merry man, but a great liar, and some thought a fool as well, and men laughed when he said the roan stallion might win. But Kol talked with him for a long time.

Gauk was the son of Kisping, the son of Bran, who was Ringan's son. They were not men of mark, but they were known for this, that they had all been born in Orkney, and so also had Ringan's father, whose name is now forgotten. Gauk was a little man, stout, with reddish hair, and rather bald on the top of his head. He had a croft far up on the hillside in Rousay, so small that it was called Calf-skin. His wife's name was Geira and she was the biggest of women, deep-voiced like a man, and so ugly that many were frightened of her.

Now Kol saw that Gauk was not so cheerful as he was wont to be, for all that he talked hopefully about the horse-fighting. And he asked Gauk what was amiss with him.

Gauk said, 'Matter enough for some to mourn over. A man could weep and rive his midriff with hiccups, and howl against hoarseness because he had not tears to wet his throat. But I am not that kind. I have suffered much, all know that, and have stood to bigger men than myself and taken their blows without flinching, and given back two for one, as Geira my wife would tell you if she could. And that takes you to half my trouble. I could hawk and sob in my throat, redden my

eyes, and beslabber my cheeks with tears to think of it.
But men would fear something too great to be told had
befallen if they saw me weeping. So I keep quiet and
say little. And it may be that things are not so bad as
they seem.'

Kol said again, 'What is amiss?'

Gauk said, 'The truth is this, that my wife Geira is
dead, and my cow is dead also, and the roof of my
house is broken in. And that is enough to be amiss
with any man.'

Kol asked how these things had come about, and
Gauk answered, 'My house is built in this way, that
stands against a turf bank, and that keeps the wind from
it. Now two days ago my cow was feeding on the bank
and saw good grass on the top of my house, where
indeed it grows well enough, for the turf I roofed it
with is now thick and the hens drop their dung on it.
So the cow came off the bank, and that is the same
height as the house, and walked on the roof. But its
feet went through and there it stuck athwart the roof-
tree. And Geira was baking bread when the cow's legs
came kicking about her ears. She was a bold woman
and strong too. If I were not so hardy myself it might
have gone badly with me sometimes when we were
talking together of matters we did not wholly agree
upon. But now, it seemed, her strength would be useful.
She went out and climbed on the turf bank and so
stepped on to the roof of my house. Then, she tried to
lift the cow, one leg at a time, out of the four holes it
was in. It was an old beast, not very heavy, and Geira's
arms were as thick round as its legs. So also was her
skin as rough as the cow's, and she was somewhat hairy
too. But she had more strength than wit. She sat
straddle-wise on the roof-tree and heaved at the cow's
rump-end, and the roof-tree broke and down they both
fell. The cow came uppermost and broke its legs, but
Geira was undermost and her breastbone cracked, and

so did her ribs. She was blowing blood through her nose when I got to her, and the cow still lay across her legs. She said she would walk again if I took another wife, and then died. And because the cow's legs were broken I must needs kill her a little later. So now I have neither beast nor wife nor a roof to my head. And yet things may not be so bad as they seem, for I am usually a lucky man.'

Kol said that Gauk had suffered a great hurt, but a man might do better than weep for what he had lost.

Gauk said he dreamt the night after his wife's death of a fox that came out of its hole and barked, and a black dog that had been digging for it turned tail and ran away.

Kol asked what meaning there was in that.

'Your horse is red like the fox, but Hoskuld's stallion is black,' said Gauk. 'The dog challenged and was beaten. So does Hoskuld challenge, and the red horse may beat him. That is why I said you should let your stallion fight. Moreover I looked closely at Hoskuld's horse, and I think he is near blind of the left eye. He has fought much, there is a scar above the eye, and he goes more eagerly to the other side.'

Kol said he did not put much trust in the dream, but he thought his horse was a good one, and if Hoskuld's horse were half-blind that would be a help.

The next day he went to Hoskuld's booth and asked if he were still of the same mind to match his stallion. Hoskuld said his horse would fight if any came into the field against him, 'But I do not see that many are anxious to try what they can do.'

Then Kol said, 'I have a young stallion that I think is good, and I should like to see how he fares against that black one of yours.'

Hoskuld laughed and said, 'If his legs are strong he is likely to fare far when he feels the teeth of mine.'

But Kol said he was content to risk that, so Hoskuld

sent thralls to bring his horse. Then all men gathered at
the outer part of the land where the cheaping-fair was
held, and there was a great crowd to watch the fighting.
Thorlief was there and he was not very willing that
things should go forward. But Ottar said there would
be little enough harm done though Kol's horse were
beaten. Thorlief said, 'Horses will fight, and sometimes
it does not stop there.'

Now Kol and Hoskuld brought their stallions out,
and some mares were tethered a little way off. Kol took
his horse by the tail and had a wand tipped with steel
to prick him on. Hoskuld did the same and also carried
a light spear. His horse whinnied loudly when he came
to the field. Now the horses run at each other, and rear
and strike out with their hooves, and bite fiercely. Kol
had no need to prick his horse, but the black was
stronger. Then Kol draws his horse to the left side of
Hoskuld's, where the black was thought to be near-
blind, and the roan bites so hard that the other turns
away. Hoskuld pricked him and drove him to fight
again. Again Kol brought his horse to the blind side of
Hoskuld's, and now Hoskuld was running on the off
side of his horse, egging him on. Kol came to the flank
of his horse and shoved quickly, and the roan bore
against the black so that he fell, and Hoskuld with him.
Then Hoskuld jumped up and was so wrathful that he
threw at Kol the horse-spear he carried. But Kol caught
it, turned it in his hand, and threw it back. And it went
through the fleshy part of Hoskuld's arm.

Then there was an uproar and men ran on to the
field. And some would have them fight, and would
fight themselves, but others held Kol and Hoskuld
apart. Thorlief came and said there should be no
brawling there at his cheaping-fair, and because he had
many men with him peace was made. Thorlief said,
'Once before, Hoskuld, I paid you atonement for a
wound you got at my son's hand, but you need ask for

nothing more. It was horse-fighting you came for, not holmgang, and now there has been enough of both. You will get no holm-ransom for the hurt you have taken, nor do I think your horse had the better of what came first.'

Hoskuld went from there ill-contented, but he could do nothing. Kol got much fame for putting down such a man, and the roan stallion was held to be as good as the black, and some thought better.

Kol would go home from the cheaping-fair. There was an ale-booth there, and when he went past Gauk came out from it and hailed him. Gauk was a little drunk. He bade Kol come with him and see what he had to show. He took Kol out from the fair.

There was a road, and sitting by the road a woman who held a cow by a rope tied to its horns. She was young and not ill-looking, though somewhat poorly clad. The cow was a good one.

Gauk said, 'See what I have got. Geira my wife is dead and so is my old cow, but now I have got a younger wife and a better beast. Things are seldom so bad as they seem, Kol.'

Kol said, 'Geira promised she would walk if you took home another wife.'

But Gauk answered, 'She talked much and often, and I heard her but little. What will be must happen, and a man cannot pay heed to everything a woman says. There is time for all things except only that.'

XIII

Harald Fairhair was king in Norway at this time. He took the kingdom when he was ten years old, after his father, Halfdan the Black, died in the ice on Rijkinswick. But many kings and chieftains fell on the land and won for themselves what they could get. Harald fought many battles with them and often had the victory. But for a long time there was much of his realm that was ruled over by other men.

The king sent men to woo for him Gyda, daughter of Eric, King of Hordaland. Gyda was the fairest of women and prouder than most. She said she would not waste her maidenhood by taking for husband a man who ruled nothing but a few fields and a handful of folk. 'It seems strange to me,' she said, 'that there is no man so high-minded he will take Norway for his own and be king over it. But if Harald can do this, and rule the whole realm, then I will be his wife.'

When Harald heard this he swore an oath that he would never cut his hair nor comb it till he had got all Norway, with scat and dues and sole rule over it, but would rather die than leave this undone.

So Harald made war through all the land that was not his, and took free land for his own, and set up earls to maintain the law and gather dues from the bonders. Many wealthy bonders came to him and said they would be his men. He had ships, and in his bodyguard the mightiest of warriors. The kings who set themselves up against him he defeated, and in their place he put earls who followed him and did him service. But many fled out of Norway and became vikings.

There was a man called Starkad. He was the son of a king in Thrandheim. That king had said he would be no thrall of Harald's, for he was as nobly born as Harald, 'And I think it a better choice to fall in battle,' he said, 'than to live and be his underling and gather scat to put in his pocket.' Then there was a battle in Thrandheim, but that king had the worse of it and got his death-wound from Harald. But Starkad fled, and men with him, and he became a viking. He harried far and wide in Norway and did great hurt to Harald and his people wherever he could find them. In the winter he fared west to Shetland, for he had friends there.

Starkad was the strongest of men, hasty in temper, rough, and unfair in all his dealings. He was a great warrior and few cared to stand against him. He had a good ship, a long-ship called the Skua, higher in the sides than most and fit for voyaging in the open sea. Those men he had with him were all the hardiest of men, great manslayers and desperate in their ways. They had sworn an oath to make no peace with King Harald, but to fight against him and do him scathe while they were able.

They took pride in many things that made them different from other men. They carried swords that were shorter than most, because they fought closer than the custom was and struck heavier blows. They took no women prisoners, and if they were wounded they did not bind the wound till the same hour the next day. None of them was less in strength than two men. They used not to lie for shelter under nesses, but would stay outside, and they did not shorten sail for a wind that made others reef to the highest row of reef-points. Nor did they stretch awnings on their ship to sleep under. They spent little time on land. Starkad said they cared not for sleeping under sooty rafters or drinking in the chimney-corner.

They would not drink sitting two together, as the custom was at feasts, but they drank all toasts in one company. Many feared them both in Norway and the islands west over sea.

XIV

Gilli the Chapman made several voyages in his ship and took Ottar with him. He became a well-known

man and was held in esteem. He had taken a wife and
lived in Rousay, and had a good household. He and
Thorlief got no little wealth from his voyaging.

Now vikings began to come again to Orkney, but
they did not trouble those at Ness nor the farm at
Ragnarshall. Mord was still grieve there. Thorlief had
many men in both places, housecarles good with their
weapons, and sturdy thralls. Gilli had good men too.
Thorlief's sons moreover were known for their
strength, and the vikings whom King Harald drove
from Norway went otherwhere than against men of
such might.

Gilli made ready for a voyage and Grim said this
time he would go with him as well as Ottar. Thorlief
said they could do as they liked, but bade them be
quickly home and not winter over sea. 'For the time is
coming,' he said, 'when men will be needed hereabout.'

But now they got little trade in Ireland or South
England, and a bad price for the goods they had. There
had been so much war that people were poor. Gilli said
that could not be helped: 'Let us go north again to
Orkney, and it may be that next year we shall do better.'

But Grim said, 'Let us rather fare east and see what
we can find there, for now that I am out of Orkney I
am minded to see what I can before I go back.' Ottar
was of like mind.

Gilli said, 'Thorlief bade us be home before winter,
and I have found that when I do according to his advice
things generally turn out well.'

But Grim said, 'He stays in bed half the day and the
other half sits over the fire. He will not miss us if we
do not go back.'

'Let us buy slaves again,' said Ottar, 'and take them
east to the Wick. These people here have no money to
buy our goods, but they will be the more willing to sell
their daughters because of that, and because there are
few husbands left for them.'

Gilli was not pleased with this, but Grim said he would nowise go home again so soon: 'I hold with Ottar. Let us go east and see what manner of men they are there.' After that he would say nothing, and presently Gilli was overruled. So they bought slaves and took them to the Wick, and wintered there.

Men took much note of Grim. He bore himself nobly, but there were times when he was rather surly and reckless. He grew somewhat quarrelsome, and fought with two Easterlings, and had the better of them. Then he was left alone and the winter passed quietly.

When spring came they made some voyages, not long ones, there where they were. They got a good lading and Gilli said, 'Now we shall go west again, and south round England, and so to Dublin. It may be that things there are better now.' So they made all ready and set sail, and had fair weather with them.

That year Thorlief stayed in his bed and would not get up. Signy scolded him and said, 'If I am not the most luckless of women, she who is must be in evil plight indeed. I have had three men, the first was a good man but not enough strong of his hands to deal with the second, who was rather a troll than a man. And the third is more useless than a bairn, for time makes him worse instead of better. If you lie there like a dead man, Thorlief, I will be minded to heap stones on you as if you were lifeless indeed.'

But Thorlief bade her be quiet. 'For I am now grown a rich man,' he said, 'and so have many things to think of that you do not guess. I must have peace to consider all fairly. But if I go outside there are men who will talk of twenty matters that do not concern me, and when I sit by the fire a wench will come with pots to hang on it or a besom to sweep the hearth, pushing me aside, and so my thoughts are upset. I am best in bed, where I can see all clearly and no one comes till it

grows dark and I must suffer you. So now bring my
porridge and say no more, or another year there will be
no porridge for any of us.'

'Sleep instead,' said Signy, 'and tell us what rede
comes in your dreaming.'

There was not much talk when Gilli did not come
back, for he was known to be a prudent man and there
were few more skilled in seamanship. They thought all
would be well with him, and with Grim and Ottar,
wherever they were. Yet Thorlief said, 'Had they taken
my advice and come back it would have been better
still.'

Much rain fell that year and the hay-cutting was late.
Then the hay lay out in the fields after it was cut, for
more rain fell. But strong winds came and dried it, and
most was brought in. None was lost at Ness, and they
had their stacks there built before other men. But at
Ragnarshall it still lay out.

Then Thorlief said that all the men at Ness should go
to Ragnarshall and help them, and so bring in the hay
quickly before bad weather came again. So they went
aboard two cutters and rowed to Firth Bay. But Kol
stayed at home, and he was the only stirring man in the
house, for Thorlief lay abed.

After the men had gone Gauk came from Calfskin and
stayed talking till it was late. He said his new cow was a
fine beast and his new wife was better still. 'I sleep warm,'
he said, 'and yet there is room in the bed. Now I know
what comfort is. Geira was a big woman when she stood
straight up, but when she lay down she seemed as big
again, and there was little enough space for me. It seems
marvellous to me that I was never overlaid, as she overlaid
the two children we had. That is what would have happened to a man no bigger than me in body who had not
had my spirit. But I held my own and thrust her away.'

Kol asked if Geira had not begun to walk, as she said
she would.

'Not a step has she taken,' said Gauk, 'nor will, I think. I buried her just at the door, so that she would not be in strange ground, and she lies there comfortably enough. My dog Bran, whom I named after my father's father, is a wise beast. He lies often on the plainstone above her, but never once has he scraped or scratched to dig her up, for she was somewhat hard on him while she lived and he knows when it is best to let a thing lie. Geira had a hard temper but she was not evil, and I do not look for her to come back and vex us. Like other women she meant little of what she said, but talked because it was her nature to. She had breath for but few words when I came to her while she lay beneath the cow, and she spoke those that came easiest.'

Signy said, 'There are also men who are given to wordiness.'

'That is true,' said Gauk. 'I have met such ones myself.'

Signy asked, 'What news have you heard?'

'Little enough,' said Gauk. 'Men are bringing in their hay as fast as they can. It is lucky for me that I have but little, for my new wife is hardly so good a worker as Geira was. But she can do what is needful.'

Signy said, 'It seems that women do most in this country.'

'They are strong indeed,' said Gauk, 'and willing to help if they are well treated. There is a gangrel woman called Mel who came by Calfskin this morning. I said she could milk the cow if she liked, and while she was milking she told me she had come from Eday the day before, and she had talked with a man who lived out on Rinansey, and he said that Starkad the Viking lay at Fair Isle with some of his crew wounded.'

Thorlief called from the shut-bed, 'What is Gauk saying there?'

Gauk went to the door of the shut-bed and told him.

Thorlief said, 'I do not know the man from

Rinansey, but the woman Mel is a liar, and you are something of that kind yourself.'

Gauk said he told truly what he had heard.

Thorlief said, 'Now I begin to think ill of having sent the men to Ragnarshall, and I would that Gilli had come home as I told him.'

'Fair Isle is far enough away,' said Kol.

'Starkad sails swiftly,' said Thorlief.

'He need not sail this way,' said Signy.

Thorlief said, 'He will not come here unless it is his luck and ours that he should come, but if I had known where he was I would not have sent the men to Ragnarshall. Starkad should be east in Norway, for there he sailed in spring. But if he is back here and has wounded men in his ship, he must have fought with King Harald and not come off the victor. And he will be in an ill mood because of that.'

Signy said, 'Everything grows big in your eyes, Thorlief. I shall lose no sleep for this tale.'

Then Gauk said, 'If Starkad and his crew should come here, Calfskin is not so far off that I could not come and bear a hand to help you. I am a man of mettle, and though it is some years since I have done much fighting, except for small matters that arose in my house, I do not think I have lost the knack of it. Thorlief says the vikings will not come unless their luck and ours hold that way, yet there is a saying that luck is one thing, brave deeds is another. Keep this in mind, that I shall be at Calfskin if any need arises. I would stay here at Ness now but that I am newly married, and so for the present time the need of me is elsewhere.'

Then Gauk went home.

The next day Kol went to the shore below Ness to see to some boats that were lying there. It had been blowing hard during the night, and now it was raining. He made sure the boats were safe and snug. Then he saw a cutter coming out of Wyre Sound towards him.

There were ten men rowing and one stood at the
steering-oar. The cutter was large and heavy, but the
crew rowed so strongly that it moved swiftly. They
seemed powerful beyond the run of men, and he who
steered was taller than most.

The cutter came to shore and those aboard jumped
out and hauled it quickly up the beach, making light of
the weight.

Kol went to greet them. They were well-armed and
he had never seen men who all seemed so reckless and
able for hardy deeds. They took short swords and axes
out of the cutter and handled them like men used to
their employment. The leader of them was richly
dressed in red kirtle and breeches, but the rain had
darkened the colour of his dress. He looked a mighty
man and ill to deal with. He was very broad in the face,
dark-hued and scowling.

Kol said, 'There is little need, I think, to ask your
name, for there is no other man like you in Orkney. If
things I have heard are true you are Starkad the Viking,
and I am glad to see you here at Ness.'

Starkad said, 'What is your name, you who are glad
to see me?'

Kol said, 'I am Kol, Thorlief's son, and men name
me Kol Cock-crow.'

'That is a good dung-hill name,' said Starkad.

Kol threw up his head and laughed loudly: 'A man
must be where he is when he is young, but I think I
shall not always live in a farmyard.'

'Who is at home here in Ness?' Starkad asked.

Kol answered, 'None but my father who lies abed
like the sluggard he is, and my mother who rates him
with a tongue sharper than wool-combs. All the men
about the place save myself alone are gone to
Ragnarshall to bring in the hay.'

'That is what we heard,' said Starkad, 'and that is
why we came.'

'You chose a good time,' said Kol, 'if your errand is what I think it is.'

There was a viking named Glum, a surly man, thick in the chest. He was a berserk. He said, 'We have listened long enough to the cockerel's crowing. Let us go to the house and see what we find there.' And he swung his sword to strike at Kol. But Starkad thrust him back.

'Let him be,' he said, 'till I ask why he was glad to see us, for he is either friendly or a fool.'

Kol said, 'I do not care much for a quiet life, and that is why the sight of such stirring men as you made me glad. Now come with me to Ness and see what cheer can be had there. For I have found it dull work sitting with none to talk to save Signy my mother, who is a shrew, and the old dotard under the blankets who is my father.'

Starkad said, 'Let us take him with us, for he can do us no harm.'

Then Kol took the vikings to Ness and spoke so well to them that they began to think him a good fellow, and that they were lucky to have fallen in with him.

Signy came to the inner door and looked keenly at them. She said to Kol, 'Who are these ugly villains that you have found, and why do you bring them here? I have seen manslayers and holmgang men in my time, but never a ruffian so ill to look at as this lout here.' She pointed her finger at Glum. 'And there are others that seem little better, and may indeed be worse if the truth about them were known.'

Kol laughed loudly and said to Starkad, 'Did I not say that her tongue was sharper than wool-combs?'

Starkad said, 'We will blunt the edge of it before we go from here.'

Then they went into the hall. There were women there, servant-wenches and Thorgerd and Hallgerda, Thorlief's daughters, with them. They crowded together and shrank into corners. Thorgerd and Hallgerda were the fairest of women.

Starkad looked at them closely, and Kol saw that. 'They are young,' he said, 'and yet not too young. But let us drink first and dry our clothes. Other matters can wait.'

Then he bade Signy bring ale for his friends. But Signy said she would bring no ale for such thieves and murderers as they were.

Glum raised his sword to strike her, but Kol stayed him. He said, 'Do not kill her till she has done some work, for she works well when she has put her mind to it. After she has brought us what we want you can do with her as you please, for in truth I have lived within sound of her tongue long enough, and I would feel no unfriendship for anyone who silenced it. But let her bring ale first.'

Starkad said that Kol was right and had his wits about him.

'Wit enough to serve my turn,' said Kol.

Signy said, 'Now indeed has ill-luck come to this house.'

But Kol said, 'Luck is one thing, deeds is another. Bring ale without more talk, or Glum will be after you.'

So Signy went for ale, and took Thorgerd and Hallgerda with her. The door of the shut-bed where Thorlief lay was open, and she closed it as she went by.

Starkad said, 'Who lies there?'

Kol said, 'The old dotard my father. Thorlief Coalbiter they call him, but now he is too lazy to come even so far as the chimney-corner.'

'Thorlief Slugabed we will name him,' said Starkad.

'Or Snoring Thorlief,' said Kol.

'Thorlief Kiss-the-pillow,' said Starkad, and smacked his hand against the table.

'Thorlief Bed-presser, Thorlief Blanket-warm, Thorlief

Mattress-mate, or what you will,' said Kol, 'and now let us keep the old winterbear where he is.'

Then he took a bar and set it against the door of the bed so that Thorlief could not get out.

One of the vikings said, 'That fire is too small to dry men so large and wet as we are.' And he took a bench and broke it on the floor, and threw it on the fire.

'Old benches burn well,' said Kol. 'Lend me your axe, Glum, that I may split this one, for my hands are hardly so strong as yours who have tugged long at the oar-looms and fought with King Harald's men.'

Signy brought ale to them. Kol tasted it and spat it out. 'That is small ale,' he said, 'women's drink and weaklings.' We want no thin stuff here, for men are here and I am become their friend. Bring old strong ale, and be quick or Glum will come after you.'

'There is sense in the cockerel after all,' said Glum.

'Sense enough to know what I want,' said Kol, and threw back his head and laughed loudly.

'What do you know of King Harald and his men?' Starkad asked.

'Nothing but this,' said Kol, 'that Harald is a king and has wide lands and rich possessions, and so is the proper kind of a man to rob.'

Starkad said that Kol should throw in his lot with them if that was his way of looking at things.

'I have been so minded since I first saw you,' said Kol.

'Then it is well that we are becoming friends already,' said one of the vikings.

Now Signy brought strong ale and the largest beakers and the men drank gladly.

Kol said to her, 'Take all those women to the women's bower and shut them in. We may need them later on. Glum will go with you and take the key, for it will be safe in his keeping.'

Glum grinned and said, 'That is the sort of employment I like.'

But Starkad said, 'See that you straightway come back with the key, Glum, for I will not have you handselling my cup or putting your fingers in the dish I have marked for my own.'

When they had drunk again Kol said, 'Why did you come here, Starkad? For I thought you were out in Norway.'

Starkad said things had not gone too well there: 'We fell in with Harald himself and five ships with him. They hid behind a ness and came on us suddenly. One ship laid us aboard and threw grapnels upon us. But we beat them off and slew eight of their forecastle-men, and cut loose their grapnels. Then we rowed away. The other ships followed close, throwing spears, and some of my men took death-wounds from that. But we were too swift for them. Then fog came down and saved us, and so we sailed westwards, for it seemed there was little more for us to do in Norway this year.'

Kol said they had had ill-luck: 'But how did you come to Ness?'

Starkad said they had come to Fair Isle and lain there for some time till most of his men were healed of their wounds: 'Then we fared south to Orkney to see if we might find men to join us, since our company was smaller than it had been. The Skua lies now in Eday. When we came there we asked what news there was, and presently a man told us there was a good house at Ness lying naked now, for housecarles and thralls had all gone elsewhere to carry wet hay from the fields. And there was no man at home save only Thorlief Kiss-the-pillow and a youngster, worthless enough, but very loud-voiced. And easy takings bring the ravens, as they say.'

'Some day I shall crow so loud that all Orkney will hear me,' said Kol.

Then they drank again and bade Signy bring more
ale. They kept her very busy and became more and
more noisy. They broke benches and threw them on
the fire, and filled the hall with their shouting. When
for a little while they fell silent they heard the lowing
of cows waiting to be milked and the women wailing in
the women's bower. Then Glum took the key from his
pocket and waved it, and the vikings jumped up and
would have gone straightway to the women. But Kol
said, 'Wait awhile till you decide who is to take Signy.
For she has worked well for us here, and it would not
be much honour to the house if she were left unsought
when the other women are bedded.'

Starkad said, 'Glum shall have her,' and the vikings
shouted and said that was a good choice and a proper
judgment. They were now somewhat drunk.

Signy said nothing, but moved her hands up and
down. She stared fiercely at Glum, she seemed black
and wild when she looked at Kol.

Glum said he would need to have some more ale
before he made love to so notable a woman. So they sat
down again and drank awhile longer. All said what a
good fellow Kol was, and swore he would be a proper
shipmate for them and they would get on well together.

Now Starkad said it was time to go to the women's
bower, and Kol said he had been thinking that for some
while: 'Let us dally no longer except to finish this ale,
and then we shall see if Glum can find the lock to put
his key in.'

So they drank up the ale and were ready to go to the
bower. Kol said: 'There is good plunder here besides
women. Come first to my father's storehouse and see
what he has there that will be useful for us to take.
There is much wadmal and other kinds of cloth, and we
need not stay long to look at it. Your weapons will do
well enough where they are, for there is none here fit
to handle them but yourselves.'

Starkad said, 'Let us see what wealth Thorlief Kiss-the pillow has got together.'

Thorlief's store-house was built a little way from the hall. It was strongly made and there were steps up to the door of it. The vikings went out, and not many took weapons with them. The sky was overcast but it was not yet dark. Kol unlocked the door of the storehouse and all went in. The outdoor air had made them more drunk and they were very noisy. They upset everything in the storehouse and began to wrestle together. One of them took hold of Kol and wrestled with him and threw him down. Kol got up and staggered from side to side. He said loudly that they must let him out, for ale was rising in his neck and he was going to spew. 'And I shall spew a great deal,' he said. Then they laughed and let him go. Kol went out and shut the door behind him. He locked it, took out the key, and ran swiftly to the hall.

Signy stood by the inner door. She had a spear in her hand and thrust at Kol when he came in but Kol put the spear aside and said, 'Waste no time on these love-tricks, for there are men outside who must be dealt with quickly.'

He told Signy all he had done. She said, 'I must be something of a fool, for your mumming deceived me, and truly I thought you were eating in Starkad's mess now. But I am glad to be put right.'

Kol took the best axe he could find, and put aside the bar he had set before the door of Thorlief's bed. He told Thorlief what had happened and said, he must rise and help. Thorlief said 'It is ill when a man can take no rest.' But he got up and found a sword and a shield and went out with Kol. He wore only a linen shirt and breeches and he shivered in the outside air, for it was still raining.

Signy stood by the door of the storehouse with the long spear in her hand with which she had thrust at

Kol. There was a great tumult in the store and Glum could be heard howling above the din, for his berserk fit was on him.

Signy said, 'It will not be long now before they break the door.'

Kol said that he would stand facing the steps, and Thorlief should stand at one side of him with Signy at the other. But Thorlief said the time had not yet come when Kol should tell him where to go, and stood himself in front of the steps, and held his shield before him.

Now Glum broke through the door, howling, and ran straight at Thorlief. Kol struck at him and missed, he went so fast. Glum had no weapon but he leapt upon Thorlief. Thorlief's sword went through his belly, but the berserk bore him down and fell on him, and was dead even as he fell. Thorlief got up slowly and said, 'Many days I am content to lie on my back, but not now.'

Five or six of the vikings came hard after Glum, but the first fell, for he had forgotten there were steps, and the others tripped and rolled upon him. Then Signy thrust fiercely at them before they could rise, and the spear went through two and pinned them to the ground. Kol hewed with his axe and struck off a man's head. He hewed again and cut off Starkad's leg above the knee, and smote backwards at a man who had risen, and the hammer of the axe took him on the forehead and he was dead of that immediately.

Now two men ran at Thorlief, and both had swords, but Thorlief took their blows on his shield and killed them both. He said, 'My arm grows stronger with age.'

Kol fought with three, and Signy held her spear so that the men it had struck through could not rise. Then she saw the uppermost of them was dead, and she pulled out the spear saying, 'As I am a woman I can deal with one.' Kol was wounded, but not deeply, yet he grew tired. Thorlief came to help him and slew one of those three who fought with Kol. Kol hewed strongly at him who was nearest and the axe fell on the man's collar-bone and shoulder-bone and sank into the chest, and the viking was quickly dead of that. Then the third man ran off, and no one followed him.

Signy said, 'You have proved yourself a good man to-night, Thorlief, but I do not know why you waited so long before showing what mettle was in you. Had Kol been minded to do nothing till he was your age, we would not have come off so well as we now have.'

Thorlief answered, 'I take no pleasure in deeds of this kind.'

But Kol said, 'I think to-night's work will be spoken of.'

XV

There was much talk about the fight at Ness, and Kol had great fame for the part he played, both in what went before and in the fight itself. It was said that Signy behaved as might have been expected, for her words had often been as heavy as blows and her tongue revealed what strength was in her. But that Thorlief should have shown himself to be stout-hearted and apt with weapons was matter for surprise in many places. Thorlief said again that he took no pleasure in what he had done, yet it was noticed that he bore himself a little more proudly than his wont was, and he said that the two men with whom he had fought at the same time were sturdy fellows, and he had had some trouble to be rid of them.

He praised Kol without stint, and yet was sometimes testy with him, and it was thought he had not been too well pleased with being called Thorlief Blanket-warm and Thorlief Mattress-mate. He stayed no longer in his bed, but moved about the house and often went outdoors. He said, 'It seems the time has not yet come when a man can be at peace and spend his time in thought. I must keep my eye on things when there is so much foolishness about.'

The bodies of Starkad and his fellows were carried a little way from Ness and buried there, and stones were piled on them. The viking who had run off was not seen again, but it was said he had fallen over a cliff somewhere. Starkad's ship, that he called the Skua, went from Eday no one knew where, though it was seen sailing southwards. Those vikings who had been left in Eday with the ship took fright when they heard their mates had been killed, for their company had already been weakened by the fight in Norway against King Harald's men. So they fled from Orkney, and no one was sorry when they went.

Thorlief's men came back from Ragnarshall when they had gathered their hay, and for some time everything was quiet at Ness.

XVI

Gauk came often from Calfskin to speak with Kol. He told many lies and sometimes there was little enough sense in what he said, but Kol liked him, not seldom laughed at him, and let him talk his fill. Gauk said that Kol was the most promising man in Orkney and ought to go a-viking to win fame and wealth. Kol said, 'There will be time for that.'

Gauk said, 'We will go together, for I have long wanted to do more stirring deeds than there is room for here, but I could find no one to my liking with whom to sail. For I would not go with trifling fellows who

creep from bay to bay and never go out of sight of the
red shore-seaweed. But when you find a ship I will be
ready, and with you on the poop and me on the
forecastle, with other picked men, I think we shall do
well enough.'

Kol said, 'But what of your wife, Gauk? Will she be
content for you to leave her?'

'She must fare as other women,' said Gauk. 'A man
cannot always be at hand to please them. I have had
two wives, and I say that a man must be given time for
other things than cosseting and holding.'

One day Gauk went early to the shore to gather
shell-fish, and had his dog Bran with him. He took a
stone and went down into the ebb. While he was busy
knocking limpets off the rocks Bran barked, and Gauk
looked up and saw, far off, two ships coming that way.
One was a round-ship, a trading-vessel, but the other
was a long-ship. He ran quickly to Ness, and they were
just stirring there. He told what he had seen. Kol took
weapons, and Thorlief bade Signy bring him his shield
and take his axe from the wall.

Signy said, 'He was less trouble when he slept.
Thorlief, I see, will be a famous man yet, if he stays
long enough awake, and there will be peace for no one.'

Thorlief and Kol went out, and men with them. Kol
looked to seaward and said, 'That is Gilli's ship come
home again.'

'Gilli had no long-ship with him,' said Thorlief.

Kol said, 'By what I have heard the long-ship looks
very like Starkad's Skua.'

'Gilli has found new friends if that is so,' said
Thorlief.

When the ships came nearer it was seen that one was
indeed the Skua. Its sides were higher than the custom
was, and the stem curved up and forward into the shape
of a gull's head, well carved. There seemed few men
aboard either ship.

Thorlief said, 'There will be news to tell.'

Then the ships came to shore and the gangways were put out. Gilli and Ottar came down from the round-ship, but out of the Skua Grim came. They were all wounded, and so were many of those with them. Gilli was lame and Ottar had his arm bound. But Grim's head was tied in a cloth.

Thorlief said, 'There must have been high words at the market.'

'We have seen more than market-places,' said Gilli. And Grim said, 'We have bought a ship that is worth more than we paid, though chaffering for it was not easy.'

Then they told what had befallen them.

After leaving Norway they had gone to Dublin, as their plan was, and sailed from there in good weather. But when they were west of Scotland they met ill winds and were blown to and fro and were in danger. They put in for shelter to one of the South Isles, but had to go from there speedily because three viking ships lay there. Then they were in peril from winds and fierce tideways and a great roost that roared like thunder. The wind changed and saved them from that, but blew so strong they were still in danger. Much rain fell, and the sky was always dark. They were beaten about for many days and grew weary, but feared to go too close to land because sometimes it fell calm under the hills and the tide might drive them ashore. And sometimes squalls blew off the hills that were worse to bear than the outer winds.

Then Gilli saw a tall headland and a high mountain beyond it and knew where he was, and knew there was a sea-loch there, safe and deep, where they might shelter till better weather came. So they steered that way and came into the sea-loch. It was night when they came into calm water, and very dark. But they went farther up the sea-loch, for Gilli knew how the land lay. They came to shoal-water and cast anchor there. Then they put up the awnings and slept. They were weary and slept long.

In the morning the Skua laid them aboard before they were waking. The Skua had come into the sea-loch some days before that, at the beginning of the storm. When they left Orkney the vikings had gone to the South Isles looking for men to sail with them, and found none. Then they had gone here and there in the sea-lochs, but the land was bare. If the weather was bad they would not venture out seawards, for their company was small. But when they saw the cheaping-ship then they thought they could take from it food and other goods they needed, and it might be some men also. So they rowed swiftly and took it by surprise.

They killed two or three of Gilli's men who woke first, and stood over the rest so that they had no chance of taking weapons. Then the vikings said they would slay no one if Gilli did as they bade, and that was to put what goods they wanted into the Skua, and with them whatever Gilli had in silver or other treasure. But if he would not do this they would kill him and all his company. Gilli thought this a hard choice, but said he would do what they ordered. Then the vikings made the chapmen carry a great part of their lading aboard the Skua, and give up all they had in treasure.

Gilli said, 'Now that we have done what you wanted we are ready to go.'

But the vikings said there was yet another matter, for their crew was too small to work the Skua and they needed some men as well as the other things.

'That was not in the bargain,' said Gilli.

The vikings said they did not do business in the chapman's way, but took what they thought fit. Gilli was unwilling to let any of his people go, and none of the men thought well of sailing in the Skua. But the vikings said if they could not take ten men alive, then they would kill ten. Gilli could not think what to answer to that, and all his crew fell silent.

Then Grim spoke, and said, 'Neither way will give us much help, but I think it better that we should lose ten alive that keep ten dead. And here is one who will go aboard the Skua if others will follow him.' And he put his hand on Ottar's shoulder and pushed him forward.

It was thought strange that Grim should thrust forward his brother in this way, but he had spoken secretly to Ottar, and Ottar had said he was willing to do what was necessary. Then Grim went from one to other of the crew and said that they should go with Ottar and join the vikings. They were not very pleased at this, but there seemed nothing else to be done that was of any use. So ten men went aboard the Skua, and the vikings let Gilli go.

Gilli sailed down the sea-loch and had few men to work the ship. They came to a small firth and Grim said, 'Let us go into the firth and anchor, for we have come far enough.'

Gilli asked what he meant by that.

Grim said, 'I spoke secretly to Ottar and told him we should come back to-night, not by sea, but walking over that hill, and try whether we could not play turn and turn about with the vikings, and this time take their ship from them. Ottar will tell those with him what we mean to do, and they will be ready to help us.'

Gilli said, 'They lie in the middle of the loch.'

Grim said, 'The loch is narrow there and we can swim.'

Gilli was scarcely glad to hear that, for he was not a very warlike man, though a good seaman. But he said he would do what Grim wished. Grim said that was well, because he had made up his mind and was not to be hindered in his plan by anyone. The men seemed willing to follow him, for Grim was a masterful man and had his own way oftener than others.

They took their weapons and went ashore. When night fell they crossed over the hill and came to that part of the sea-loch where the Skua lay. They took off their outer clothes and swam as quietly as they could. Grim and three more got aboard. Then the vikings woke and there was hard fighting. Ottar and those with him had no weapons and were tied by the feet. But they pulled down one of the vikings, took his sword, and cut themselves loose. Then they killed one or two with bare hands, and some got weapons. Gilli and the others came aboard also. The vikings were unready and had no leaders, but Grim shouted to the Orkneymen and egged them on. Grim slew two men and wounded others. Ottar stood with him and was the death of two more. Gilli did well, and the Orkneymen pressed harder as the vikings fell back. Then those vikings who were left alive and not too badly wounded jumped overboard and swam to shore.

When day came Gilli's men rowed the Skua down the sea-loch, and found their own ship where they had left it. They were few men to work two ships, but Grim said that nothing would make him go back to Orkney without the Skua. 'A long-ship is more to my mind than chapmen's vessels,' he said, 'and what we won by night should not be hard to keep by day.'

Gilli said they would have to wait for good weather and a fair wind. They lay in the firth four days. Then they set sail and came home without more trouble.

When he heard this story Thorlief said they had done well to take so good a ship and fight in such wise in the darkness.

'Many trifles happen at night,' said Grim.

Kol asked how he had chosen the ten men who should join the vikings and stay in the Skua.

Grim said, 'Eight of them could not swim well. Ottar

was one of those. And two had corns on their feet and so could not walk fast enough to come over the hill.'

Thorlief said, 'I see that you two can make plans as well as fight.'

Grim was much talked of for this deed, and he grew somewhat overbearing. But he and Kol got on well together. The Skua was hauled up on shore and put in a shed with Gilli's ship.

XVII

The wound on Grim's head was slow to heal, for it had been a shearing stroke and had taken off much of the skin. No hair would grow on that part of his head afterwards, and he had a large bald patch there. For this he was now called Skallagrim.

That winter he talked often about going a-viking. He had a good ship now, and he thought it would be strange if he could not find a crew to sail with him. When spring came he would go southward, he said, or, it might be, east into Norway where Harald was still fighting for his kingdom and where a man should be able to reap profit for himself out of the bickering of others.

But Thorlief said, 'It would be foolishness to interfere with Harald, for he is a great man and will come into his own before long. Either leave him alone or become his man and fight for him.'

Signy said, 'There is another whom it would befit my sons to fight against more than against King Harald. I have heard that Ivar the Boneless still lives in England and is no better thought of now than he was while he dwelt here in Orkney. But he is a mighty man, they say, and men fear to pick a quarrel with him. I think it would not come amiss to Skallagrim's fame if he did something against Ivar.'

Thorlief said, 'That is an old matter now and stale in the telling. You would do well to forget Ivar as I have forgotten him, for there is no sense in brooding on what happened long ago.'

'Blood that is spilt will not dry clean away like water,' said Signy. 'Ivar killed Bui my husband here at Ness, and Bui is yet unatoned. For Ivar took back the gold ring he gave, and that was but small weregild for such a man as Bui though I had kept it. Moreover there are certain things I have against Ivar on my own account, and now that my sons have shown themselves to be men of fame I am not minded to keep quiet about them.'

Skallagrim said, 'I do not see that much would be gained by bringing suit against Ivar while he and those with him are masters of half England.'

Then Signy asked Kol whether he would take up the quarrel.

Kol said, 'What must be will come to pass. I am in no hurry about this matter you speak of.'

Then Signy said scornfully, 'You are sons of your father, wise men all, and he had better make room for you in the chimney-corner.'

Kol and Skallagrim liked that not at all and took it moodily. They were rather silent for some days.

Two weeks after Yule Gauk came from Calfskin. He brought his wife with him, his cow, and Bran his dog. Gauk was greeted well, and they asked him why he was flitting his house like this in the middle of winter.

Gauk said, 'Had I been a lone man with none to think of but myself I had stayed where I was, for I am not easily frightened. Nor when I am frightened do I count that much, for a man can put up with fearful things. But that is not the way with these others. Calfskin is a fruitful place and and it is well that Bran here is not a bitch, or there would be no room to move. As things are my cow is in calf and my wife is

with child, and for them to be frightened again as they
have been these last two nights might spoil all.'

Signy asked what had been happening.

'It comes to this,' said Gauk, 'and there is no need to
make a long tale about it, for all can be explained in
few words as well as in many, that Geira has been
walking.'

'That was to be looked for,' said Kol.

'May be it was,' said Gauk, 'Yet I am he whom it
most concerns, and I did not look for it. Nor do I like
it now that it has happened. It is easy to be wise about
another man's troubles, but if you were in my place I
do not think you would take things so calmly. Geira
was a good wife as such women go, but she was often
ill to argue with, and now that she is dead her ghost
seems worse in temper than ever. She rode the roof last
night and the night before, cracking rafters with her
heels, and came down to thunder on the door. I was in
dread lest I see her, for she was never fair to look at,
and for my wife's sake as well as my cow's I judged it
best to leave Calfskin for a while till she grows quieter
or till a champion can be found to deal with her. It
would be a matter of some fame to overcome such a
woman.'

'You have found the right house if you want
champions,' said Signy. But Kol was silent.

Then Skallagrim said, 'I will see what can be done to
stop Geira walking if you think it my part to do so,
but it seems to me that Kol is more friendly with Gauk
than I am.'

'Calfskin is a small place to fight for,' said Thorlief,
'and if Geira walks no further it might be as well to
leave her alone. There is a croft on this side of the hill
that Gauk can have, where he would live as comfortably.'

Gauk thanked him for that. 'Yet I would be glad to
stay at Calfskin if something could be done to make

things quieter there,' he said. 'For I have grown used to it, and my kinsfolk lived there a long while before me.'

Then Kol said, 'I will go and argue with Geira, for there is no happiness to be got from shutting our eyes to such things or running away from them.'

Gauk said, 'I will face her gladly if you are there also, for danger is halved when a friend is with you.'

The next day Kol went to Calfskin, and Gauk with him. The weather was cold, a gale was blowing, and there was heavy rain. Gauk said, 'It will be marvellous if Geira walks on such a night as this.'

Calfskin was a small dwelling with two rooms only. At one end was the kitchen with a shut-bed in it, at the other end was the byre and a stall for the cow in it. There was also a little stall in the kitchen where a calf could lie. There was a door at each end and a passage from the kitchen to the byre.

Kol said that Gauk should sleep in the bed, and he would lie on a bench before the fire.

'That is poor comfort for a guest,' said Gauk.

Kol said, 'Geira would be put to shame if she got into the bed and found me there.'

'It is worse than shame I shall suffer if she lays her head beside mine,' said Gauk.

Nothing happened that night nor the night after, and Kol said, 'It seems I have come on a needless errand.'

But Gauk answered, 'She was always loth to go in the rain.'

On the third night there was a hard wind but no rain, and the moon shone between dark clouds. 'We shall have no peace till morning,' said Gauk.

Kol lay down on the bench and had a sword beside him. About midnight there was a heavy trampling on the roof, Geira went to and fro upon it, roaring louder than the wind. The rafters cracked and turf fell on the floor. Then Geira came down and ran round the house, beating on the walls. She thrust against the door and it fell inwards. She put her head round the doorpost and peered this way and that. Her head seemed big as a troll's, but it was dark and Kol could not see what she looked like. She came into the room and was quiet at first, and then began to howl and break thing up. Gauk pulled-to the door of his bed. Geira heard that and ran towards him. Then Kol struck at her with his sword, but she turned quickly and hit his arm with a cudgel she had. Kol let fall his sword, for his hand was useless and numb.

Then Geira seized him and he could do little against her, she was so strong. She got him into the passage and tried to pull him through into the byre. But Kol put his foot against the wall where it jutted, and braced himself. He had not much power in his right hand. Geira got her arms about his ribs and pressed on him till his breath went. She was big as a troll, stronger than two men, and there was a foul smell about her. She carried him into the byre and put him with his back to the side of the cow-stall, that was made of a flagstone set endways. She bore on him till his backbone was near to breaking.

Now Gauk came at her from behind, but not very briskly. She turned and gave him a buffet that laid him flat. Then she would have trampled on him, but Kol grappled her. His breath had come back to him and there was more strength in his arm. But still Geira was stronger, and now she began to pull him to the byre-door. Kol set his foot against the door-post and braced himself there, and Geira could not move him. She tugged hard and howled with anger. Then Kol quickly put down his foot and heaved himself forward as Geira pulled. She was not ready for that, and they fell against the door and broke it, and tumbled outside. Kol was uppermost and got his hands in Geira's throat. But she struck at him and struggled hard.

Kol shouted to Gauk that he should bring his sword,

and Gauk came quickly. Then Kol took the sword, and it was a short one, and set the point of it on Geira's throat. But now the moon came out, shining through the clouds, and shone upon Geira. Her face was huge and ill to look at. She was like a troll, and her eyes were troll's eyes. Her skin moved on the bone beneath it, and her eyes were like deep pits full of black water, and the moon rolled in them. Kol felt a weakness come over him, and his hand shook on his sword.

Geira said, 'I wish there will be no luck for you when this light is shining, and what you fear now you will fear more in time to come.'

Then Kol drove the sword into her throat, and presently she lay still.

'This was well done,' said Gauk.

'I am in two minds about that,' said Kol, 'but now I am weary and can do nothing else but sleep.'

So he went in and lay on the bench and slept till morning. He was bruised wherever Geira had gripped him, and very sore and stiff. When it was light he and Gauk went out to her, where she lay on the ground, and she was heavier than they could move. She was all smeared with the mud in which she had struggled and fought with Kol.

Gauk looked at her and said, 'It is strange what a man will take to his bed. I am not the only one who has found there are worse things than cold to lie with.'

Kol bade him find men who should help to carry her. Those whom Gauk brought were not very willing to touch her, but Kol drove them with his sword, and they took her a long way to the shore and put her down there. Then they made a fire and burnt her, and covered her ashes with boulders. And Gauk said she would trouble them no more.

Kol said it was not likely she could walk again: 'But I feel no better for this deed, though it was a good one, and I could wish, Gauk, that you had lived unwed when Geira died.'

There was much talk about this exploit, and Kol was praised for what he had done. It was said he had become the most promising man in Orkney. But he seemed little glad of it, and Geira's ill-wishing began to work upon him. He was sometimes afraid to go abroad in moonlight, because now and again there returned to him his fear of Geira. And in bright moonlight a kind of blindness came to him at times, as when her eyes had dazzled him, so that he would stumble as if he walked in utter darkness.

XVIII

Skallagrim spoke more and more about going a-viking, and Signy egged him on. But Thorlief paid no heed. When spring was nearly come Skallagrim said he would go now and look for a crew. But then Thorlief said flatly he could not sail that year.

'The ship is my own,' said Skallagrim, 'and I shall go when I choose.'

Thorlief said, 'Then you will sail alone and sail hungry, for neither men, money, nor foodstuffs will I give you.'

'There seems little sense in that,' said Skallagrim, 'for you cannot expect me to stay at home all my life and plant cabbages.'

'There will soon be heavier work than that,' said Thorlief, 'and you will not have far to seek it.'

Skallagrim said, 'I am little suited for a peaceful life, and I can do best for myself when there is not digging but fighting to be done.'

Thorlief answered, 'I think before long there will be fighting enough here in Orkney to keep you busy.

Were you to sail southwards this year you might find peace, but from Hoxa to Rinansey there will be no peace. For now this has happened, that Harald is king over nearly all Norway, and the lesser kings and their men, who will not be his men, are killed in battle before him or take ship and sail west over sea. Many have gone to Shetland, many have come here. And now more will come, because Harald is a great king and none can withstand him. Let him fight one more battle, and that a good one, and he will rule the whole realm. But from the greatest battle some escape, and they will flee westwards and look for land here. And so there will be fighting, for since so many of those who fled King Harald have sat down here already, there is little land left untaken. Dog eats dog when there is no other prey. Stay here in Ness and you will find work enough for both axe and sword, and more, it may be, for your shield.'

'And maybe such talk is woman's talk,' said Skallagrim. 'Yet you have a name for wisdom, and because of that I shall do what you say and wait here for those whom Harald is too slow to kill. But if they do not come I shall not take your rede again.'

'Nor will you if too many come,' said Kol.

XIX

That year King Harald fought the battle of Hafursfjord, and drove before him the ships of the men of Hordaland and Rogaland, of Thelmark and Agdir, with their kings and leaders. He captured many ships and slew many men. But a great number fled, and not a few took refuge in Shetland and in Orkney. And before winter came some sailed east again to raid and harry in Norway. But they wintered in the islands west over sea.

Then Harald was king of all Norway, and he remembered Gyda the Proud, who would not marry him when his rule had been no more than half the land. He had by this time other wives, yet for pride he sent men to Gyda to woo her for him. And now she said she would marry him, since he was king of the whole realm of Norway. So the wedding was made.

But Harald still kept the oath he had taken, that he would neither cut his hair nor comb it nor shave his beard till he had got all Norway for his own, with scat and dues and sole rule over it. And his head was like a cock of hay, wind-swept, and his beard was like an old straw brush.

Gyda said, 'It is time you took shears and a comb and did something to make that tangle less.'

But Harald said he was still bound by his oath, for he had been cheated of certain dues, and men sent to gather his scat had been robbed by vikings who dwelt or wintered west over sea in Orkney and in Shetland.

Gyda said, 'You have ships. Can you not fight for what is yours in Orkney as well as in Norway:'

Harald said it was in his mind to go there and bring the islands under his rule: 'But now it is not many weeks till winter, and the vikings must wait my visiting till another year.'

'When I dwelt in Hordaland,' said Gyda, 'I was told that King Harald Shockhead lay out in his ships winter and summer alike. They said King Harald had no liking for the chimney-corner and the smoky beams of an ale-hall, but loved weapons rather, and to reap the winter-corn of hail. And now I see that my lips must be swept by the besom of your beard and the tangle of your hair fall on my cheeks for another year, because all that was lies, and you do not care for cold sailing, but, like other men, keep your ships in harbour till the days grow warm.'

Then Harald laughed, and yet was somewhat angry,

and said he would sail straightway west to the islands
and bring them under his rule: 'Then I will shave my
beard, and you, Gyda, shall comb my hair till it is
smooth enough for your liking.'

Gyda said, 'That is well said, and I will comb your
head as clean as you comb the islands.'

Harald made ready his ships, and though men
murmured against faring oversea at that time of year
the king made light of their grumbling and said they
would said the faster with strong winds to help them.
'And we shall keep Yule in Orkney and drink the
vikings' ale for our reward,' he said.

Then his fleet set sail, and he had a great company of
men with him famous in war, and many berserks who
were in his service. Earl Rognvald of the Mere, called
the Wise in Council, went with him, and other men of
mark. They came speedily to Shetland and took the
vikings there by surprise, slaying many and burning
their homesteads. There was none left in Shetland fit to
bear arms or wreak war against the king when Harald
had worked his will upon those islands. And when that
was done he said it was time to fare south into Orkney.

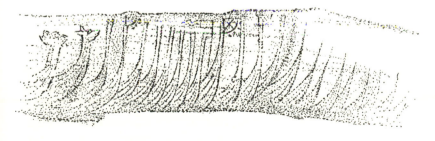

XX

There was a man called Rani, a landed man of
Thelmark in Norway. He was a brother of Hadd the
Hardy and fought with him against King Harald in

Hafursfjord. When the battle turned against them Rani brought his ship out of the fight and fled to sea. But Hadd was slain by one of King Harald's forecastle men.

Rani came oversea to Orkney. He was a kinsman, though not close-standing, of Hoskuld of Aikerness. He brought his ship to Aikerness and it lay there within sight of Ness, and Rani lived ashore with Hoskuld.

Now there began to be some bickering in Orkney, for there had been a great flight before Harald, and all about the islands were ships of those who had got clear of his battle. Some came to Orkney because they had kinsmen there, and they found quarters without much seeking, for their kinsmen were mostly those who wintered in Orkney and in the summer season sailed to harry in Norway. But others would take land, and there was not much good land left to take. So there was brawling between the newcomers and those who had settled there before them. Yet the manslaying was not much between so many men, for it seemed to most that the greatest gain was to be got by harrying in King Harald's realm, and the newcomers were sturdy men who would bring great help to that. There was more thought of viking than of land-settling among those then in Orkney.

But Thorlief Coalbiter would have nothing to do with King Harald's enemies, nor took as guests any who had fled from Hafursfjord. Neither at Ness nor at Ragnarshall could they find hospitality. Ottar Bui's son lived at Ragnarshall with Mord the grieve, and had men well-armed with him to guard it against the Easterlings. And at Ness Skallagrim and Kol went always armed, and there were housecarles and sturdy thralls made ready to fight if need be.

Skallagrim was not altogether of the same mind as Thorlief, and sometimes said they would do better to throw in their lot with those who meant to go a-viking against Harald. But Thorlief said, 'Let us wait awhile

and you will see something to put you in another
mind. For if Harald is the man I think he is he will not
long suffer his enemies to live untroubled, though they
dwell here in Orkney.'

Skallagrim answered, 'You said there would be much
fighting here this summer, but no one has so far come
to argue with me.'

Thorlief said, 'That is because all men know you are
ready to answer them angrily. It is a good thing to be
so able to fight that none doubts it and no challengers
come to put you to the trouble of proof.'

Signy said little but often muttered angrily as she
went about her work. She did not like to see men living
quietly at home, but thought they should always be
somehow busy with stirring deeds. Yet now she could
not guess which way the cat would jump, and so held
herself from egging them to take one side or the other.
But it went ill with her to keep silent.

Hoskuld of Aikerness talked often with Rani his
guest. He was not much pleased to have him there, but
he hid that feeling and spoke fairly to Rani, for Rani
was a man of note, strong in battle, and his crew were
many and well armed. It cost Hoskuld much to keep
them, but it seemed to him that Rani could be brought
to do something that was beyond his own power, and
that was to hurt Thorlief of Ness. For Hoskuld still
nursed a grudge against him and his sons.

There came a time when Hoskuld said, 'I count that
day a good one when you came here, Rani, for I find
pleasure in talking to such a man as you, and all say
that my honour is much increased by having you as my
guest. Yet often this comes into my mind, that you
cannot feel very comfortable here at Aikerness, for my
hall is hardly so great as those you are used to, and I
am not able to entertain you according to the style you
kept in Thelmark.'

Rani said, 'A landless man cannot pick and choose,

and I think you have done all you can to look after my comfort.'

'That may be true,' said Hoskuld, 'yet I would gladly see you in some place that went better with your fame. There is a hall called Ragnarshall beside the Bay of Firth, not many miles from here, that would suit you very well.'

'That hall is Thorlief Coalbiter's,' said Rani, 'and he has men well able to keep it for him.'

'Yet there are good men in your crew,' said Hoskuld. 'Moreover Kalf Skeggison in Birsay has for his guest Ospak the Red, who also fought at Hafursfjord, and all Ospak's men are quartered there. Now I do not think that Kalf has meat and meal to keep Ospak's men all winter, for his land is nowise so good as mine, and what I have is hardly enough to entertain you in a fitting manner. And your men are no more in number than Ospak's. So it seems that Ospak will soon be looking for another home. Now what I think is this, that you should join forces with Ospak and take Ragnarshall for your own, where there will be plenty for all, and you can spend the winter in comfort.'

'There is something to be said for such a plan,' said Rani.

Hoskuld said, 'It would be well, then, if we went to Kalf Skeggison's and talked with Ospak to see what he says on the matter.'

'What need is there for hurry?' said Rani. 'Let us think for ourselves before we ask others their thoughts.'

But Hoskuld said, 'If we dally here Ospak will have other plans made, he will have gone elsewhere, or some who are swifter than we are to make up their minds will have fallen on Ragnarshall and taken it for themselves. For it is a good place and many think greedily of it.'

So Hoskuld had his way, and they rode to Kalf Skeggison's. Then they made a plan together, that Rani

should take his ship and go by sea to Firth Bay. But
Ospak would find horses for himself and his men and
ride to Ragnarshall, and come upon it from the hill
side. Then Rani asked Hoskuld if he would come with
them and help. But Hoskuld said he could not do that,
for he lived too near Ness and it would be easy for
Thorlief to take vengeance for anything he did against
him. He said they must swear to tell no one that he
knew of this plan or had done anything to further it,
for it would not go easily with him if that became
known.

Rani and Ospak the Red said they would tell no one.
But Kalf Skeggison said, 'I find it hard to keep tidings
of any sort to myself. Yet I shall do my best, Hoskuld,
to say nothing of this, for indeed you might be in some
danger if Skallagrim came to hear of it, or Kol Cock-
crow.'

Three days after that, those at Ness saw the men go
aboard Rani's ship. It was a white day, there was
neither sun nor wind, and they rowed swiftly. There
were about sixty men in the ship.

Thorlief stared hard at the ship and said nothing. But
between the others there was great talk and argument
about where Rani might be going.

Not that night, but in the middle of the next night,
Ottar Bui's son came to Ness in a small boat, and four
men with him. They were all wounded. They told what
had happened at Ragnarshall. They had seen Rani's ship
come into the bay and guessed he had come for no
good purpose. They had armed themselves, all the men
who were there, and waited outside the hall till Rani
should come to them. When Rani came they had some
talk, and Rani said plainly he had come to fight for the
hall, as he needed a house to live in through the winter.
Then Ottar's men took bows and shot some arrows,
and killed two of the Easterlings. After that the
Easterlings fled downhill to their ship, and Rani did

nothing to stop them. So Ottar's men followed and came at the Easterlings on the shore, and fought with them by the ship. But now other men came riding over the hill, and these were Ospak the Red and his company. Ottar saw that nothing could be done against so many, and bade his men look to themselves and flee while there was yet time. But Mord the grieve and many others were killed. Of those who escaped most fled along the shore and some hid themselves in rock-pools where the seaweed grew thick and covered them. Ottar lay in a tangle of ware till night fell. Then he came out, wet and stiff because of a wound in his thigh, and found the other four. They took a small boat then, and so came home to Ness.

Now Skallagrim cried out and said they must arm themselves and go straightway to Ragnarshall and fall upon those who were there. Kol took an axe from the wall and a helmet, and men ran quickly to fetch their weapons. There was a great stir in Ness, and all were eager to make no talk about it but to go then and there to take their revenge on Rani and Ospak the Red.

Skallagrim said, 'I do not think they will live long in Ragnarshall, or die far from it.'

Then Thorlief said, and his voice was louder than its wont, 'Put down your axes. Your hands are sweaty with heat, and your grip on them is too loose to work much harm on those who are many in numbers and can make plans before they fight. There will be no running against them in the darkness, nor in daylight either, but we shall stay here and look to ourselves and what we have got here, and wait awhile till we see what comes to pass. For the tide turns, and it is easier to row with it than against it.'

Then Skallagrim grew angry and said he had been put

Eynhallow and Rousay

off before but now he thought there was no case to be
made for sitting still.

'Nor is it the time to talk and think of next year,'
said Kol, 'But this is the season for doing something.'

Thorlief said, 'We shall do nothing against Rani and
Ospak the Red till a better season comes than this one.'

'When Starkad the Viking lighted on us you dealt
properly with three or four of his men,' said Signy.
'Has your strength gone from you, that you cannot do
to Rani what you did to Glum?'

'I saw greater need for stirring myself then than I do
now,' said Thorlief.

'Must you wait till men come into your house and sit
down on the benches before you rise to deal with
them?' said Skallagrim.

Thorlief said, 'Men might come fast enough into my
house if you took everyone who is here to fight at
Ragnarshall. For Rani, before he went there, lived with
Hoskuld of Aikerness. Hoskuld is no friend of ours. I
think it was Hoskuld who put into Rani's mind the
thought to take Ragnarshall from me. And if Hoskuld
saw Ness lying naked, with all its men fighting
elsewhere, Hoskuld would not be ill-pleased at such a
chance to do some mischief against me.'

'Then let us go to Hoskuld first,' said Kol. 'I think
his house would burn as well as another's.'

Skallagrim said in a surly way, 'Hoskuld or Rani or
Ospak, I care not which comes first. But some of that
sort I will deal hardily with before long.'

'The proper time will come,' said Thorlief. 'Let us
wait till then.'

There was much grumbling at Thorlief's words, but
he would not be moved, and nothing was done against
Rani and Ospak, nor against Hoskuld. Men thought it
strange that so great a household should sit quiet and
take no steps to bring the Easterlings to account for
their robbery and man-slaying, and some said that Kol

and Skallagrim could not be the men they were held to be. Neither Kol nor Skallagrim would much talk to those about them, and spoke nothing to any strangers who came there.

XXI

It was then about harvest time. Before winter came news was brought that King Harald lay in Shetland and fought with the vikings there, and ever had the better of it, so that there were like to be no vikings left when he had worked his will upon the islands. When the Orkney vikings heard that they marvelled, for to few had it seemed that Harald would come to seek them out, and none had thought he would sail oversea now when the winter nights were falling. There was much stir and talk among them, and those in the West Mainland and the north isles said that Rani and Ospak the Red should be their leaders, and they would fight under their banners against King Harald. Then Rani and Ospak sent word speedily that all who had fought against Harald before, and were nowise minded now that he should rule over Orkney as he ruled in Norway, should come with their men to that neck of land between the West Mainland and the East Mainland, and there they would fight with him.

Many listened to the word and came with their men, and their ships lay in Scapa Bay, and some in the outer bay north of the neck of land. But some of the bonders did not come, and said they had no quarrel with Harald and cared not who ruled the islands so long as they were left in peace. Hoskuld of Aikerness was one of these. He said he had lived quietly with his neighbours all his life, and as he had done no man wrong he saw no cause why Harald should do wrong to him.

When Thorlief heard that Harald was in Shetland he said, 'The time grows ripe. This is the time I waited for, and I would have been content to wait longer that this. Now we shall make ready to greet Harald, and we shall become his men. These others can neither stand against him nor live at peace among themselves. But Harald is a wise and mighty king. He will settle things here well, and it may be I shall find some quiet again under his rule.'

Skallagrim said he was not inclined to be anyone's man, but all turned against him and said that Thorlief had spoken well and shown himself to have been wise from the beginning.

Then Skallagrim said, 'I may as well agree with you in this, for it seems that Harald is not the man to hang back from fighting, and perhaps I will get what I want under his banner.'

'See that you get back Ragnarshall from the thieves who have taken it,' said Signy.

'I make no doubt of that,' said Thorlief.

Then Thorlief bade Skallagrim make ready his long-ship, for the Skua had lain all summer in its shed, and Skallagrim did that gladly. Thorlief armed his house-carles and certain bonders' sons also. He sent for Gilli and his men. Then they had a fitting crew for the Skua. But Ottar was to stay in Ness with some few men, and guard it if need be. 'But I do not think there will be any danger now,' said Thorlief. 'Sparrow-hawks do little hunting when the eagle is aloft.'

While they were busy with the Skua Gauk came down from Calfskin, and his dog Bran with him. He had a thick leather coat, and on his head was a very old rusty helmet. He had a shield and a long sword at his side.

He said to Kol, 'Now I have come to join you as I said I would when fitting occasion arose, for such men as we do not lightly go into battle, or for a little cause.

Nor, being in, do we come thence lightly. And I have brought Bran my dog, who will bark well if there comes a sudden onset by night, though there is another reason than that why I brought him. For he has never been used with children, and when my wife puts down the bairn from her breast Bran is like to tear him. So we thought it best he should come with me, where there will be no sucklings to worry him. He is a good dog and bites shrewdly.'

Skallagrim was not very willing that Gauk should go in the Skua, but Kol spoke for him and said he was a likelier man than some they had.

He said to Gauk, 'That is a long sword you have. You will do mischief with that.'

'It has done mischief before now,' said Gauk. 'It was my father's sword, and it is called Leg-biter. It was always too long for him, for he was a littler man than I am, and often when he carried it in his belt it would go between his legs and trip him. His legs were cut and scarred from ankle to mid-thigh, and all by his own sword, for he never fought anyone else. It is a good blade, and I fear now it will be the bane of many.'

'It is well that you are on our side,' said Kol.

Then they launched the Skua and rowed past the Green Holms to the south end of Eday, where they might see King Harald coming from Shetland, and lay there under a ness. Thorlief was grown rather stout, and no byrnie would go on him. His helmet sat somewhat uncomfortably on his head, and his face was white beneath it, for he still went little out of doors.

Presently they saw King Harald's ships, and there were near fifty of them. They were great ships. Shields hung on the gunwales and on the prows were dragons' heads. The wind was behind them and their sails were white and red. Thorlief bade row into the middle of the sound to meet them. When they came near, those on the king's ship let down their sail. There were many

men on that ship, all men of might and famous in
battle. The king's berserks stood by the mast. They
wore wolfskin coats and looked marvellously grim.

Then Thorlief greeted King Harald.

The king said to Earl Rognvald the Wise, who stood
by him on the poop, 'Who is that fat man with a face
as white as curds?'

Earl Rognvald answered, 'I cannot tell, but it seems
to me that he has the look of a prudent man, and those
in his ship are well armed.'

Then the king bade Thorlief come aboard, and asked
who he was and what was his errand.

Thorlief said, 'I am Thorlief, son, Ragnar Hairybreeks, and I live here in Rousay. I have come, I and
my sons, to be your men and to do what you will us to
do in Orkney.'

The king said, 'In his time there were few men so
famous as Ragnar.' Then he said, 'That is a good ship
you have there, but I think I have seen it before.'

Thorlief said, 'That may well be, for it was Starkad
the Viking's ship, who was no friend of yours. Starkad
came here and fought with me. Kol, my son, slew
Starkad, and Skallagrim, my son, took his ship from
those among his crew who were left after the fight at
Ness. You had an enemy the less because of the deeds
we did there, Harald.'

But Harald said, 'Yet I have friends with me here
who can deal with all my enemies, and I have no need
of friends I do not know.'

'You will be none the worse of our help,' said Kol.
'It may bring you a day nearer to that harvesting of
your hair men say you are eager for.'

And Skallagrim said, 'There are those among your
enemies who are my enemies also, and I am not
inclined to let you have the slaying of them alone.'

Then the king laughed and said he had room among
his friends for such men as they seemed to be. And he

bade them go back to their ship and sail beside him. Then the whole fleet hoisted sail again and drew into the bay.

Thorlief told the king that the vikings had gathered to give him battle, and the king sent men ashore to get what news they could. But he and the rest of those who were with him let fall their anchors and stayed all night in the ships. In the morning the men came back and said that Rani and Ospak the Red were over against Scapa Bay, and many ships were in the bay, some drawn up on the sand and some anchored not far off.

Then Harald took his men ashore and marched over the neck of land to Scapa. Rani and Ospak had drawn up their battle a little way in front of the bay. There was flat ground there, and the sea was behind them. Harald ordered his line and set his berserks in the middle of it, and his own banner there with them. And he said that Kol and Skallagrim should fight beside him, for he would like to see if their deeds were as bold as their words. But Thorlief did not come into the battle.

There were berserks on either side of Kol. He looked at them and said, 'Even a deaf man might guess there was something toward.' For the berserks were biting their shield-rims and howling.

Then the battle was joined. It was a loose battle, for the king's berserks broke the vikings' line, and they scattered and fought in groups here and there. Rani's men and Ospak's did well and there was hard fighting where they were. King Harald said to Kol and Skallagrim, 'Let me see now what you are fit for.' So the brothers went there where Rani was and thrust their way to him. Kol slew a man. Skallagrim said to Rani, 'Did you sleep well in Ragnarshall, Rani?'

Rani said, 'No, for the beds were lousy.'

'A bird will find its own nest,' said Skallagrim. 'It seems you chose the pigsty to sleep in.'

Then he thrust strongly at Rani, and Rani took that

on his shield, and hewed at Skallagrim. They fought
fiercely and threw away their shields, for they were cut
to pieces. Rani took his sword in both hands and swung
at Skallagrim about the height of his knees. Skallagrim
leapt nimbly and the sword went under him. Then he
hewed at Rani and the blow fell on his right shoulder,
for Rani was a little turned away, and cut far into his
chest. And that was the Easterling's death.

Kol said, 'Now let us see where Ospak is.'

Skallagrim said, 'The weather grows warm again.' So
they put off their byrnies and went forward in their
shirts. But when they came where Ospak had been he
was dead already. Some of the vikings had fled to their
ships, so they followed and fought with them on the
beach. Gauk kept always close behind Kol and said he
would guard his back. Kol fought with two men and
killed one. The other thrust at him with a spear,
somewhat from the side, but Kol stood away from that.
Then Gauk came from behind Kol and cut off the
man's arm.

'Leg-biter did something there,' he said.

Ivar, Earl Rognavald's son, was killed by a spear in a
fight that grew near to one of the ships. Many grieved
to hear that, for he was the most promising of men.

It was dark before the battle was over, for it scattered
far and wide, and Harald bade that none should be let
go who might be taken. But some escaped, for the
king's men, coming newly from their ships, were not
very fleet of foot. There were some prisoners, but not
many. Kol saw a man he knew, who was a prisoner.
This was Kalf Skeggison, who had taken Ospak the Red
as his guest, and he was wounded. He called loudly to
Kol, and they spoke together.

Kalf said, 'I have always found it hard to keep things
to myself, and I should not like to die without telling
some last piece of news.'

'What news is that?' said Kol.

'There were some who should have come to fight along with us here,' said Kalf, 'but chose rather to stay at home. And one such, whom you know, is Hoskuld of Aikerness. For Hoskuld was Rani's kinsman, and it was he who egged on Rani and Ospak to take Ragnarshall for themselves.'

'That we had guessed, but did not know certainly,' said Kol.

'There are other things I could tell you,' said Kalf, 'but a kind of weakness is coming over me. It is a pity that a man should die who is still full of news.'

'A pity indeed,' said Kol, 'but what you have told will be of some use.'

Harald and his men rested that night and slept in their tents. But when daylight came the king divided his force and sent some in ships to the outer isles, some to the north and some to the south, and others he bade take horses and ride through the Mainland. And where they found open enemies they should kill them. But all others they should warn, and bid all householders attend a Thing that was set for a certain day.

XXII

Kol went with that band that rode through the West Mainland. On the third day they came to a farmstead called Overabist, and that was not very far from where Hoskuld lived. Harald's men said they would stay the night at Overabist. But Kol said that he had an errand of his own that he must do, and he took Gauk with him and rode on. But they tied the dog Bran to a bench and left him in the house, for Kol said that barking would not help them this night, and as for biting he thought they could do what was needed themselves.

It was midnight when they came to Aikerness. It was

very dark and there was a hard frost. They left their horses a little distance off and went forward on foot. There was a turf dyke to the north side of the house, and some low bushes grew in the shelter of it. They stood there and Kol said what he was minded to do. Now they heard a noise behind them, and Gauk said, 'There is someone hiding in the bushes.' He took his sword Leg-biter and thrust with it into the midst of them.

Kol said, 'How many did you kill with that stroke?'

But Gauk said, 'It is dark and I cannot see. Nevertheless my sword went through something, though it did not feel like a man.'

Then they heard the noise again, as though some one were creeping through the bushes and making the branches rustle. Gauk thrust swiftly here and there, and cut downwards when the noise did not stop.

'I think there is more than one,' he said, 'but they are too nimble for me to get at them.'

Kol groped with his hands among the bushes, and found something. He picked it up and held it close to his eyes. Then he laughed and said, 'It is Hoskuld's shirts you have been slaying. They are frozen stiff. It was the wind moving the bushes under them that made the noise, and now they are cut into ribbons.'

'It were better had Hoskuld been inside them,' said Gauk. 'Yet Leg-biter did what it could.'

Then they went to the door of the house and Kol beat upon it. A man came to the door and asked what they wanted.

'We have come to see Hoskuld,' said Kol. 'Light torches and bid him get up.'

The man blinked and peered into the darkness. He could not see who they were. He said it was late in the night to come visiting.

'Hurry, and do what I tell you,' said Kol, 'or it will be the worse for you.'

Kol and Gauk stood in the porch. Presently Hoskuld came to the inner door, and had his axe with him. There was some light behind him, but it was dark in the porch and he asked who were there and what they wanted.

Kol told him. He said, 'Gauk has been fighting with some of your shirts and we have come to see what atonement you will ask for them.'

He threw the shirts in to Hoskuld and they were all cut and rent.

Hoskuld said he could not see why they had done that.

Kol said, 'As things were, indeed, it served no purpose. But many people would be pleased had you been inside the shirt when Leg-biter went through it.'

Then Hoskuld swung his axe and struck hard at Kol, but could not see him very well because of the darkness. Kol moved backwards. The axe missed him and stuck fast in the door-post, and before Hoskuld could pull it free Kol gave him his death-stroke.

Kol went into the hall with Gauk at his back. The men had risen from their beds and were taking weapons. But they were still in some confusion.

Kol told them he had killed Hoskuld. 'And that was because he was my enemy and also King Harald's. Now Harald's men are round about the house and ready to bring fire to it and burn all within if you do not straightway do what I say. And that is to swear you will become King Harald's men, and do according to his laws and live under his ruling.'

All swore that readily. But some of the women, seeing Hoskuld where he lay dead, began to wail and mourn him loudly. Kol spoke with some of them, but Gauk bade him leave them alone: 'For the more you speak the faster they will weep,' he said. 'Kindness draws out their tears as the moon does tides. Let us leave them alone and before long they will forget whom they are mourning. For Hoskuld was not a very good man.'

Kol and Gauk rode back to Overabist, and when they came there Kol told what had happened. The other men said he had worked quickly and done well. They asked him what he would have done had Hoskuld's people not believed him when he said that Harald's men were round about the house.

Kol answered, 'A man can always tell lies at night.'

XXIII

All men went in good time to the Thing where they had been summoned by King Harald. Earl Rognvald of the Mere stood by the king, and Thorlief Coalbiter next to him. The king said that those who had been killed in battle had been his enemies, and those who had fled from it and escaped were his outlaws. But with those who had become his men he would live in peace, and they should pay scat and dues for their land according to its worth. For the men who had been killed while fighting for him full atonement must be paid, and that should be taken from the goods of those who had fled from Norway and become vikings, and from the Orkney-men who had sided with them. And to Earl Rognvald, because Ivar his son had been killed, should be given the earldom over Orkney and to him must all men pay their scat. And now if any were in doubt about what rights they had, or laid claim to any land, they should bring witnesses and put their case before the earl. And what land was untaken should also be made known to him.

It was a long time before these matters were settled. The Thing lasted three weeks, and then there were some who went from it unsatisfied. But Earl Rognvald was wise in his dealings with men, and Thorlief did much to help him. The king made certain grants to those who had come to his aid. To Thorlief he gave back Ragnarshall and all its lands, and Hoskuld's farm at Aikerness also. For these he must pay scat, but for Ness he need pay nothing. To Kol and Skallagrim the king gave good gifts, an spear set in gold and a rich helmet to Skallagrim, and to Kol a sword with much gold about the hilt and a full suit of clothes of scarlet cloth.

Harald found a good house for himself in Orphir. A hill called the Ward Hill was behind it, and to the front of it lay Scapa Flow. There the king stayed all winter and had many men with him. He kept Yule there, and that was a great feast. Kol and Skallagrim were with him all this time, and the king held them in much honour. But Thorlief went home to Ness and lived there.

There was a man called Erling Gleam. He was one of the king's forecastle-men. He was young in years but already of the greatest fame, mighty in the use of all weapons but light-hearted and not quarrelsome. Kol and Skallagrim were much in his company and they were close friends. Those three were accounted the most promising of men.

When spring came and the nights grew longer Harald said it was time to fare south into the South Isles, for there were vikings there also whom he was determined to destroy. So his fleet was made ready and they sailed together out of Scapa Flow. They sailed through Hoy Sound and across the Pictland Firth, and had a fair wind. Then they came into Scotland's firths.

Skallagrim sailed in his own ship, the Skua, and the king gave him a crew. But Kol became one of the king's forecastle-men and ate in the same mess with Erling.

Then the king harried in all the South Isles and

fought with the vikings there and had everywhere the
victory. He took much goods and had great strand-
slaughterings. He went south to Man, but the people
there had heard of King Harald and how none could
withstand him, and fled before he came. Some fled to
England and some into Ireland, and they flitted all their
goods with them. So when the king came to Man the
island was bare of both men and goods and he got
nothing there.

After that the king sailed north and came to Orkney
some weeks before harvest. And now he would go east
again to Norway, for besides that there were other
matters there he must see to, it was now time he said,
that he was shaved and shorn. For he had won sole rule
both in Norway and the islands west over sea, and all
his enemies were destroyed. But he would not cut his
hair till he came home to Norway, and there Gyda
should cut it for him.

Earl Rognvald of the Mere said he would go with
King Harald and give up his earldom in Orkney. He
had a brother whose name was Sigurd. Earl Rognvald
said he would give his Orkney earldom to Sigurd, and
the king said they could arrange that matter as they
liked. So King Harald made Sigurd Earl of Orkney
insted of Earl Rognvald.

Then the king made ready his ships and went aboard.
He gave many good gifts to his friends. He gave Kol a
long-ship of twenty benches, and to Skallagrim he gave
a gold ring of great price and a silk mantle richly
emboidered. Erling Gleam said he did not care about
going back to Norway but would rather stay some time
in Orkney. Harald was not very well pleased with that,
but nevertheless he said that Erling could do as he
pleased, and to him also he gave a long-ship, like in size
to that he had given Kol.

Then the king set sail, and a great host with him.
And Earl Sigurd ruled in Orkney.

XXIV

Earl Sigurd took the house that Harald had found in Orphir and dwelt there. He was a strong man, very brisk and stirring in his ways, and a great warrior. He was a restless man and stayed little at home. He treated his friends well when he was in a good mood, but he was not very trustworthy. He would often look hard at a man, and turn surly because he thought the man was lying to him.

Skallagrim and Kol and Erling Gleam were all in his bodyguard and had the greatest of honour from him.

Earl Sigurd made ready ten ships and went south to Dublin. Olaf the White was king there, and his queen was Aud the Deep-minded. Their son was Thorstein the Red. He also was a restless man, not willing to stay much at home, but rather taking his pleasure in fighting and going abroad. He got on well with Earl Sigurd and they talked much together. It was said that Thorstein had never been so friendly with any man as he was with Earl Sigurd.

The upshot of their talking was this, that they should join together and make war in Scotland. So Earl Sigurd went home before winter and the next year Thorstein came north with a large force, and Sigurd was ready with many ships and a great company of men. Then they fared into Scotland and fought three battles there, and had the better of it in all of them. They took Caithness and Sutherland for themselves and held all the land as far south as the river Oikel. They built a burg there and held it against the Scots.

Kol and Skallagrim got much praise for the part they took in those wars. They were always there where the fighting was hardest, and few could stand against them. They were well matched in strength and skill, and none could truly say which was the better man. But this difference was noticed between them, that Skallagrim

fought with bitterness and would throw off his byrnie
because he could not come quickly enough to his
enemies. But Kol took things more easily, and yet
fought as well, and often laughed loudly in the press of
battle as he put by a spear-thrust or held his shield
against fierce hewing.

But there came a time when Kol was laughed at and
made a mock of. Earl Sigurd was in the burg they had
built on Oikel-bank, and the Scots were gathering to
attack them. But Thorstein the Red was in another part
of the country, west from there in the mountains. And
Sigurd thought it best that he should come and help
them against the Scots, for they had got together a great
force. So he sent out a small party to find Thorstein,
and bade them ride hard both night and day. There was
a full moon at that time, so darkness would not hinder
them. Kol and Erling Gleam were in command over the
party.

They rode that day and part of the night, and came
into a narrow glen. It was dark then, for the sky was
cloudy. So they halted awhile to rest their horses and
wait till the moon came out again. But while they were
resting a band of Scots fell suddenly on them, for they
had ceen the Orkneymen riding and come swiftly over
the hill to waylay them. The Scots were all marvellously
fleet of foot, and ran through the heather quicker than
horses could go upon the road. And now they whooped
suddenly in the darkness and rushed upon the
Orkneymen, and the Orkneymen were surprised and
hard put to it to defend themselves.

But then the moon came from behind the clouds and
there was a bright clear light in the glen. At that the
Orkneymen did better, and made a ring and faced
outwards, and held off the Scots. But when the moon
shone upon him Kol was afraid. That fear came upon
him that he had felt when Geira, Gauk's wife, stared at
him before he killed her, and the moonlight dazzled

him as the moon shining in the troll-wife's eyes had dazzled him. He remembered the ill-wish she had spoken, that there would be no luck for him in that light and that the fear he felt then would be greater in time to come. So now his spirit failed him, and he fell on the ground and pulled his cloak over his head, and hid beneath his shield.

The Orkneymen looked over their shoulders and called to him to come and help. But Kol did not answer. Then they mocked him and shouted scornfully over their shoulders, and turned again to fight with the Scots. But Kol lay on the ground and shook beneath his shield.

Presently the Scots were beaten off. Kol's fit went from him a little after that, and the Orkneymen rode forward. Kol was somewhat behind them and covered his head with his cloak. He would talk with no one. But when the men spoke jeeringly of him among themselves Erling bade them be quiet, 'For none knows what is in his heart.'

They came to where Thorstein was and he sent men back with them to help Earl Sigurd, and there was a battle at the burg on Oikel-bank. Kol fought bravely there, but he was not so cheerful in fighting as he was wont to be. Yet no one could say that he seemed any whit afraid or shrank from going where the battle was hardest.

For a long while there was talk about his cowardice in the fight in the glen, and many jokes were made about it. But when Sigurd was told he said nothing, nor would Skallagrim speak much on that subject. He said, 'There is a fit that comes upon him,' and most men took that word and spoke no more about it. Kol kept much to himself at that time.

XXV

Earl Sigurd and Thorstein the Red fared north to
Orkney before Yule, and Kol and Erling Gleam went
with them. But Skallagrim stayed in the burg on Oikel-
bank, and he had sufficient force under him to guard it
against the Scots.

Kol said he would like to spend Yule at Ness, and
would have Erling go with him. Sigurd said that could
be as they liked. So Kol and Erling went over to
Rousay and found a good welcome there. They kept
good cheer at Yule and there was no stint of ale, but
great fires were lighted in Thorlief's hall and many
toasts were drunk. There were games in the hall and
every kind of merriment. All said that Erling was the
properest of men. He was comely to look at, stronger
than most, and friendly with everyone. He had a ready
tongue, but did not find fault with anything.

Signy was well pleased with the way that matters
were going, and was seldom heard scolding. She said
that Thorlief had been wiser than she thought, and now
things had turned out as he said they would. And Kol
and Skallagrim were living in a stirring way as she had
wished them to. Yet she was not wholly content, but
two or three times took Kol apart and spoke to him of
her feud against Ivar the Boneless.

She said, 'Now that you and Skallagrim are men of
such fame it would be easy for you to go south into
England and see whether something might not be
done against him. For I shall not live contented nor
die happy unless he is dead before me. You are both
greater men than Ottar, who should by rights take up
the feud. But now Ottar is lame of that wound he
got at Ragnarshall, and I do not think he will ever go
far from Ness again. It is your part and Skallagrim's
to seek out Ivar and kill him. For I suffered much
from him, and many things that you do not know,

and the hatred I feel against him will not be forgotten.'

And another time she said, 'Are you all frightened of Ivar, that you will not go against him? Must I seek him out myself, an old woman, with a bed-stick in my hand, and beat him flat as though he were a knot in the blankets? For I think there is more pith in me than in any of you youngsters.'

But Kol said that always that what must happen would surely come to pass. There was time for everything, and he would make no more promise than that. Yet he often thought of what Signy said, and it seemed likely to him that the time would come when he must go into England and look for Ivar the Boneless.

Now before Yule was over it began to be seen that Erling talked often with Hallgerda, Thorlief's daughter, and sat with her in the hall and spoke closely to her. Hallgerda was the older of Kol's sisters. She was the comeliest of girls, tall and very fair. She spoke well in a soft voice. She was quiet and well-behaved.

One day Erling took Kol aside and spoke to him, and said, 'Always till now it has seemed to me that there were two sides to the matter of taking a wife, one good and the other nowise so good. But now I do not feel like that, but I am wholly of one mind, and that is to have Hallgerda your sister in marriage. And because we have been friends I hope you will speak for me, Kol.'

Kol heard that gladly and said he would be very willing to speak for Erling. He said, 'There has been whispering of this matter already, for we have not been blind while you were sitting in the corners.'

Erling said, 'I may be somewhat deaf, for I heard no whispering. But I am not blinder than you, since I saw very clearly what I wanted, and that as soon as I came into your house. And now go and say what you can for me.'

So Kol went to Thorlief his father and spoke to him as Erling had asked, and praised Erling greatly.

Thorlief said, 'I have nothing to say against Erling, for he seems to be a proper kind of man. But still I do not know much about him.'

Kol said he came of famous stock. His father was a landed man in Raumsdale and close friends with King Harald.

'So I have heard,' said Thorlief, 'but Raumsdale is not very near at hand.'

Kol said that Erling was the noblest of men and a good match for any woman in Orkney.

But Thorlief said, 'Hallgerda will be heir to more than a little, and I am not inclined to see her wed without giving her a dowry that many would consider a great one.'

Kol answered that Erling was very well off in loose goods, though he had no land.

Then Thorlief said he would talk matters over with Erling, for he would not set himself against that which both Kol and Hallgerda seemed to wish so long as a fair settlement could be made. So he talked with Erling and said he thought well of him but had not wholly made up his mind about Erling's suit. 'For there is this difficulty,' he said, 'that when Hallgerda marries her portion will not be small, and I think it best that her husband should not come empty-handed.'

Erling said in a pleasant way, 'It is a wife I woo, not money.'

'That I had hoped,' said Thorlief. 'Yet many a woman looks more fair when she is well dowered.'

Then Erling said he was not without goods of his own, and he said what he had. Thorlief thought it over, and the upshot was that they came to an agreement about what sums should be paid down by each side. And when they had agreed they shook hands and took witnesses to their agreement.

Then Thorlief betrothed his daughter to Erling Gleam, and it was decided that the bridal feast should

be at Ness a week after harvest. For when spring came
Erling must go on warfare again with the earl in
Scotland.

Not long after that Erling and Kol went from Ness
and rode back to Orphir, where Earl Sigurd was. And
the earl greeted them gladly and gave them a good
welcome.

XXVI

Thorstein the Red was still with Earl Sigurd, and
when the nights grew longer they made ready to go
south into Scotland again. They took a great force,
leaving few men in Orkney, and crossed the Pictland
Firth with a north-west wind. They rode through
Caithness and found things quiet there. But they came
to the burg at Oikel-bank where Skallagrim was there
was a different tale. For Skallagrim said he had been
plagued all winter by the Scots.

There was a Scots earl whose name was Melbricta.
He was called Melbricta Tusk, because he had a buck-
tooth, very big and ugly, that stuck out from his mouth
on one side and he could not close his lips over it. Earl
Sigurd had made peace with Melbricta, and the Scots
earl had sworn to do nothing against those men left on
Oikel-bank, nor to interfere with them in any way. But
now Skallagrim said that Melbricta had driven off their
cattle and taken sheep from them, and when Skallagrim
sent out men to look for the cattle the Scots had
waylaid them and shot upon them, and slain two men
with arrows. But when he sent word to Melbricta,
asking why he had not kept the oath which he had
sworn, then Melbricta said he knew nothing of these
matters, and his men had taken none of the Orkneymen's cattle.

Sigurd was nowise glad to hear that, and went straightway with many men there where Melbricta had his house. Melbricta came out and gave him a good greeting, but Sigurd made no answer.

Then Sigurd asked the Scots earl why he had done those things against Skallagrim though he had taken an oath to keep peace with him. And Melbricta laughed and said he had done nothing. He was a tall man, burly in his build, and he spoke with a loud voice. He was very daring and skilled in battle, and ugly to look upon.

Sigurd said, 'The cattle did not stray of themselves.'

'I know nothing about that,' said Melbricta. 'I am not your cow-herd.'

'And those men who were killed did not come to their death without other men taking a hand in it.'

'Unless he dies in the cradle a man has but little chance of coming to a peaceful end,' said Melbricta.

They talked together for some time, but Melbricta spoke only in a flyting way and would give no proper answers to the earl.

Then Sigurd said, 'I do not think we shall come to an agreement about this matter, for you have no good will towards me, and I am not minded to be put off by jeering words.'

Melbricta said nothing to that, and Sigurd stared hard at him, knitting his brows and frowning.

Melbricta said, 'There is always another way when words fail.'

'That has come into my mind also,' said Sigurd.

Then they made an arrangement that on a certain day each would go with forty men to a place they agreed upon, and they would settle their quarrel there. But they should not bring more than forty men, and that was the bargain they made.

Earl Sigurd rode back to Oikel-bank and was somewhat moody. The day came when the quarrel was to be settled, and those forty whom the earl had chosen he made to keep peace with Skallagrim, and now he might break the agreement to bring no more than forty into battle with him.

'That is hard to tell,' said Skallagrim.

Sigurd said, 'It is foolish to trust a man who has once shown himself to be a liar.'

'A man may have lied yesterday and still speak truth to-day,' said Skallagrim.

'If I take not forty but eighty men into battle I shall be forearmed against treachery,' said the earl.

Skallagrim answered, 'That is an ill rede and will bring you no fame. Moreover the Scots will see that you have a greater company, and not wait for you to come at them.'

'I have a plan for that,' said Sigurd.

Then he bade other forty take weapons and make themselves ready. And when the first forty were mounted he said that every one of them should take a man behind him, and they should ride to the battle two on every horse.

But when a man came to mount behind Skallagrim, Skallagrim would not let him, but made his horse rear and strike out with his hooves.

Then the man went to Kol and said he had come to ride behind him. But Kol said, 'I would not sleep two in a bed without choosing my partner, nor will I ride two on a horse unless with someone a great deal more handsome than you are.'

Earl Sigurd was ill-pleased with that, but did not say much about it. They rode away from the burg, and there were two men on every horse except those that Kol and Skallagrim had.

Erling Gleam stayed behind in the burg.

Now they came to the place that had been appointed for the battle, and Melbricta Tusk was there before them. He had forty men with him and no more.

As Sigurd and his men came riding Melbricta looked

long at them and said, 'Now Sigurd has cheated us. I see
four feet of a man on every horse, and so they must be
twice as many as we are.'

Some of those who were with him said it would be
best to ride away while there was still time. But
Melbricta said, 'Rather let us harden our hearts and
make sure of this, that each of us takes a man for
himself before we die.' So the Scots made ready for
battle.

When Earl Sigurd was that he bade those of his men
who were mounted behind the others get down from
their horses, and half should go to one side of the field,
and half to the other. But the forty mounted men
should ride as hard as they could upon Melbricta and
break his array. Then the dismounted men should come
in upon either flank.

So Earl Sigurd rode against Melbricta. But Kol and
Skallagrim would not charge with him, but took their
horses to a side of the field and sat on them there and
watched the battle.

There was hard fighting, but it did not last long, for
the Scots were much outnumbered. Many of Earl
Sigurd's men were wounded and some were killed. But
of Melbricta's men not one was left alive. Earl Sigurd
had their heads cut off and tied to his horses' saddles as
a sign of triumph, and Melbricta's head was tied to his
own saddle.

Skallagrim and Kol rode slowly to him while his men
were busy with this matter. Skallagrim said, 'Melbricta
fought well for a man who was such a liar.'

Sigurd was angry at that, and asked why they had
done nothing to help. 'Has it come to this,' he said,
'that now you will sit like crows and wait till the battle
is over before you come near?'

Kol said, 'It seemed to us that you had plenty and
more than plenty to do what you came to do.'

Sigurd said, 'Once before this you lay flat on the

ground while there was fighting to be done, and when
you were called a coward for that I did not hear it. But
now it seems indeed that you are not so fain of fighting
as you used to be.'

Kol grew red with wrath when he heard that, yet he
answered nothing. But Skallagrim said, 'It is true that I
am somewhat tired of fighting for other men, and after
this, I think, I shall fight in my own cause or not at
all.'

Sigurd said, 'I have an answer for that, but it can wait
awhile without spoiling.'

Then he bade his men ride back to Oikel-bank. He
was in no good mood, and spurred hard, and rode at a
gallop. Melbricta's head hung from his crupper and
swung to and fro. Sigurd spurred again and struck his
calf against the great buck-tooth, and grazed his calf and
broke the skin of it.

They came back to the burg and sat down there and
drank much ale for the victory they had won. But Kol
and Skallagrim took no share in the feasting and kept
apart from Earl Sigurd.

In a little while the wound in his calf grew hot and
painful, and his leg was swollen. That grew worse and
the earl lay in a fever, and nothing that was done would
help him. His leg began to mortify and was green to
the knee, and a foul smell came from it. Then the
mortification spread upwards and came far into the
thigh, and when it was a hand's breadth from the groin
Earl Sigurd died of it.

Then he was buried there not far from the burg, and
a howe was cast upon him by Oikel-bank.

Thorstein the Red asked the Orkneymen if they
would stay with him and hold what they had won
against the Scots. But the Orkneymen said no, for they
would rather go home and see how matters might fall
out there. So they gathered their goods and rode
northwards, and came to their ships. Thorstein stayed

where he was and had the Dublin men still with him.
But all the others went home to Orkney.

Then Guthorm, Sigurd's son, became earl, and he
was a quiet man and took no pleasure in war. He was
weak in his body and often ailing. Kol and Skallagrim
thought there was nothing to be gained by being in his
bodyguard, so they went home to Ness. And Erling
Gleam went with them.

XXVII

It was then harvest time, and after that preparations
were made for the wedding of Erling and Hallgerda.
Many guests were invited, and all the men in Orkney
who were of the greatest mark came to Ness.

There was a man called Thorkel Neb. He was a
wealthy man and lived over by Hamla Voe. He had
been long in Orkney and was well known to Thorlief.
When King Harald sailed west over sea Thorkel had
been one of those who became his men. His wife's
name was Bergliot, and she was a brisk managing kind
of woman. Her tongue was sharp and there were often
high words between her and Thorkel. They were both
invited to the wedding.

Signy asked Bergliot if she would help look after the
guests, and Bergliot said she would do that blithely, for
she hated to sit idle when there was work about. Then
Signy and Bergliot carried water to the guests, and
towels, and let them wash their hands. When Bergliot
came to Thorkel her husband he dried his hands in the
middle of the towel. Bergliot snatched it from him and
said, 'The edge is good enough for you, leave the
middle dry for others.'

Thorkel said, 'There was a gangrel woman came to
the house one day and asked if Bergliot had not a pair

of old shoes to give her. Bergliot found her the shoes, but took the laces out first, because they had been newly put in.'

Thorlief Coalbiter sat in the middle of one bench, with Ottar and Skallagrim on either side. Gilli the Chapman sat next to Ottar, and inward from him were many men of mark. Outwards from Skallagrim was Einar, Thorlief's youngest son. He was still small and weak in his body, and no one paid much attention to him. Then came other of Thorlief's neighbours, and Gauk of Calfskin sat at the end of that bench.

Erling Gleam sat in the middle of the bench over against Thorlief, and had Earl Guthorm at one side, with many of the Earl's men inwards from him. Kol sat on his other side, and those next to him were men who had fought with Earl Sigurd in Scotland.

Hallgerda sat on the cross-bench with all the women about her. She wore the finest of clothes and sat there very quietly.

Now meat was put on the table, and Signy and Bergliot bore ale to the guests. There was great feasting and much merriment.

Signy behaved well and was lavish in all entertainment. But she looked somewhat grim, and when she was not talking her lips were pressed tightly together. She said, 'Hallgerda has a better wedding that I ever had, though I have had two, and a third that was something of the same sort.'

Thorkel Neb heard that and said, 'It is not the bride ale but what comes after that makes a woman think well of marriage.'

Bergliot his wife said, 'Must you always be thrusting your long nose into matters that do not concern you? Both the bride ale and what came after might have been better in your case.'

Thorkel got much laughed at for that. He turned to Thorlief and said, 'Now I am minded to put Bergliot

away from me and take another wife, for I have had
enough of her sharp tongue. You still have a daughter
left unwed, Thorlief. Would it not be a good thing if
we had a second marriage now and I also became your
son-in-law?'

But Thorlief said, 'One at a time goes fast enough for
me.'

Thorkel would not be put off, and went to everyone
saying he was tired of Bergliot and would keep her no
more. He kept saying to this man and that, 'You have a
daughter now. How old is she, and is she comely? For
if she is comely I will have her to wife?

And always he was told, 'So-and-so has a daughter
who is far more comely that mine. Go to him and say
what you want, for he will surely be glad to have such
a man as you for a son-in-law.'

So Thorkel went from one to the other, and while he
was questioning them he got somewhat drunk. For all
men plied him with ale.

Many toasts were called, and there was some talk of
what they would do when next spring came. Skallagrim
said, 'I will go on warfare with you, Earl Guthorm,
wherever you like, so long as there is good hope of
fame or profit to be got.'

But the earl said nothing to that, for he was not
minded to go anywhere.

Skallagrim said, 'Then I will go a-viking on my own
account, as I have meant to for some years. And Kol
will come with me, and Erling Gleam.'

Then many others said they would sail with him, and
pledged themselves to him. Thorlief looked at them and
said, 'These are my neighbours whom I know well. But
ale is another man.'

Now presently Gauk of Calfskin went outside and
came to the back of a shed. It was very dark and he
stumbled against a man who lay there on the ground.
He bent down and felt about his face, and knew by the

long nose that it was Thorkel Neb. Then he tried to lift him up and found that he was all wet about the chest.

Gauk wiped his hands on the grass and ran to the hall and cried that vikings had come upon them, for Thorkel Neb lay outside and had been murdered. So there was a great stir and men found their weapons and ran out. Gauk took his sword Leg-biter and went with them. But it was dark and they could not see. Then torches were brought and they found Thorkel where he lay behind the shed. And it was not blood on his chest but spew, for he was dead drunk.

But Gauk was still peering about in corners and thrusting with Leg-biter. For he also was not wholly sober. Then the other men came to him and said what they had found, and laughed at him. But Gauk said, 'It is well to think the worst, for then a man is always ready.'

He went in and spoke to Kol, and said, 'We will go a-viking together when spring comes. I did not fight in the earl's wars in Scotland, for it seems to me that kings and earls have always enough men to fight for them, and I do not like to be one amongst many. But when you and Skallagrim go I shall come with you. Then we shall all be picked men, and we may expect to do well.'

Kol promised that Gauk should go with him when he sailed, and told him to put Leg-biter aside for the present time, since Gauk was carrying it rather carelessly: 'For now there is none but friends here, and it is better that you should go swordless than they be legless.'

Gauk put Leg-biter on the wall, and went back to his bench, and told everyone that he was Kol's greatest friend and that Kol would go nowhere without him, 'For he knows a proper man when he sees one.'

Now Thorkel Neb was brought into the hall, for it was cold outside. But Bergliot would not go near him. She said, 'I have nothing to do with him now, and if he

takes another wife then I will find another man.
Women older than I am have done well for themselves.'

Signy stood by her and said that was true enough:
'For now we know more than we did when our cheeks
were smooth, and knowledge does more than looking.'

But all this while the earl sat quietly, and Thorlief
talked long with him.

The wedding-feast lasted five days and Thorlief got
great fame for his hospitality. Then the guests went
home, and to many of them Thorlief gave góod gifts.

Erling took Hallgerda to that house at Aikerness
where Hoskuld had lived, for Thorlief had given it to
her. But he had made this condition, that Hallgerda was
to manage all money matters, and half of all the goods
they had between them were to be hers.

Erling and Hallgerda loved each other very dearly,
and they lived in great content.

XXVIII

Kol and Skallagrim began to make their plans with
Erling Gleam for the viking voyage they intended. Each
had a good ship, but their difficulty was to find proper
crews. There were men who had fought with them in
Scotland who would go, but Earl Guthorm was not
willing to let too many sail out of Orkney in their
service, and would take no interest in the voyage
himself. Then there were many bonders' sons who
offered to join them, and these were strong and likely
men, but few of them had seen much fighting or been
abroad before.

Thorkel Neb came over from Hamla Voe. He went
much about the country at this time, since he got little
peace at home, where his wife was always talking about
his bad behaviour at the wedding. Thorkel said he

would sail with them and bring so many men. Thorkel was a good man with all weapons and had before this been on warfare both by sea and land.

Kol and Erling thought his offer a good one, and said they would be glad to have him with them. But Skallagrim was not pleased, for he did not think he could get on with Thorkel, and said privately that he would not have him sail in the Skua. There were some others who seemed willing to join them, but Skallagrim was hard to please, and because he did not much welcome their offers they said no more about it.

Because he was still short of men Skallagrim asked his father to help, and let certain of his housecarles go with them, who were hardy men and likely to do well. Thorlief had kept himself apart from all their talk and pretended to know nothing of what was going on.

Now he said that none of his men should sail with them, and he would give them no advice except this, that they would do better to give up all thought of faring abroad and stay at home instead.

Skallagrim said angrily, 'That is always your advice, and I might have known what it would be when I asked you. I have listened to you before now, and done what you wanted, because then there was something to be said for the side you took. But now there is no reason in what you say, and there is nothing to be argued against the voyage except your dislike of such things and your will that all men should think like you and live by the fireside like you.'

'Many a time I have seen arguments, for or against a thing, that you were blind to,' said Thorlief, 'and I have a good reason for saying that none of my men shall sail with you, if you are still of a mind to go when the time comes.'

Now Signy took sides with Skallagrim and asked Thorlief what were his arguments against the voyage, and what his reason was for refusing to help. 'For though you see many things while sitting in the chimney-corner,' she said, 'some of them are trifles that no proper man would bother about.'

Thorlief was slow to answer, but at last he said, 'Earl Guthorm is a weak man both in mind and body. If he dies there will be trouble in Orkney, for vikings will come again, and the bonders will quarrel among themselves. Even though he live there will, I think, be trouble before long. For he is not man enough to rule these people. Therefore we should keep our strength at home, and not waste it abroad, since there may soon be need of it to hold what we have.'

Signy and Skallagrim both answered him with scorn. They said a man would have little sense who stayed at home because he was afraid some other man might die. As to there being unrest while Guthorm still lived, that might well be. 'But what use is there in sitting here and dreading it?' said Skallagrim.

Signy said, 'Bold men have often better luck than timid ones, and I think that Kol and Skallagrim now show good sense and their manhood too in setting out on this voyage. I do not yet know where they mean to go, but since they are eager for fame I think it will be into Northumbria, where an old enemy of ours is still alive. Nowise could they win greater fame than by killing Ivar.'

Skallagrim said she was wrong in that, for they meant to go west of Scotland and then harry in Man and Anglesey. He said, 'That chapman who was here in summer said that Halfdan was now king in Northumbria, and Ivar was with him. We cannot do much against him while things are like that. But from Anglesey and Man we may win something with three ships.'

'You will not have three ships if you are counting on me to give you a crew,' said Thorlief. 'Though you two cannot settle where to go, I have this settled, that my men do not go with you.'

Thorlief would listen to no arguments. Then they went again to Earl Guthorm. But neither would he give them any more men. Kol and Skallagrim and Erling were then in such state that they had three ships, but of good men only enough to make two crews.

Kol said, 'It will be better to sail with two ships only and have all proper men in them, than to have three ships with some weaklings aboard, or men who cannot fully be trusted.'

Skallagrim and Erling thought the same about that, and they planned to take the Skua and Erling's ship, that was called the Scarf, and leave Kol's ship behind.

Erling asked Kol if he would sail with him in the Scarf, and Kol said he was very willing to do that.

But Skallagrim said, 'I will not take Thorkel Neb in the Skua, for I cannot get on with him. Let Kol come with me, for we suit each other better than most, and Thorkel can go with you, Erling.'

Erling did not answer at once. Then he said, 'I would be better pleased to have Kol with me, but since we have had difficulties enough I will say nothing more, and Thorkel shall be my shipmate in the Scarf.'

Both Kol and Skallagrim thanked him for that. Skallagrim said, 'I am not an easy man to deal with. You and Kol I can agree with, and I am not often minded to quarrel with you. But other men tempt me much to go against them, and with many I cannot sit in the same room and be quiet.'

Now there was a great stir at Ness and Aikerness till those ships were made ready. They were new-painted and brought down from their sheds, and all their tackle was seen to. The Skua was a ship of twenty-five benches, the Scarf of twenty. They were both well built and seaworthy. The Skua was much higher in the sides than the Scarf, for Starkad the Viking had built it as much for faring in the open sea as for coastwise voyaging. There were few ships so noble to look at, and

none better to sail in. But the Scarf was also a good
vessel and Erling was well content with it.

Skallagrim saw that all his men were well armed.
They had each man a sword, a shield, and an axe. Many
had byrnies or leather coats so thick and tough they
might turn off a hard stroke. There was also put on
board a store of spears for throwing and thrusting, and
sufficient bows and arrows. Then water and meat were
carried down, stock-fish, fresh beef and salted beef, ale
and hard bread and meal and cheese. Sixty men were to
sail in the Skua, so they had a good store of food. Yet
not a great store, for they could take more when it was
needed from the seaward farms and homesteads in
Scotland's firths.

Gauk came from Calfskin and said that Kol had
promised he should go with them when they sailed. Kol
said there was still room for him.

'And I hope, for my dog Bran,' said Gauk, 'for I
cannot leave him at Calfskin. My wife has another child
and Bran will not bear the sight of it. He growls so
fearfully that all who hear him are frightened, save the
child only, and he takes pleasure in every kind of noise.
But he would get no pleasure from Bran's teeth, and so
the dog must come with me. He behaves well in a ship,
and his coat is clean except for a few fleas. But it is the
nature of a dog to have fleas.'

Skallagrim said, 'It might be easier for all if you and
your dog both stayed ashore, since you cannot be
parted.'

'The truth is this,' said Gauk, 'that I am something
like Bran in that I find little comfort in a house full of
bairns that are for ever wet and yelling to be dried.
They shout well, my children, for they are all healthy.
And so it would suit me to leave them for a while till
they are a little older. I take no interest in wiping them
and watching them suck. Warfare and matters like that
are my proper trade, I think, and if any men are nimble

enough to dodge away from Leg-biter and take to running, why, Bran will be there to bite their heels.'

Kol spoke again for Gauk, and they agreed that he could have the dog with him.

Thorlief sat by the fire and would take no part in the preparations. He spoke once more to Skallagrim, and once to Kol, and asked them to put off their voyage to another year. But they would not.

Thorlief said, 'It has never hurt you to take my advice before. Why do you refuse to listen now?'

Skallagrim said, 'The deepest well goes dry at last.'

'You will think of that again,' said Thorlief, 'when your judgment is seen to be wrong, and mine is proved to have been right.'

'Too long time is spent in all this judgment,' said Skallagrim. 'No man's wit is a match for luck, and if luck goes against us it cannot be helped. But I am willing to risk that, for I am not afraid even of the worst luck. And now, so long as I am able, I shall do what pleases me most.'

Thorlief was silent then.

Kol said, 'Skallagrim is right. For wisdom is not the only thing to be sought. It is better to fight well in a foolish cause than to be so wise you never fight at all.'

Thorlief said no more to them till the day came when they were to sail, and the two ships lay together at Ness. It was still early in the year. Then he said, 'Do not sail to-day, but wait till the weather grows better.'

It was a clear day and cold, the sun was shining, and there was a fair breeze. Skallagrim said, 'I see nothing wrong with weather like this.'

Thorlief said, 'The wind has come from the south-east to north-east. It will go into the north, then towards the west and so against you, and blow to a storm before you lose sight of Hoy.'

Skallagrim said, 'Now you are talking like a Finn wife,' and would not listen to him.

Signy said loudly, 'I wish he speak true and the wind go against you and blow you east, not west, of Scotland, so that you come into England's sea and come to where Ivar is, and so kill him. For Bui my husband is unatoned and there is shame on you all so long as Ivar lives.'

Thorlief bade her be quiet, but Signy turned on him and said fiercely, 'Keep your own tongue still, for what have you to do with men who go upon the cold sea and ply their axes abroad where luck may send them? When did you ever give warm meat to the wolf or set the ravens screaming over carrion? When did you go where swords met the shell-thin edge of a sword? Sit by the fire, Thorlief. But my sons shall walk with bloody brand and whistling spear, and the wound-bird shall follow them into Ivar's hall.'

Skallagrim said shortly, 'We go to Anglesey and Man, and like enough the wound-bird will follow us there. But we do not mean to go into Northumbria nor to look for Ivar.'

Then he told Signy to say no more. But they could not keep her quiet, and when no one would listen she went away by herself and sat on a rock at the sea-shore.

Now Kol and Skallagrim went aboard, and all their men. Thorkel Neb went aboard the Scarf. But Erling Gleam stood by the gang-plank and Hallgerda was with him. She said, 'I cannot come with you farther than this, Erling. But my heart will follow you. I would come much farther if you were faring by land and that green were green grass. But only my heart can go far and fast enough to bear you company at sea.'

Then Erling went aboard and the gang-plank was drawn in. Now both crews took to rowing, and the sea grew white under their oars. But when they came out of the shelter of land they shipped their oars and made sail.

XXIX

The wind was in the north-east. There was calm water in the sound between Eynhallow and Rousay, but when they came from under the lee of Rousay there was a lively sea running. The Scarf lay somewhat astern of the Skua.

All the men were in good spirits and spoke cheerfully about the voyage. With such a wind they would soon cross the Pictland Firth and come to the west side of Scotland. Because of the rising sea Skallagrim bade them take in their shields, that hung outside on the gunwales, and stow them away.

They sailed westwards along the north coast of the Mainland of Orkney, from Costa Head to the Broch of Birsay, and came speedily to the Broch with the wind on their starboard quarter. When they had passed it they altered course to the south-west, and the wind was squarely behind them.

Skallagrim had his crew busy shifting some ballast, for the Skua was rather by the head. The men worked with a will. They were all good men, very sturdy and warlike, and most of them well used to ships. A few of them were young, and this was their first viking cruise, but some were oldish men who had sailed in many seas, far east in the Baltic and south by Spain, harrying there under famous captains. Some had fought in King Harald's wars, and two had sailed with Biorn Ironside, Ragnar Hairybreeks's son.

The Skua was sailing faster than the Scarf, and Erling's ship fell more astern. Skallagrim bade his men take a reef in the sail, that they might not part company.

Now they were farther from the land, and on the larboard side they could see all the west coast of Orkney. It stood like a wall with breaches here and there where the sea had broken down the cliffs and made small bays and geos. It was a bad coast to be wrecked on. It had a friendless look to all except the sea-birds, and they nested on the cliffs in great numbers. There were gulls of all kinds, scarfs and puffins, and eider-ducks, and trimly flying kittiwakes. In some places the cliffs were white with their droppings.

Erling's ship came up and sailed abreast of the Skua. The men shouted to each other across the sea between them, and waved their caps.

It grew more difficult to steer, for the wind was rising and did not blow steadily now, but came in hard gusts and then fell for a little while to a light breeze. The gusts became stronger all the time, and then the ships leapt forward with foam curling before them and hissing along their sides. The masts creaked, the stays stretched taut, and the sails stood out hard and round. And the wind was backing into the north.

There came a long fierce gust, and afterwards for some time a light and pleasant breeze. The sun shone brightly and the farther sea was blue with thin white crests on it. Then another squall came, darkening the sea and flattening the waves. It came swiftly, spreading

like a fan, and struck hard on the ships. And now the
wind came out of the north.

Kol said, 'It seems that Thorlief was right when he
said it was a backing wind.'

But Skallagrim said, 'We shall be over the Firth
before it can back far, and there is plenty of shelter on
the other side.'

The day became darker and the sun was covered. To
the west a brown mass of clouds appeared, growing
larger and reaching into the sky. And now when the
wind slackened there was the faint far-off noise of a
greater wind. But Skallagrim held to his course and
Erling sailed a little distance away, on the weather side
of him.

Kol said, 'I think it were best if we turned and ran in
towards Hoy and took some shelter under the high
land there. For if the wind grows stronger while we are
in the open Firth it may go badly with us.'

Skallagrim rubbed his chin at that, but did not
answer.

Then two or three of the older men on board came
to him and said the same thing, and while they were
disputing they saw Erling wave to them from the Scarf
and point landwards.

'Have it your own way,' said Skallagrim, and
changed his course and stood in towards Hoy.

That is the highest land in Orkney. There are two
hills there, black and rugged, and most often there is
cloud about their tops. On the west side the cliffs come
sheer out of the sea. From the Kame of Hoy to the
Sow they are more than a thousand feet high, and
straight as a wall. Then they fall lower, and the coast
turns in to a bay called Rackwick, and from there runs
south-east. There is no landing-place on that side of
Hoy except Rackwick, nor can a landing be made at
Rackwick when the wind blows strongly from the west.

The ships were well to the west of Hoy and

somewhat south of the high cliffs. They could see into
Rackwick. Now they sailed for the shelter of Hoy and
had the wind on their larboard quarter.

But before they were near land it fell away
altogether, and they tossed about in the sea without
steering-way. A light squall came and filled the sails. It
raced on and left them tossing again. But another came,
stronger than the first, and behind it the sea was all
dark and the wind came steadily and blew gale-strong.
And now the wind had gone farther round and came
from the north-west.

It blew so strongly they could do nothing but run
before it.

'This is a poor course for Man,' said Kol.

Skallagrim said, 'Now we can find no lee under Hoy.
We must run through the Firth and take shelter east of
Scotland.'

Kol said, 'There will be ebb-tide in the Firth.'

'Tide or no tide, that is the way we must go,' said
Skallagrim.

'Erling will fare worse than us,' said Kol. 'He has less
freeboard.'

'Erling must fare as he can,' said Skallagrim, 'for
there is nothing else to do.'

The Scarf fell somewhat astern of the Skua again when
they ran into the Firth and came against the tide. The ebb
runs eastward there and is a strong tide. With the wind
against it there was a heavy sea and the Scarf laboured in
it. Erling set men to bale. The sea rose wildly and the
waves fell in confusion between the wind and the ebb.

Now the gale broke on them in all its strength and
roared about them. The Skua drove before it, beating
the tide, and plunged in the heavy sea. It was not easy
to steer it then. Kol often looked backwards to the
Scarf. There was little comfort in Erling's ship, for the
steep waves broke about them and they shipped a lot of
water. The men there baled steadily.

There are two islands in the Firth called Stroma and Swona. They are small islands, not high, but rocky. At the north end of Stroma and the south end of Swona there are fierce roosts. The roost of Stroma is called the Swelkie, and that of Swona the Tarf. There the tide boils and tumbles in great whirlpools, so that even on a calm day the waves leap up, white-hooded, and in stormy weather no ship can live there. Skallagrim's course lay midway between Swona and Stroma.

The Skua came nearer to the islands, and on the larboard bow the waves of the Tarf rose fiercely and the wind flung the spray from them in a great cloud. But on the starboard bow the Swelkie of Stroma boiled like a giant's cauldron, and it looked as though the sea lifted itself in great ridges and leaped out of huge holes.

Skallagrim had two men with him at the steering oar. They brought the Skua's head round to the north a little, and so ran some while with the wind rather on the quarter, and came safely by the north edge of the Swelkie.

Now the Scarf followed them. But Erling's ship lay deep and laboured in the sea, for though the men baled they could not keep it dry, and it was hard to steer.

They came by the edge of the whirlpool and a curving wave took the ship and twisted it inwards. Another wave caught the stern and flung it high, and the ship was drawn into the roost. The mast broke. The Scarf rose high like a rearing horse, and the sail dragged down one side. It was thrown sideways and fell on its side. The men clung to the thwarts, but some were hurled into the sea. Then a confusion of waves leapt upon it, and broke it and beat it down, and the Swelkie of Stroma sucked the Scarf under, and Erling's crew with it, and drowned them.

Kol saw it sink and gave a great cry, and made as though he would jump into the sea. But Skallagrim caught him by the arm. 'There is time enough to drown,' he said.

'Erling is drowned,' said Kol.
'So may we all be,' said Skallagrim.

XXX

The Skua ran eastwards before the wind and the sea.
When they had come through the Firth the tide carried
them northwards. Then they left the islands far behind.
The sail was reefed to the highest row of reef-points and
showed little more than half its size. So strong was the
wind that the mast would bear no more than that. Yet
they had to carry what sail they could to keep before
the seas that rose high over the stern and hung like
black cliffs above them.

Three men stood at the steering-oar and bent all their
strength on it to keep the Skua before the wind. There
was great danger of broaching. Skallagrim stood by the
steersmen and would not let them look over their
shoulders at the waves that followed them for fear they
should flinch from their great height and the gulfs that
seemed like to swallow them. He shouted to the
steersmen to look straight in front and never turn their
heads.

But Kol sat in the fore-room with his cloak over his
head and mourned for Erling. After some time
Skallagrim came to him and said, 'There are things
more befitting a man than to weep for the death of his
friends.'

'That may well be,' said Kol, 'but now I am in no
mood for wisdom, nor to think what is best. My heart
is full of grief for Erling, and I have no room for any
other thought.' And he would not be comforted.

It grew dark, but the storm did not lessen. They

could see nothing of what lay ahead and little that was behind them, though the broken tops of the waves still showed half-white, and about the stern of the Skua there was white boiling foam that now raced alongside and lipped the gunwales, and now was sucked back and swallowed in the throat of a rearing billow. The wind shrieked in the rigging and howled overhead. Sometimes in the trough of a wave the sail hung flat. Then with a great bang the wind would fill it again, and the Skua reach forward with a lurch.

The men stood here and there, braced against the thwarts, and looked outwards, though they could see nothing. No one slung his hammock. In the baling-place some worked steadily with scoops.

In the middle of the night Kol came to Skallagrim where he stood under the break of the poop. The men at the steering-oar were beside him there. The poop sheltered them, but was no higher than a man's shoulders. Kol looked backwards and in the darkness could still see the half-white ragged edges of the waves that followed them. The sky was quite black. He said nothing, but he and Skallagrim stood there together.

The Skua groaned in its flight, and timbers creaked. With a surging hiss it drove onwards. The wind bellowed as it staggered to the top of a wave, and howled as it lay for a moment in the stillness of their valleys. There were no stars, and Kol could hardly see as far forward as the mast.

Skallagrim stared this way and that, but he was little better than blind in such darkness. He rubbed his eyes, and that did not help.

Now he looked aft over the poop and saw a line of whiteness in the sky. He said, 'The sky is breaking and daylight is coming.'

Kol turned and looked hard at what Skallagrim had seen. It was a narrow whiteness high above them. Kol

took Skallagrim by the shoulder and thrust him to the
steering-oar.

He said, 'We have reached the end of our voyage, I
think, for it is not morning that you see in the sky, but
the white top of a mountainous wave. Our luck will be
no different from Erling's.'

But they took hold of the steering-oar with the other
men who were there. Now for a little space of time a
heavy stillness lay on the Skua, for it was in the lee of
the giant wave and sheltered from the storm. There was
no creaking of timbers nor any noise in the rigging. But
they heard the hiss of the wave coming, and a growling
in the lower waters, and when one man spoke to
another his voice seemed loud as shouting, and what he
said was heard from end to end of the ship.

The wind was out of the sail and it hung limp from
the yard. The wave took the stern of the Skua and
thrust it forward. The sail filled with a bellow of wind
and the ship lurched under it. The men at the steering-
oar heaved on it with all their strength to keep from
broaching, but the weight of the ship came forward
against the pull of the oar and the oar broke. Then the
bow swung round to larboard, and the ship heeled over,
and the sea came in over the lee gunwale.

The body of the wave was under the ship and lifted
it and bore it on its back. But the crest of the wave
broke over the ship and covered it with a stormy
whiteness and filled it to the thwarts. The ship was
thrown high in breaking surf. Then the wave raced on,
darker than the sky, with a grey mane of foam behind
it, and the Skua sank sullenly in the trough.

Hall the Icelander was the name of a man who had
been at the steering-oar. When the oar broke he fell
against the gunwale, and as the ship heeled over and the

Aikerness

wave broke upon them he was carried overboard. The
Skua was water-logged, and a second wave, a small one
followed the great one, half-broke across it as it lay
unmoving. And Hall was washed aboard again. He had
fallen out on the starboard side, and now he came in
upon the larboard.

The ship was full of water. Hall said, 'It is not much
better here than it was out there, but still I am glad to
be with my friends again.'

The sea was a little calmer after the giant wave had
passed, and the wind grew less. Kol had let go the sheet,
and the sail flew loose, cracking like a whip. Skallagrim
fetched another oar and put it in the steering-crotch.
They made fast the sheet. He and Kol got the ship
before the wind again, but it was heavy and sullen with
its weight of water and would scarcely move to the oar.
The other steersmen who had been there when the first
oar broke had fallen so hard they lay stunned.

All hands baled, not only from the baling-place but
from all the rooms between the thwarts. They baled
with helmets and their shoes and whatever they could
find, but the water would not grow less. For the ship
lay so deep that waves constantly broke upon it.

Skallagrim bade Hall the Icelander come and help
him at the steering-oar. Hall was a good seaman, though
surly sometimes and inclined to be quarrelsome. He
said, 'If we can keep afloat till morning we may live to
see our wives again. Heavy weather makes me think
kindly of women, though a fair breeze drives all
thought of them away.'

Skallagrim said, 'Hold this oar and it will keep you
warmer than holding a woman ever did.'

'Indeed it does not lie still for very long,' said Hall.

Kol stood beside them with his shoulders bent. He
shivered when spray flew over him and the spray-drops
beat on his back like hail.

Skallagrim said to him, 'Why do you not help

those who are baling, and do something to save your life?'

But Kol answered, 'What is the use, when the sea pours in like this? We are drowned men, as Erling was drowned.'

'Hallgerda will weep for Erling. There is no need for you to mourn him too,' said Hall.

Kol did not answer, but stood with his head bowed, and shrank from the cold.

Gauk of Calfskin came aft to where they stood, and pulled Bran his dog with him by a thong. Neither seemed very well pleased with their luck, for Bran whimpered and howled, and Gauk leaned on a thwart and retched before he could speak.

Hall, mocking him, said, 'Here is a proper sailor. You can see that Gauk is not sorry he left Calfskin, a smoky fire and a narrow bed, to come a-viking and live bravely like this.'

Gauk said, 'It is true I did not think the sea would treat us so roughly, but he who travels widely will meet both good and evil. I am sorry for Bran, however, since he has to swim hard to keep his head out of water, and three times I have saved him from being washed overboard. But if I can tie him up here he will be safe, and then I shall have more time to look after myself.'

'Kol says we are drowned men already,' said Hall, 'so it is too late to worry about trifles like that.'

Gauk stared first at Hall the Icelander, then at Kol. He said, 'I had not looked for our voyage to end so soon.'

He spoke again: 'There will be much weeping in Rousay for this, and when the women spread their shifts on the grass to bleach their faces will be as white and wrinkled as the clothes. It grieves me to think of that, and it grieves me to think of my own fate, for I would be glad to live awhile yet. Yet men must be ready for anything, so I shall wait here with you and

Bran to see what will happen. The sea can make me no colder than I am already.'

Kol took a gold ring from his arm and broke it in two, and gave half to Gauk. 'Take this,' he said, 'so that gold may be seen on you who are my friend when we come to be guests in Ran's hall.'

Gauk took the gold first in one hand, then in the other, weighing it. It was a good ring and heavy. Gauk seemed more cheerful.

'But this is riches,' he said, 'and there are places where I could make better use of it than in Ran's hall. If it were not for the wife I have in Calfskin already I could marry some well-born woman since I own so much wealth as this. Come, let us go and bale steadily, for now I have a great desire to be on land again.'

Skallagrim said to Kol, 'Go with Gauk, for this is no time to stand idle, unless you are so frightened that you cannot move.'

Kol answered, 'I am not frightened, but many a man in such a state as this would think death a likelier thing than life.'

Gauk put the broken ring in his pocket. 'Come and bale,' he said, 'for life is precious to us who are men of wealth.'

'Ran will work faster than we can,' said Kol. But he went with Gauk and found a scoop and laboured with it.

'He takes Erling's death too sorely,' said Hall.

'No one dies of another man's wound,' said Skallagrim. After a long time he said, 'I shall be glad when day breaks.'

XXXI

It grew light, but there was little in that to make men cheerful, for then they saw clearly what damage had been done. They still baled, more slowly for they were weary, and water washed to and fro on the bottom boards. But the ship was lighter now and steered well. It rode safely in a high sea. There was less wind and the waves were not breaking so much. But the sea was still so steep and dangerous that they could do nothing except run before it, though that course took them where they had no thought of going, and already they were far east of Orkney and to the north of it.

Skallagrim mustered his crew and counted them. There were four missing who had been washed overboard in the night, and no one had seen them. Two of them were Easterlings, good seamen, and two were Orkney bonders' sons.

That was a great loss, but worse was discovered, for their water-casks were broken, and most of their store of food was either lost or spoiled. The open cask that stood by the mast was there still, but now it was full of salt water. Two greater casks in the mainhold were smashed to pieces. One had broken loose from its fastening and crushed a man's foot as it rolled about. That was Reidar of Wasdale, an Orkney man. The bones of his ankle were broken and the small bones of his foot also. The staves of the other cask had been smashed by a loose spar. So now they had no drinking water on board.

Very little food was left unspoiled. The water in the baling-place was thick with meal, and sacks of meal lay sodden on the boards of the mainhold. A tub of salted beef had been broken and the meat trodden underfoot. The new-killed sheep were all lost, and much stock-fish.

But the chest of the high-seat, that stood in the fore-room, between the mainhold and the poop, was unbroken. Skallagrim said, 'We are not so badly off while we have that. We can do without food and water for some little time, but without swords and axes we would be of no account.' For all weapons were kept in the chest.

The figure-head, carved like a skua, had been carried away.

'We can do very well without that,' said Hall the Icelander. 'There is small use in showing off when there is no one to admire your finery.'

Before midday the Skua was so dry there was no need to bale except from the baling-place. Kol worked there and would not stop.

Skallagrim had things made shipshape as far as he could, and gathered what food there was and brought it into the fore-room. Then the men were tired and most of them lay down to sleep. Their leather sleeping-bags were wet, and many had been lost overboard. Some of the men lay on the bare boards, but the ship plunged and moved so violently that they were thrown about. Then they tied themselves to thwarts, but still they rolled to and fro and groaned in their sleep.

Gauk had taken a small cask of ale aboard with him and hidden it in the forward part of the ship under the forecastle-deck. He took Bran and went there and broached the cask. After he had drunk a great deal of the ale he felt sick, for in the bows he was continually thrown from side to side. So he fell on the boards and spewed all he had drunk.

Now Hall the Icelander came there to look for something and saw Gauk spewing. And Bran was licking up the vomit and barking gladly, for he was very hungry.

Hall watched them for some time and then he went from under the forecastle-deck and bade Kol come to him, who was in the baling-place just aft of there.

When Kol had come and seen what was going on, Hall said, 'No wonder you are wealthy people in Orkney, for now I see that you waste nothing there.'

'Gauk was always good to his dog,' said Kol.

'But is the dog so good to him?' asked Hall. 'When Bran has eaten his fill does he throw it up for Gauk to have his turn of it?'

'Gauk is more dainty than that,' said Kol. 'Do you not see how he has brought ale of his own aboard?'

'Let us take what is left in case the dog gets too much,' said Hall, and picked up the cask and took the cup from Gauk's hand. Gauk lay there and said nothing.

'We will drink his health,' said Kol, and Gauk groaned loudly.

Then Kol and Hall the Icelander drank what was left of Gauk's ale. They turned to go aft when they had finished, and Bran followed them. But Kol said to him, 'There is no use in following us, for we are not generous like Gauk.'

Skallagrim was still at the steering-oar, and another man with him. Kol told him to go to his own place under the poop and sleep there, 'For now I will take the oar and steer awhile.'

'Is your heart whole again?' said Skallagrim.

'My thought plays about Erling as the tongue will play on a broken tooth,' said Kol, 'but you yourself said that a man had more to do than to mourn for his friends.'

'That is true,' said Skallagrim. 'And even the worst-cut hair will grow straight again at last.'

XXXII

There was no sun that day, nor the following day, and no stars by night. The sky was dark and cloudy and the sea rose fiercely still. Always they ran before the wind, for no other way was safe. Kol stood by the steering-oar when daylight came again. And now the wind lessened and the ship ran easily, but it was very cold. That morning there was a rime of frost on the gunwales and the thwarts, and the wet sleeping-bags were half-frozen. The men were stiff with cold and their arms and legs were fretted under their wet clothing.

There was much talk about where they were and in what direction they should steer. Skallagrim called the chief men in the ship to him, and they argued for a long time as to what must be done. One of these was Hall. He was named Hall the Icelander because he had been with Ingolf Arnarson on that voyage when Ingolf sailed to Iceland and was the first man to settle there. He had been on many viking cruises and also on trading-ships. He knew the firths both of Norway and Scotland, and all the sea from Iceland to south England, east by England and west about Ireland. He was a good man, but stubborn in his opinions.

He said the wind had gone into the south-west when they left the Pictland Firth, and now they were far to the north.

Skallagrim said he thought the wind had kept due west, and so they could not be very distant from the southern part of Norway.

'If we hold to our present course,' he said, 'we shall come in about Hvinfjord, or sight Lidandisness, or perhaps we are a little south of that and shall come to Denmark.'

But Hall said that could not be. 'It is so cold that we must be a great way north of that. My sleeping-bag was frozen stiff about me when I woke, and I have a feeling that there is ice not far away.'

There was a man called Thord. He was a great burly man, red-faced and strong as a bull. He had fought with Earl Sigurd in Scotland and been the death of many there. But he was not much used to the sea. Now he laughed at Hall and said, 'Do you think there must be icebergs near because your feet are cold? There is no ice in this sea. Your wits must be wandering and you think you are still sailing out of Reykjavik.'

'What do you know of this sea or any other sea?' said Hall. 'Because you have set fire to three or four pigsties in Caithness, and killed half a dozen long-legged lousy Scots, and are feared by a few thralls, you think you know all there is to know. But now you are at sea and little better than a bairn. I doubt if you know enough to water to leeward now.'

Thord was angry at that, but Skallagrim bade him be quiet.

'Nevertheless I do not believe in Hall's icebergs,' said Thord. 'I myself do not feel cold, and if his feet are frozen I can give him some thick-knitted stockings to keep him warm. Let us wrap him up well, since he is not a strong man, and then take our own councel and hold our own course.'

'Keep your stockings to trample in your farm-dung,' said Hall. 'I say there is ice near, for I can smell it.'

'Worse than ice is what I smell when you stand to windward of me,' said Thord.

Then Hall leapt at Thord and took him by the throat, and they wrestled together. But Kol pulled them apart.

Deaf Gylfi was the name of the oldest man on board. He had been one of Harald's forecastle-men when the king came to Orkney, and he had fought with Harald in all his battles both by sea and land. He was a great warrior but he had been as great a spendthrift, and now when he was old he was no richer than he had been as a young man. He was still strong, long in the arm, cunning and fierce in battle. But he was very deaf and he spoke in a thin high voice, not easy to hear when the wind was blowing loudly.

While Thord and Hall were arguing he had said more than once, 'What are they talking about? I can hear nothing. Why do they not speak louder?'

Some of the others told him that Hall thought there was ice near by. But Deaf Gylfi said, 'Eh? Speak up, man, for I cannot hear what you say.'

Now he said, 'I do not know what all this talk is about, nor why Hall and Thord are fighting. But surely it is foolish to wrangle about some trifle or other when we are running into danger. There is ice not far away, for I smell it clearly.'

But no one paid any attention, for Gylfi's voice was very thin and small.

So they continued to argue, and now more men said they thought it not unlikely that Hall was right, for they too considered the wind was in the south-west and was blowing them past Norway into the northern sea.

Eric Arnison, who was rather a grumbling man, said it all came of sailing too early in the year: 'If you had asked my advice I would have told you not to sail for three weeks yet, or even four. Then we would not have run into that great storm nor have been in danger of ice.'

Deaf Gylfi heard that, for Eric had a loud voice and he stood beside Gylfi when he spoke.

Gylfi said, 'That was my rede also, but no one listened to me. And by night, if we sail on this course till then, we shall have ice-floes tearing our timbers.'

'What,' said Skallagrim, 'do you also smell ice?'

Gylfi turned red in the face and shouted as loudly as he could, 'That is what I have been saying all the time, but no one pays any heed to me. I smelt ice when I woke and I have been telling you so all morning.'

'If there is ice near we cannot be far from land,' said Kol. 'For it must be glacier ice, broken and carried out to sea.'

'And to which side is the land?' said Thord. 'There has been so much talk of west and north that now I am lost indeed, and hardly know if my rump or my head is uppermost.'

'To the starboard side,' said Kol.

'Then let us steer that way,' said Thord, 'for I am tired of the sea and would rather a land all frozen than these black waves.'

But Hall said, 'It will be safer to hold for the open sea, as there will be no ice there.'

Skallagrim said, 'We have no water and little food. We are hardly in good shape to fare far from land.'

'There will be rain,' said Hall, 'and we have some food left. Better go hungry for a few days than break our timbers on ice-floes in the darkness.'

Hall's rede was judged to be the best, so they turned to larboard and the open sea. The wind was fresh now, but not heavy. They trimmed the sail fore and aft and sailed with the wind on the larboard beam.

They found a little dry kindling and made a fire, and stewed beef in sea-water, and some made porridge. But the porridge and beef were both very salt to the taste, and those who ate much of them suffered greatly from thirst. There was some hard cheese, but that also had been soaked by spray. And there was very little ale left.

The night was dark again, with no stars. Kol slept for some while in his room under the poop. He woke after midnight and walked the length of the ship. His legs were stiff and chafed by his wet clothes. He felt along the weather gunwale and found it was covered with ice, and there was thick ice on the forecastle-deck.

He stood by the steering-oar and gave a hand to the steersman. That was Deaf Gylfi. After some time the wind grew light and puffy, and the sky turned grey. It began to snow. There was not much to begin with, but presently the wind freshened again and the snow fell fierce and heavy. It filled the air and covered the ship. It flew wildly and covered Kol and Gylfi with thick clots like fur. Gylfi seemed to be talking, but Kol could not hear what he said. He turned white all over. They steered blindly by the feel of the wind.

It grew calm again and the snow stopped. For a little while the sky half-cleared and a few stars shone. Then Kol saw the ship like a winter field, with hummocks of snow where the men lay in their sleeping-bags, and those on watch beating their arms and throwing off white mist.

Clouds covered the stars. No more snow fell, but instead it grew colder and colder. The wind blew fitfully and spray leapt over the weather gunwale, freezing as it fell. Towards morning Kol felt the Skua labouring, heavy on the steering-oar, and listing to larboard.

Skallagrim and the others woke when it grew light. Then they saw such a thickness of ice on the weather-side that it bore down the ship, and a great hummock of ice on the forecastle-deck made it heavy by the head, so that it could hardly rise clear of the sea. On the thwarts and the bottom-boards snow lay frozen. The ship was covered with snow and ice.

Skallagrim opened the chest of the high-seat and gave out axes to break away the ice. They filled the water-butt by the mast with it and put some in cooking-pots, kindling a fire and making porridge with fresh water. That was some use they made of it, and those who had suffered badly from thirst became more cheerful.

When all the ice had been cleared from the ship it rode easily again. Now the wind fell away altogether. It was a white day. Mist lay all round them, thick as curtains, and it was still very cold.

Reidar of Wasdale, whose ankle had been broken in the storm, was frost-bitten in that leg from the thigh downwards. They took him out of his sleeping bag and rubbed his leg with sea-water. Even when they touched the broken bones and made them grate together he felt no pain. The ankle was bruised and swollen. Skallagrim strapped the bones as well as he could, and took off his shirt, that was dry now and warm, to wrap the leg in. Reidar did not complain much about his bad luck. He said, 'There is nowhere to walk here, so I do just as well lying still.'

Now Kol said, 'Let us take the oars and row, for that will make us warm.'

But Eric Arnison said, 'What is the use of rowing, and which way should we go? For no one now can even guess at north or south, unless Hall smells them as he smelt the ice.'

Hall stood silent for some time. Then he said, 'I think that way is south. But ask Deaf Gylfi. He has been longer at sea than I have, and perhaps he will know.'

Kol spoke loudly to Gylfi, and presently the old man knew what he wanted. He pointed with his finger and said, 'There is the south. I have been saying that all morning, but no one pays attention to me, no one heeds me now.'

The way he pointed was nearly the same as Hall had shown. Skallagrim said, 'When two guess alike truth may not be far off.'

So they took the oars from where they lay in crotches under the gunwales and began to row. Many of the oars had been broken or lost in the storm, but there were enough left to row twenty a side.

The sea grew white under their strokes. The breath of the rowers came from their mouths like a thick mist, and the chop of the oars, the creaking of their straps against the thole-pins, made a noise that seemed pleasant enough after the silence in which they had lain. Some of the younger men had been ill at ease, sulky or disheartened by their bad luck, and some, like Eric Arnison, had begun to grumble and say the voyage had been wrongly managed from the start. But now they became more cheerful and called to each other, jesting roughly. They grew hot and steam rose from their damp clothes. Deaf Gylfi stood at the steering-oar and held the Skua's head southward. He sang a song while he steered. The tune was rather gloomy but few people heard it.

A man called Gyrd grunted as he tugged at his oar. He said, 'My hands have been wet so long they are grown soft.'

Gyrd rowed on the starboard side. Over from him on the larboard thwart was Olaf, Deaf Gylfi's son by one of King Harald's bondwomen. He had come to Orkney the year after his father. Olaf said, 'I do not mind much about soft hands, but my backside has been in a puddle for three days and now it also is blistering.'

'What,' said Gyrd, 'not wit enough yet to keep your breeks dry?'

'He is still young,' said Hall the Icelander, who was rowing in front of Gyrd. 'The young keep their ears shut, but everything else is wide open.'

'I was old enough to please Huld of the Dykeside, which is more than you did,' said Olaf.

'Thorlief's young bull thought much the same when he mounted Brindle my cow,' said Hall. 'But no calf came to prove it.'

Olaf got laughed at for that and was silent for some while.

Gauk of Calfskin was rowing two thwarts behind

Olaf. He said, 'Blackie my cow dropped the prettiest calf in Rousay before I left home. It is a good place where I live. Everything grows well there and is very fruitful. The hens lay steadily, my ewes generally have twin lambs, and my wife has three children though she has not been long with me.'

'There may be four when you get back,' said Thord, who had been Earl Sigurd's man.

'I do not think so,' said Gauk, 'for she is still suckling the youngest.'

'But this voyage may last a long time,' said Thord, 'and many birds will seek an empty nest.'

'I have no fear of that,' said Gauk, 'for she loves me well and is a simple kind of woman. Moreover the three children sleep in the one bed with her while I am away, so you cannot say the nest is wholly empty.'

Eric Arnison rowed on the larboard thwart over against Gauk. He disliked Gauk because he was so friendly with Kol, and he would have been glad to hurt him in some way. Now he said, 'There is little meat left on board and we shall be hungry before long. If anyone asks my advice when there comes to be talk of what we must do, I have a good plan in my mind.'

'What is that?' asked Gauk.

'Why,' said Eric, 'we must kill Bran your dog and eat him.'

'That you will never do,' said Gauk angrily, 'for he is the best of dogs and has more wit than some men aboard this ship.'

'Who do you say has less wit than that ragged cur?' said Eric.

Gauk answered, 'Well, I do not think that you are one of the cleverest men to be found here.'

Those sitting near Eric bagan to laugh at him, and Eric grew angry. 'If I had no more wit than you have I should be sorry for myself,' he said loudly.

'Read this riddle, then, to show your wit,' said Gauk.

'Four ganging, four hanging, two showing the way, two keeping the dogs off, and one ever dirty lags behind. Read my riddle, Eric!'

But Eric said there could be no meaning in such nonsense.

Gauk said, 'I see meaning enough.'

'Tell it then,' said Eric.

'Blackie my cow,' said Gauk.

Eric grew more wrathful then because of the laughter of those about him, and because they said that Gauk had had the better of him there.

He spoke shortly: 'Blackie your cow will not save Bran your dog from the cooking-pot.'

'Bran will not come to any hurt,' said Gauk, 'unless he drown with the rest of us.'

'Wait till we get hungry and begin to think of the broth he would make,' said Eric.

Gauk said hotly, 'Bran is my dog and mine alone. I think more of Bran than I do of most men, and Bran will fill no belly except his own. Better you were killed to feed him than that he should die to feed you.'

Eric rose from his thwart and ran at Gauk. But Bran lay under Gauk's seat and took Eric by the ankle while Gauk thrust at him with his oar so that Eric toppled over on to the rower in front. Now there was confusion on both sides of the ship, for Eric's oar, that he had let go, fouled the man in front of him, and the man before Gauk was knocked off his thwart.

Skallagrim came forward angrily and rated them. He spoke harshly and said, 'Is there not trouble enough without fools like you adding to it? I will have no brawling here, nor will I listen to what you have to say for yourselves. For I know that each will try to prove himself right, and I know that both of you are in the wrong, since all are in the wrong who find quarrels of their own when our whole company is in danger, and nothing save the good will of all and their even temper can bring us safely out of it.'

'The danger we are in is no concern of mine,' said Eric hardily. 'It was you who bade us start so early in the year, Skallagrim. It was you who brought us into danger. And now it is your business to take us out of it.'

'I mean to do that,' said Skallagrim. 'Now take your oar again, Eric, and row with the others.'

'I have rowed enough,' said Eric. 'Since none knows where we are going, I do not feel like using my strength to no purpose.'

Skallagrim had no weapon with him, but with his fist he struck Eric so heavily on the jaw that Eric fell, striking his head against a thwart, and lay stunned. Skallagrim let him lie where he fell and bade another man take his oar. Then they rowed on.

When night fell Gylfi said he could steer no longer, for in the darkness he grew confused and could not tell which way the Skua was heading. So Skallagrim let them ship their oars. Then the awnings were spread and the men lay under them, close together for warmth, and slept till morning. Hall and some others kept watch. There was no wind, only a long swell rising slow and easy.

XXXIII

That night Kol tossed and struggled greatly in his sleep. Skallagrim woke beside him in the room they had under the poop, and for a long time watched him wrestling and heard him sigh and mutter fiercely. But he did nothing to rouse him or break his dream.

In the morning Kol was weary when he woke and loath to rise. But he went out and stood in the fore-room, leaning against the chest of the high-seat, and looked to sea. Skallagrim came and stood beside him.

Kol said, 'I dreamt of strange things last night.'

'You were restless for a long time, and thrashed your arms about, and spoke angrily to someone,' said Skallagrim.

Kol said, 'I dreamt first of Signy our mother. She stood on the shore at Ness and cried to us, "I wish the wind may go against you and blow you east, not west, of Scotland, so that you come into England's sea, and come to Ivar's hall and so kill him. For Bui my husband is unatoned and shame is on us all so long as Ivar lives." '

'I have remembered that too,' said Skallagrim. 'Yet she is no Finn wife to bid the winds blow and storm come.'

'Then she said, "The wolves will eat well and ravens scream over carrion, for my sons walk with bloody brand and whistling spear, and the wound-bird shall follow them into Ivar's hall." '

'We are far to the north of England now,' said Skallagrim, 'and no one knows where the next wind will carry us. Yet it may be southwards, and since we scarcely know left from right we may come into Northumbria as easily as into Denmark. Thorlief would say that ill-luck is the right end of ill redes.'

Kol said, 'Then I dreamt of the storm and Erling's death. I saw the Scarf sink in the Swelkie of Stroma. I heard the cries of men drowning, and Erling called loudly to Hallgerda. But I could not hear what he said. Then mist and fog fell upon us and for a long time I saw nothing clearly. But I grew tired and my body was cramped and sore. The noise of breakers and gulls crying followed that, it was dark, and I could see no shore. Yet the Skua was wrecked there. And afterwards there came a man tall and white-faced, walking quickly but in a loose shambling way, and he carried an axe bigger than most men carry. He was ugly as a troll and his hair was wolf-grey. He, I think, was Ivar the Boneless. There was fighting before he came, and fighting after, and it seemed as though somewhere a house was burning in the darkness.'

'What then?' said Skallagrim.

But Kol stared seawards and would not answer.

'Was Ivar killed?' said Skallagrim.

'There were many dead,' said Kol.

'By whose hand did Ivar die?' asked Skallagrim.

'I am not sure about that,' said Kol, and would have gone forward into the main hold.

But Skallagrim took him by the arm and said, 'Tell all that you saw, for I am not frightened of anything you can say. Dreams are not always true.'

Kol looked at him: 'I saw you dead, Skallagrim, and I felt my own death-blow.'

'No one can escape his luck,' said Skallagrim.

'Yet dreams are not always true,' said Kol.

'That is so,' said Skallagrim. 'But Ivar was also dead?'

'Ivar was dead,' said Kol.

'Then things may fall out fairly well after all,' said Skallagrim, 'for Signy was right in saying that Bui's death should be atoned, and that some shame lay on us for doing nothing.'

'I had meant to do something when the proper time came,' said Kol, 'but I did not think the time so near at hand.'

Skallagrim said, 'There would have been good plunder to be got in Man. I feel a kind of anger against my mother for wishing the storm on to us and wind-driving us into Northumbria.'

'We are not there yet,' said Kol. 'The sea is wide and our landfall may be anywhere from Iceland to Frisia.'

'England is midway between them,' said Skallagrim.

Now the men were all sitting at the oars ready to row, and Deaf Gylfi came to Skallagrim and said he

could not steer that morning, for he was tired from all
his work yesterday.

'I have also a pain in my bowels,' he said, 'and it is
not easy to stand upright.'

'Get Hall the Icelander, then,' said Skallagrim, 'for he
can smell the south as well as you.'

'Hall is sleeping,' said Kol. 'He was on watch last
night.'

Skallagrim said to Gylfi, 'Tell me where the south
lies and I will steer. You can sit beside me and keep me
right.'

But Gylfi turned away as though he did not hear.

Skallagrim shouted to him.

Gylfi put his hand to his ear and said, 'Eh? Speak
louder, Skallagrim, for I am somewhat deaf nowadays.'

Skallagrim shouted again.

Gylfi looked round him, first one way and then the
other, and said slowly, 'The north seems to be
thereabout, and so the south must lie there.'

Now Hall had wakened and come aft, and when
Gylfi stretched his arm in such a direction Hall said he
was wrong, and that the south was there. And he
pointed far from where Gylfi had pointed. He said to
Gylfi, 'Your wits went astray while you slept, and now
you are lost as though you had lived all your life in a
fog.'

But Gylfi pretended to be too deaf to hear him and
would not argue.

The sea was still calm and mist lay closely round
them. The sky was covered, and a little way from the
ship the sea itself was white as the mist above it.

The men waiting on the thwarts began to argue
among themselves. Some laughed and some turned to
speak angrily to those behind them.

Skallagrim said, 'We will take your advice, Hall.'

But Kol said, 'Let us follow that gannet, for I think
he knows better than either of them where land lies,

whether it be south or north.' And he pointed to a gannet flying a little ahead of them.

It was heavy with fish and flying low. It had passed so close to the Skua that they could see the buff patch on its head and the blue ring round its eye. It dived straight, and came up with a fish. It flew farther and dived again.

'It follows the fish,' said Skallagrim.

'It is nearly full. It flies home,' said Kol.

Skallagrim said nothing for a little while, but watched the gannet. It flew low along the water and disappeared in the mist.

'We will go that way,' said Skallagrim, 'though I do not know if it is better than any other way.'

Hall grumbled a little, but Skallagrim took the tiller and they followed the gannet.

After some time they saw it again. It was swimming now, but it rose heavily when they came near it, and flew forward. It flew in the same direction as before.

'It is going home,' said Kol.

XXXIV

When it grew dark the men stopped rowing. They had had little to eat all day, and no water to drink. There had been only enough water left to make some porridge. Yet because the air was cold and full of mist they did not suffer very much from thirst. They were hungry though, and by nightfall tired with rowing.

The ship lay quiet, and the sea was a flat calm. Kol put up his hand and bade the men stop all their talking. He went forward, listening to something, and called Skallagrim and Hall to him. They came and listened also. Then Kol said, 'What do you hear?' 'Nothing,' they said.

Kol said, 'My ears are better than yours, for I hear water lapping the shore and the tide moving on a stony beach.'

'It may be,' said Hall, 'yet my ears are good and I hear no sound at all.'

'Let us row that way,' said Skallagrim, and bade the men to take to their oars again.

They rowed for some time and then stopped once more to listen. And now both Skallagrim and Hall heard, far off, the low muttering noise that Kol had heard. They told the men that land was near, and the men rowed on again, very cheerfully although they were tired.

Presently a man called Ragi cried out that his oar was caught in something, and when he pulled it in they found a great mass of seaweed on the end of it.

'We are not far now,' said Skallagrim, and all listened and heard the shore-sound except Deaf Gylfi.

But while they rested for a little while, and left the oars hanging loosely from the thole-pins, the oar-blades went slowly forward.

'The tide is running out,' said Kol. 'It has turned against us, and we must row hard or it will beat us.'

So Skallagrim bade the men give way, and egged them on and made them forget they were weary, and the Skua went swiftly landwards.

Then another noise was heard, the light noise of wind, and Gauk, who was rowing bow oar on the starboard side, felt a cold breeze on the back of his neck. The mist cleared and black catspaws came over the water.

'Put your strength into it, men,' said Skallagrim. 'We have wind and tide both against us now.'

The men grunted and heaved at the oar-looms. The sea grew choppy and small waves leapt against the bow. The mist was blown away and all the sky cleared. The night was not very dark. The moon shone through a cloud and Hall, who was standing on the forecastle, cried that he could see land ahead.

Skallagrim egged the men on. They heaved hard, and those who were not rowing stood before them and thrust on the oar-looms as the rowers pulled.

But the wind blew more strongly against them.

Clouds came quickly over the sky, and the out-going tide ran faster. Skallagrim at the steering-oar could hear the harsh breathing of the rowers. Sweat ran into their eyes, and their arms grew heavy.

Now a fierce gust of wind came against them, whitening the sea, and their stroke faltered. A man tumbled from his thwart and his oar fouled those in front of him. The Skua fell away from the wind and all was confusion. The squall passed, but the men had no longer strength to row.

Kol said, 'We had better make sail and go coast-wise along the land till morning.'

They hoisted the sail, reefing it high, and set it fore and aft. With the wind on their starboard beam they sailed swiftly, heeling over till the sea lipped the leeward gunwale. The sky darkened under heavy clouds and men were set to watch for any sight of reefs and to listen for the noise of breakers.

When daylight came there was no land to be seen. But that morning they saw the sun, and it rose on the larboard quarter.

'We still fare southwards,' said Skallagrim.

There was some talk about turning back to look for the land they had come near to on the night before, but because the wind still blew freshly and would be against them if they turned, and because they did not know if the land were a large one or nothing but some small islands, there was not much to be said for such a course, while many lands lay to the south, and if they held in that way they must reach somewhere if they did not sink first.

'And I do not think that drowning will be our luck now,' said Skallagrim.

'It is more likely we shall starve or go mad from thirst,' said Thord.

'Rain will fall before long,' said Skallagrim, 'and there is still some meal and stock-fish.'

XXXV

On the following day there was more fog. It was not now a white mist, but dark banks that moved slowly over the sea. Now and then a light wind came that filled the sail and scattered the fog. But in a little while it would grow dark again, and the Skua rolled heavily in a windless swell.

Many of the crew were out of heart. Their limbs were cramped and chafed with long wetting. They had been thrown to and fro in the storm, and were bruised with falling, and it was hard to find rest in the ship, for it moved continually to the sea. Some of the men had sea-water boils, their eyes were sore, and their beards stiff with salt. Their cheeks and their clothes were white under a rind of salt. And this day they finished what was left of their food.

They watched the sky for rain, but no rain fell. Nor could the sun break through the clouds and the fog.

Eric Arnison said again that they must kill Bran, Gauk's dog, and now many of the men listened to him and thought that was a good plan.

'Of what value is a dog that we should starve to keep him alive?' said Eric. And two men went to lay hands on Bran.

But Gauk stood against the gunwale between two thwarts and had the dog at his feet. Bran was hungry as any man there and he had grown somewhat fierce. He

was a great strong brute, grey-coloured and lean, and he
had teeth like a wolf. He bit the hand of one of those
men who came to take him, and Gauk struck the other
on the head with the broken haft of a boat-hook. But
more came to help those two, and a great brawling
grew over the dog.

Kol came forward from the poop to see what was
amiss and Gauk called to him for help. Kol thrust aside
the others and came to where Gauk was with Bran
fighting at his feet.

'What has gone wrong now?' he said.

Gauk said they were trying to kill Bran to make soup
of him.

'He is somewhat lean to make broth,' said Kol.

But the men were angry and said it was not right that
they should starve while there was a dog who might
make a good meal for them.

Gauk said, 'Bran and I came aboard together, and
Bran was taken on the same terms as I was. For I told
Skallagrim that he was a brave fighter and would be of
use to us whether those who came against us stood
stoutly or turned to flee, since he is fast in pursuit and
bites hard. And so it is no fairer that Bran should be
killed and cooked than that I should be hewn down, or
any one else, to make broth for the others.'

Kol said that Gauk was in the right: 'Bran is his dog
and you have no more claim to him than Gauk has to
any of your property. And if any lay hands on him,
not Gauk but I will deal with them. Now let there be
no more brawling here.'

Some of the men still muttered. Eric Arnison said,
'Cook us some breakfast, Kol, and we will be quiet
enough.' But Kol made no answer to that.

Hall the Icelander sat down beside Gauk. He had
taken no part in the tussle. He said to Eric Arnison, 'If
you are hungry pull your belt in tighter. Have you not
wit enough to know that?'

Gauk was now well pleased with himself. He felt very safe, moreover, and was inclined to mock at those who had gone against him in the matter of Bran. He said to Hall, 'Do not talk to Eric about his wit, for he has little of that, and is ill at ease when people say anything about it. He could not read a riddle of Blackie my cow that I told him, for he had never noticed that a cow's tail is generally dirty.'

'I doubt if yours is any cleaner,' said Eric.

Gauk said, 'I saw in summer-time a household awake and merry at sunset. The gentlemen drank their beer in silence, but the ale-butt stood and screamed.—There is another riddle, Eric. Read me that one.'

Eric said, 'I take no interest in such bairnly things.'

But the men about him pressed him to answer and laughed at him when he could not.

'I think I could read it,' said Hall.

'It is a sow with its litter,' said Gauk. 'I learnt it from my father one night at Calfskin when he sat drinking his beer, but not in silence, for he was a merry man and sang between cups.'

Gauk grew quiet and somewhat sad to think of Calfskin. 'I wish I was there now,' he said, 'with my wife setting a dish of bacon before me, a bowl of ale, and a cheese of Blackie's milk. Calfskin is a fine place, and I have a good wife. She would be sorry to see my hands all sore from rowing, and this boil on my neck. I remember sitting on a bench, a day or two days before we sailed, watching her spread clothes on the grass to bleach. She wore an old loose gown, and when she bent down with the clothes her breasts leaped out. "Cover them quickly, lass," I said, "lest some man should see them and be moved to desire of you." "There is no man here but you," she said. "And am I too dull to have a desire?" I said. "Cover them again, or your bleaching will be spoiled." She was still suckling our youngest bairn. There is no fear that he will grow hungry like his father.'

'Do not speak of women,' said Thord. 'The sea has made us salt enough without thought of such matters.'

'Indeed it is not altogether comfort I take from remembering Calfskin and my wife,' said Gauk. 'I am glad that Bran is here with me.'

After that Gauk would never let Bran go far from him, for fear that someone might kill him. And at night he took Bran with him into his sleeping-bag.

There came a long spell with no wind blowing, and Skallagrim bade the men take to their oars. But they grumbled and said what was the use of rowing?

Thord said, 'We are weak with hunger. Our hands are blistered with rowing and cracked with salt. Why should we work to no purpose? For you cannot know where you are steering.'

But Skallagrim would not listen and ordered them again to go to their thwarts.

'As you will,' said Thord, 'but I do not think I shall go to sea again, unless I am to be captain.'

There were two men called Thorgils and Thorgrim. They were brothers. They sat still when Skallagrim bade the crew take oars, and did not move though all the rest obeyed.

Skallagrim said, 'Why do you not do as I tell you? Or are you fools, so that you do not understand the meaning of words?'

Thorgils said, 'It is not we who are fools.'

'Give us something to eat, then we shall work,' said Thorgrim.

Skallagrim took the haft of the boat-hook that Gauk had used, and struck them with it. He struck Thorgils on his left cheek and Thorgrim on the right. Then the brothers got up and sprang at Skallagrim, but Kol and Hall the Icelander caught them and threw them down.

'Now will you row?' asked Skallagrim.

'It seems we had better,' said Thorgils.

But Thorgrim said, 'You will not often persuade us that way.'

So the men rowed for a time, but they put little heart into it and the ship moved slowly.

Reidar of Wasdale, whose ankle had been broken, still lay in his sleeping-bag. He did not complain of his hurt and kept as quiet as he could. But sometimes he was so cold that his teeth chattered noisily, and sometimes he shouted with fever. He would shout boldly as though he were in battle, and then speak more quietly to some girl, and bid her not to weep for him. But when he came out of his fever he would ask those about him if he had spoken anything, and tell them to pay no heed to it, 'For I am fond of jesting and often say things that have no meaning.'

Now Kol came to him and asked if he was not any better.

'Much better,' said Reidar, 'for now my legs feel neither pain nor cold, so that half of me is very comfortable.'

Kol said that if rain fell he would bring him something to drink.

'The men of Ness were used to offer their guests better cheer than water,' said Reidar.

'But now the ale-cask is empty and the meal-chest bare.'

'Nor can we blame the housewife for that,' said Reidar. 'Let me sleep awhile, Kol. I will dream of plenty, and if I can be troubled with waking again I shall tell you how I feasted.'

That day passed slowly, and the best men were those who kept silent. For there was little to talk about save thirst and hunger.

Some time before nightfall a black cloud rose and they could see rain falling from it into the sea. The Skua lay in its path. Then the men took the awning and spread it all over the ship, and waited for the rain to come.

It fell heavily, and when the cloud had passed the awning was full of a great pool of water. They filled what butts and casks they had from that. Then the men cupped their hands and drank eagerly. But quickly they spat the water out again, for it was brackish. The awning was so full of salt that it made the rain-water in it no better than sea-water. But a few men drank of it, and they fell sick during the night and grew nearly mad with thirst.

There was much ill humour after that wasting of the rain. Some sat quiet and surly, others were loud in their anger.

There was one man who talked much to those near him. He said it was possible to drink sea-water mixed with urine. Hall the Icelander said he had heard of that, but he had never tried it himself, nor did he think well of the idea.

But the man took a baling-scoop and dipped it in the sea, and half-filled it. Then he made his water in it.

Skallagrim called to him to know what he was doing. The man told him. Skallagrim said, 'Come here and let me taste it first, and I will give you a toast.'

Then Skallagrim took the scoop and threw it overboard.

The wind blew steadily that night and they sailed before it. No one know for certain in what direction they were going. But for a little while the sky cleared and they saw some stars, and by them they thought they were heading southwards.

XXXVI

In the morning Kol went to speak to Reidar of Wasdale, but when he pulled open the sleeping-bag he found that Reidar was dead. He had died in the night and had not called to anyone to be near him. He was a man of good heart, easy to get on with, and many were sorry for his death.

Skallagrim said they should bury him there at sea, so they took a large stone from the ballast and tied it to his sleeping-bag with thongs, and put Reidar overboard with the stone at his feet.

He sank at once. But then the stone came loose, and Reidar rose again because of the air that was in his sleeping-bag. The ship lay in a flat calm and Reidar floated a little way off. All the men stood at that side of the ship and looked at him, and some were uneasy and said there was ill luck in that, when a man would not sink but came out of the sea again to look at his messmates.

Then Hall took an oar and reached far out with it, and got the blade of it on Reidar, and so, a little way at a time, pulled him to the side. They lifted him aboard and the water ran out of his sleeping-bag, and some came out of his mouth when they turned him. His eyes were open. They were pale and staring. Some of the men took another stone from the ballast and tied it to him, but the leather thongs were stiff with so much wetting, and the men's fingers were cold and numb so that it was not easy to tie it fast. But they put Reidar back into the sea, and saw no more of him for some time.

The wind rose, filling the sail, and the Skua moved slowly before it. The wake spread thin and white behind them. Then Olaf, Deaf Gylfi's son, looked aft over the poop and cried suddenly that Reidar was following them. They looked where he pointed and saw Reidar floating in the water, moving a little up and down.

The stone had loosened again, and when its weight had gone he had risen and come up under the Skua, lying under the bottom while the ship was becalmed.

Then when the wind blew and the ship moved before it, he floated free.

But Skallagrim said they should pay no more attention to him, and presently he was out of sight.

There was little stirring that day on the ship, for all were weary with hunger and the pangs of thirst were on them, and most men sat unmoving, saying nothing. But Olaf, Deaf Gylfi's son, went here and there busily about the ship, asking men if he could not do something for them. He coiled ropes away and made things tidy, and would have people talk to him. But they bade him be silent and sit still.

There was a man called Haeng who made some noise. He had drunk salt water many times, though the others stopped him when they could. But he would rise in the night and go to the baling-place and drink, and now he was mad. He roared and ran to and fro, and would not be quiet. He went on the forecastle-deck and said he would throw himself into the sea and go where Reidar was, for Reidar was a good man to drink with. But Thord took him down from there and held him till his fit passed.

Towards evening Haeng got up, shouting, and ran to the side. Deaf Gylfi tried to stop him now, but Haeng struck him in the face and leapt overboard.

Some of the crew made as though they would turn the ship to pick him up, but Skallagrim bade them do nothing in that way, and took the tiller himself and held straight on. He said, 'Haeng would not be helped for long though we brought him aboard again, and we should nowise be helped. We have troubles enough without him roaring in the ship.'

Eric Arnison said, 'Haeng ate in my mess, some time ago that is, when eating was still in fashion, and I do not care to see a messmate drown without doing something to help him.'

'Care as you will,' said Skallagrim, 'but stand away from the steering-oar.'

The brothers Thorgrim and Thorgils stood nearby.
Thorgrim looked at Skallagrim and said to his brother,
'He has a big voice indeed. No wonder we are afraid of
him.'

Thorgils said, 'The colts ran away when it began to
thunder, but the old mares stayed where they were and
took no hurt.'

Skallagrim paid no heed to them.

Presently Thorgils called loudly, 'Skallagrim, where
are we now? It is time we saw something of that
plunder you promised us when we sailed with you.'

Thorgrim said, 'We should have brought fishing-gear
instead of swords and axes.'

Kol came there and bade them be quiet: 'Lest I show
you where you are, and that will be on the broad of
your backs.'

Thorgils said, 'We are talking with Skallagrim, not
with you, Kol.'

Skallagrim bade Kol stand away, 'For I can look after
this matter myself.'

'There is that voice that fills me with fear,' said
Thorgrim. And he let fly a noise from his breech.

Then Skallagrim leapt upon him and took him under
the arms and threw him heavily. And he turned to
Thorgils, who stood grinning, and struck him in the
face so hard that he fell.

Most of the crew came aft to see what was afoot, and
Skallagrim bade certain of them take Thorgils and
Thorgrim and hold them fast.

Then he said: 'I am not a man whose temper is an
easy one, and if men turn against me or thwart me I
find it hard not to answer them roughly. Yet since we
came aboard this ship and the storm broke on us I have
spoken softly and used everyone with what mildness I
could. For then it was luck that turned against me, not
men, and there is no use in being ill-humoured because
luck is ill. But if Thorgils and Thorgrim, or Eric

Arnison, or any other of you, seek to make more trouble than that which we suffer already, I shall not hold in my anger but I shall deal with such ones as they deserve.'

Thorgils said, 'My brother and I are somewhat restless men, Skallagrim. We came with you in the Skua because you said there were stirring times ahead, and there would be enough fighting to keep us from thinking of duller matters. But now we have seen nothing but much rolling to and fro in the sea, we grow more hungry every day, and we have come to our wits' end for want of something to do.'

'We are all in the same plight,' said Skallagrim. 'But I do not think our luck will continue as it is now, though whether it will turn to better or to worse I do not know. It cannot be long before we sight land, but there are not many lands that will welcome us in peace. We may not have long to live, but it is not likely we shall die by drowning. My brother Kol dreamt not long ago of battle and burning by night. Ravens were screaming and there was warm meat for the wolves.'

'That will suit us very well,' said Thorgrim, 'but let it come soon, Skallagrim. For this sitting-still troubles my patience and I do not know how much longer I can bear it. My tongue, moreover, is so swollen by thirst that presently I shall not be able to speak.'

'We can suffer that loss without mourning,' said Skallagrim.

XXXVII

Rain fell during the night. The awning was spread again to catch it, and now there was so much rain that the salt was washed out of the canvas and the water was sweet for drinking. The men quenched their thirst and everyone grew more cheerful.

They stood in the rain and washed the salt from their hair and their beards. Then they stripped off their clothes and bathed themselves all over, and let their clothes soak in the rain, for they were caked with salt. But the rain still fell and before morning they grew cold, though in a way they were more comfortable because the salt itch had gone and their clothes were soft and supple now.

When morning came the rain stopped and the wind blew strongly, but from another direction. The sun rose and the day grew bright.

'Now the wind is in the north-east,' said Hall.

Skallagrim said, 'Let us abide by luck and run before it. We sail fastest that way, and if there is land ahead we shall come to it the sooner.'

'That seems good advice,' said Hall, 'since I can think of no better myself.'

It seemed as though another gale were springing up, but there was clear sunlight and the crests of the waves shone brightly in blue water. The men were in good spirits now, for they no longer suffered from thirst. They were weak from want of food, yet fine weather did something for them.

'There are few things better than sunlight and a good fire,' said Hall.

Before darkness fell they saw many seagulls, and that was considered a sign that land was near.

'We must keep a good watch to-night,' said Skallagrim, and sent Kol and Hall the Icelander on to the forecastle.

The sun set in front of them, and then the wind blew stronger till a gale was blowing. It was not very dark that night, for there were stars in the sky and thin fast-moving clouds.

Presently Kol cried out that he could see land ahead.

'And it does not look good land to come ashore on,' said Hall, peering into the darkness. 'For there are cliffs and I see no break in them.'

Skallagrim came forward also, and then they held off from the land a little. But with the wind on her quarter the Skua laboured and was hard to steer.

They drew closer to the land, for the tide was with the wind and drawing them inshore. They could see the waves breaking on the cliffs, dim-white and huge.

'We have not often had dry clothes since leaving Ness,' said Kol, 'and I think we shall get them wet again before long.'

Now Skallagrim opened the chest of the high-seat and gave out the weapons that were in it, so that everyone was fully armed. 'For it seems as though we shall go ashore in a hurry,' he said, 'and there may be no time to come back for what is forgotten.'

Skallagrim spoke very cheerfully as the men came for their weapons. Thorgils and Thorgrim came with the others. Thorgils said, 'Can you swim well in broken water, Skallagrim?'

'Why,' said Skallagrim, 'must I carry you ashore on my back?'

'We shall be no laggards when land is near,' said Thorgils.

'I look for much from you two restless men.'

Thorgrim said, 'If we strike others as hard as you have struck us, Skallagrim, we shall do well enough.'

Hall came quickly and said they must hold from the land as far as they were able, and try to weather a certain headland: 'Else we shall be broken on the cliffs and few of us can hope to save our lives.'

But the wind blew so strongly that they dare not bring it on their beam.

'Then we must drown either in deep water or in shoal water,' said Hall. 'Choose as you like, for I have no choice in the matter.'

Now Kol shouted there was a break in the shore, north of the headland, and it seemed like the mouth of a small river.

'Do not speak about drowning, Hall,' said Skallagrim. 'We shall soon be on dry land now.'

So they steered for the river-mouth. There were breakers on both sides of it, and the waves rose high between them. But they did not break there. Skallagrim stood at the steering-oar and had two men with him. Now the land grew tall and black before them. They came near to the mouth of the river and seemed to run in upon the back of a wave. But there was a sand-bar across the river and the keel touched on it. Then the ship slewed round and fell into broken water, and struck on a reef there.

It rose and fell again, grinding on the reef, and the mast broke, falling in a great tangle with the sail. The sea swept over all the ship. It lay on one side and the waves broke on it, pounding it hard.

Some of the men were thrown overboard when the Skua struck, and of these a few came into calmer water inside the reef and swam ashore. For the ship lay close in under the headland. But others were beaten against the rocks and so killed, or else, being stunned, they drowned. But most clung to the ship for some little while.

The Skua lay on its beam-ends, somewhat slant-wise on the reef, and the men held fast to any hold they could. It was too dark to see clearly, and the noise of the storm, of the sea breaking, and the ship grinding on the rock, was so great that even the loudest man's voice could hardly be heard. Yet Kol and Skallagrim went from one end of the ship to the other, helping some who were in more danger than the rest, and seeing as they were able what should be done.

The stern of the ship lay towards the landward end of the reef, and there were some men who climbed out that way and tried to come ashore along the reef. But the sea broke over it so fiercely that they were swept away.

Then Kol went to the bow and saw that it lay over deep water to the inside of the reef, and the water there was somewhat sheltered and calm. So he went back along the ship and by signs told the men where they should go. That was not easy, since the ship lay so awkwardly. Gauk of Calfskin had most trouble, for he held Bran by a thong and the dog was frightened and would not go anywhere willingly. But Kol helped them, and presently they got to the bow.

When the men came there they jumped overboard and swam ashore. Bran was eager for that, and he and Gauk jumped together.

Hall the Icelander was in the bow holding to a rope. He put his mouth to Kol's ear and said he thought that all the men who jumped from there had gone safely ashore.

Kol asked if Skallagrim had gone, but Hall said he had not seen him. Now there were left there only Kol and Hall, and the brothers Thorgils and Thorgrim.

Kol made as though he would go back along the ship to look for Skallagrim, but Thorgils stayed him and said that he would go. It was dangerous now, for the ship was breaking. Yet he climbed swiftly from thwart to thwart and came aft to the fore-room, and found Skallagrim there. He was down in the lee-side, where the water came deeply, looking for weapons that had been lost. He had ten or twelve swords tied with a thong, and now he found a spear and two axes. He gave these to Thorgils, carrying the swords himself, and they went forward again.

Kol and Thorgrim and Hall the Icelander were waiting for them. Skallagrim made them divide the weapons he had found between them, and carry them as well as their own. Then they jumped together and swam to shore, and came there safely.

Most of the crew were waiting for them on the beach. Skallagrim counted them and found that forty-

two had come out of the wreck. Some of them were
cut and hurt where they had fallen.

The moon came out between the clouds, and they
saw a great wave rise and fall upon the ship, breaking
high over the reef. When it passed there seemed to be
little left of the Skua.

'It was a good ship,' said Skallagrim, 'but no wood
grows that can stand against the sea when fair-haired
waves waken in the gale, and the white-hooded ladies
play upon the reefs.'

XXXVIII

Many of the men lay on the sand as though they
were too weary to move. They were weak from hunger
and cramped with being so long aboard ship, and now
the last of their strength seemed to have gone in the
wreck and their struggle to swim ashore. Some were
already fast asleep. All had weapons lying beside them,
however.

But some were eager to move inland at once to see
what they could find. Thorgils and Thorgrim were
among these. Their legs were so stiff that they could
move only with difficulty, yet they would not rest, and
Skallagrim had trouble to keep them where they were.

Thorgils said, 'All that worries me now is this:
suppose I come into a house and find a cup of ale, a
bowl of broth, and a woman, which shall I take first?'

'Take the broth before it cools,' said Thorgrim.

'Take the woman before she runs,' said Thord.

'Yet if I took the ale first I should have a better
appetite for the others,' said Thorgils. 'It is not an easy
matter to settle. Come, Skallagrim, and let us put it to
the proof to see which is best.'

There were high banks on either side of the river,

and not far away a steep path led upwards. Skallagrim took those men who were strongest and went with them up from the stream. When they came to the top they saw the ruins of a stone building that might have been an abbey. There had been a small town there, but it had been burnt. Charred timber lay in the street that had gone through the town, and there were no walls standing. The stones of the abbey were black.

'I do not know what country this is,' said Skallagrim, 'but it seems that matters fall out much the same as elsewhere.'

Kol said, 'If vikings have been harrying here there may be little left for us to take.'

'Plain fare suits a hungry man,' said Hall. 'We have no ship to go farther and seek better, so we cannot be dainty.'

Skallagrim had been walking about looking at the ruins of the abbey and the town. He said, 'This has not been newly done. It is a long time since these houses were burnt.'

'Do not waste time over ruins,' said Thorgrim, 'but let us look for what still lives.'

Now Skallagrim said it would be best if a small party went first to see what could be found. Thorgils and Thorgrim said at once they would go with that party. But Skallagrim said they must fare cautiously and not start fighting on their own account: 'For it is likely that we shall have fighting enough, being few in numbers and in a strange land, and now what you must do is to see where we can get food and drink, since none of us is as strong as he was wont to be. So go quietly and do not stay long away, but as soon as you have found a house or a farm that seems to be small or not well guarded, come back and tell me.'

Then Skallagrim asked Hall if he would go with Thorgils and Thorgrim and two other men who were still strong on their feet and not too worn with hunger. Hall said he would go willingly, and would see that Thorgils and Thorgrim did nothing that was unwise.

Kol said that he also would be glad to go. But Skallagrim said it would be better if he stayed with the crew awhile: 'For Hall and his people may not come back, and another party will have to go out. Then it will be your turn, Kol.'

So Kol and Skallagrim went back to the beach, but Hall and those with him set out on their errand with what speed they could.

Skallagrim roused some of the men and bade them search about the shore for the bodies of those who had been drowned. Most of them had come either into the river or on to the landward end of the reef. Some they buried in the sand and some they piled stones upon.

Kol and Skallagrim talked together. Kol said, 'What land is this, do you think, that we have come into?'

Skallagrim said, 'I do not know, but it seems likely to me that that which our mother wished has come to pass, and we are in North England, in Ivar's country.'

'I also have been thinking that way,' said Kol. 'and it may be that my dream foretold what will now happen to us.'

'You saw Ivar lie dead,' said Skallagrim.

Kol said, 'There were more than Ivar whom life had left.'

'A man cannot go against his luck,' said Skallagrim, 'and for myself I do not much care what befalls us so long as we face it well and gain some success before we die.'

'I am glad to feel earth beneath my feet,' said Kol.

'I do not think there is much to be said for living a long while, till there is no warmth in life except that which comes from lying under the blankets,' said Skallagrim.

'I am curious to see Ivar,' said Kol. 'Luck has often

gone against him, yet he has lived and become famous.'

'The man who kills him will be much spoken of,' said Skallagrim.

Then they lay for some time and said nothing. Presently Hall came back, and two men with him.

Skallagrim asked him, 'What have you found?'

Hall said, 'A farm, quiet and standing by itself. We killed a man there, and two thralls who slept too soundly to be of much use to him. There is meat and meal there in plenty, and enough ale to wet our tongues.'

'Did you ask what country this is, or did you kill too quickly to have time for speech?'

'I spoke to one of the thralls before I quietened him, and he said we were in Deira.'

'Ivar's country,' said Skallagrim.

'My dream was a good one,' said Kol.

Skallagrim said, 'Where are Thorgils and Thorgrim?'

'There were women about the farm,' said Hall, 'and Thorgils and Thorgrim seemed unwilling to come back with us. So we left them to guard the house.'

'Let us hope the women took their minds off the ale,' said Skallagrim.

Then he gathered all his men and they set out for the farm with Hall guiding them, and came there before daylight.

The house was well built and of a fair size, with a good steading. The main room in the house was large and furnished in a suitable way. A fire burnt there, and a woman was cooking food at it. Thorgils sat on a bench near by, and had a very old woman sitting beside him. He spoke much to the woman who was cooking, bidding her take pains with what she was doing, 'Else I will visit you with certain other pains.'

The old woman laughed loudly and said, 'Beat her, man, beat her as she has often beaten me. It does me good to see her humbled like this.'

The woman who cooked was the mistress of the house. She was tall and not uncomely, though now her face was red with weeping and her clothes were somewhat untidy.

Thorgils said, 'Stir up the fire now, for when the broth boils we shall go back to bed.'

The old woman cackled shrilly, but her mistress turned and struck at Thorgils with a ladle. He caught her by the wrist, however, and vexed her with his laughing.

Thorgrim sat on the other side of the room, and had a young strong-looking serving-woman beside him. She was busy mixing dough for bread. She seemed rather sullen, yet she listened to what Thorgrim was saying and looked at him in a sidelong way.

When Skallagrim and the men came in Thorgils and Thorgrim greeted them noisily and said there would be good cheer for all.

'We have set things moving,' said Thorgils. 'Thorgrim and I have done what we could to make the women friendly towards us and eager in our service. There is moreover a sufficiency of food for us all.'

Some of the men went to the fire and took the ladle from the women there and supped the boiling broth. And though they burnt their mouths they would not stop till Skallagrim drove them away. Others took handfuls of the dough the serving-woman was mixing, and ate that. But Skallagrim made them stand away and wait till food was ready for all. The room they were in was too small for the whole company, so half he sent into the barn, and bade them stay quietly there and not show themselves about the farm. And he told three or four men to go and keep watch from the farther outbuildings and from a hedge that sheltered the house.

'You need not worry yourself about keeping a watch, Skallagrim,' said Thorgils. 'This is a lonely place and far from any neighbours.'

'I am the best judge of what is needed,' said Skallagrim.

Then the food was made ready, and there was plenty for them all, of broth and mutton, and cheese and butter-milk and bread. There was not much ale, and they drew lots for that. Then when they had eaten their fill they lay down and slept, all except those who kept watch. And Skallagrim bade them see that the women did not run away.

XXXIX

They lay quiet that day and the following night, waking only to eat and fall asleep again. No one came near the farm. There were cows to be milked, and some of the men helped the women do that, and drank the milk while it was still warm.

On the second morning Skallagrim took Kol and Hall the Icelander apart, and told Thorgils to bring the women to them.

He asked them in what piece of the country they
were, and what men of note lived near by, and whether
any company of the Danish army were in the
neighbourhood: 'For I take it that Halfdan calls himself
king here, and has some part of the army with him?'

The mistress of the house pressed her lips together
and would answer nothing, nor would the serving-girl
speak while she was there. So they took her away by
herself to question her, and they found she was too
stupid to tell anything that was useful. But the old
woman nodded her head and laughed when her mistress
was threatened with a stick, and seemed well pleased
with the way that things had gone.

Skallagrim said, 'It does not look as though we shall
learn much from these women, since one is stubborn
and the other a fool.'

Kol said, 'You have not asked anything of the old
one yet.'

'I think she is so old that she has lost her wits,' said
Skallagrim. 'I cannot see much to make her happy, yet
she has done nothing but laugh since we came here.'

'There may be a reason for that,' said Kol, and spoke
kindly to her.

The old woman said, 'This is the first day for many a
year that I have not been beaten by that one there.'
And she took a stick that was lying near and struck her
mistress over the shoulders.

'What can you tell us of this country?' said
Skallagrim.

'More than she could, since I have lived longer,' said
the old woman. 'It is a good country, but full of bad
men. Our own people were weak and bad, and you
foreigners are strong and bad, and which are the worse I
cannot tell. There were good men once, in the abbey
by the river-mouth, but they are gone now. For old
folk and good folk can do little to help themselves. It is
an ill world, it seems, and I am glad of this chance to

enjoy myself for once.' And she struck her mistress several times with the stick.

'Is there any town near here?' said Skallagrim.

'York is not far for a man with a horse fit to carry him,' said the old woman. 'But it is too far for me to have any interest in it, for I have never seen it and never shall. Where do you come from? Judging by your beards it is some time since you left home.'

'From Rousay in Orkney,' said Kol.

'Some men from Orkney came here a long while ago,' said the old woman, 'but I think they are dead now, all but him who brought them here.'

'Who was that?' said Skallagrim.

The old woman laughed and cackled: 'A bonny man with a pale face like yours, tall like you, but not bald like you nor young like you.'

'What do they call him?' said Skallagrim.

The old woman stood up and began to walk to and fro in a shambling way. She carried her head high, but her arms hung loose and her feet seemed to slide on the ground. 'He walks like that,' she said, 'and they call him Ivar the Boneless.'

Kol and Skallagrim were silent for a little while. Then Skallagrim said, 'Our mother is going to have the best of this business, as I thought.'

'That seems likely indeed,' said Kol.

'Where is Ivar now?' asked Skallagrim.

'Had you come a few days earlier you would have seen him,' said the old woman, 'for he was here last week.'

'But where is he now?'

'Unless he is at his hall in Eastadale I do not know.'

'And how far away is that?'

The old woman pointed inland and said, 'A long way. It may be twenty miles or it may be more. I am no great traveller and cannot say for certain, but that is what I have heard.'

Then Skallagrim asked how many men had been with Ivar when he came to the farm, and how many he kept in Eastadale.

The old woman scratched her head and began to mutter and to count upon her fingers: 'He had twelve or fourteen with him when he came here, but he will have more than that in Eastadale. He will have a great company there, I think.'

'How many?' said Skallagrim. 'Forty perhaps?'

'It may well be that he has forty,' said the old woman.

'Or perhaps sixty?' said Kol.

'He is sure to have as many as that,' she said.

'Or even a hundred?' asked Hall.

'Who can say?' answered the old woman. 'Ivar is a great man and the worst man, great or small, in this country, so he is likely to have as many men as he wants.'

The mistress of the house said, 'He has more than enough to deal with your ill-looking crew.'

'Hush, chatterbox,' said the old woman, and struck her on the cheek.

'I can tell you about the Danes' army also,' she said, 'for one of Ivar's men spoke of it while he was here. Part of it is now in Tyne valley, and that is a long way to the north, though how far I cannot say, for I have never been there. And Halfdan, who calls himself king and is Ivar's brother, is there also. But most of the army is in the south part of Mercia, a great distance from here, and is making ready to fight against a king in Wessex called Alfred, with whom they have fought already. Ivar fought against him but always had the worse of it, so now he will go no more against Alfred, but sits in his own country and works evil among his neighbours.'

Then Skallagrim sent the three women away.

'Now,' he said, 'it is clear enough what we must do.

The men are well fed and well rested now, and in good heart. Let us march against Eastadale without dalay, and deal with Ivar as roughly as we can.'

'I see no need for that and not much profit in it either,' said Hall.

Skallagrim said, 'I am minded to humour my mother in this, for it has always been her wish that we should take up her feud against Ivar, and now that he is near at hand I think it right that we should do what we can.'

Hall said, 'And do you think the same, Kol?'

'I have long said that I would deal with Ivar when the time came,' said Kol.

'Well then,' said Hall, 'if you two mean to humour your mother I may as well humour you and come with you. For I do not fear death. I have already done most things that a man may do, except die, and I have found nothing so far that a brave man need be frightened of. So I do not see why death should make me afraid, since it is nothing out of the common, but something all must face in due season.'

'Let us warn the men to make ready,' said Skallagrim.

XL

The old woman said there was a path over the moor to Eastadale that they could follow even by night if they were careful and walked with their eyes open. There were a few horses at the farm, and Skallagrim had them brought in so that some might ride, taking it in turns to rest if they became weary.

They waited for the moon to rise before they set out. The moon was full and gave them a good light when the clouds did not cover it.

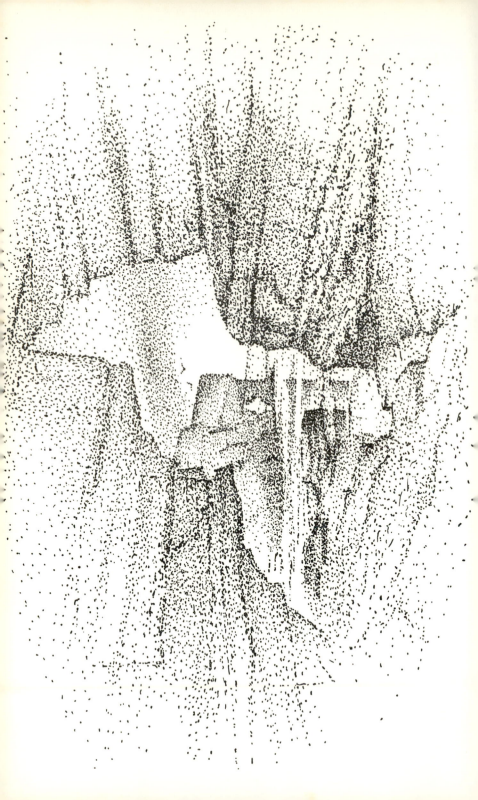

Now the old woman said, 'If you leave me here with my mistress she will kill me for what I have said and what I have done to-day.'

Skallagrim said, 'What else can we do? For you cannot come with us.'

The old woman said, 'Tie her up, then, so that she cannot interfere with me while I pack together a few things and make ready to go away. I have a daughter living somewhere to the south of here, and if I can find her she will take me in and look after me.'

Skallagrim bade two of the men get thongs and bind the mistress of the house by her hands and feet.

Then she began to scream and beg them not to do that, for if they left her helpless the old woman would murder her.

Skallagrim said, 'I must help her who helped me,' and told the men to tie her up.

She screamed still, but then the old woman took a knife and held it to her throat, and her mistress was silent. The old woman cackled loudly and told Skallagrim it was time now for him to go, 'For you have given me all the help I need, and you will do yourself no good by staying here longer.'

But the mistress of the house whimpered and rocked to and fro in fear when she was left alone with the old woman.

The Orkneymen went by the path they had been shown, and marched quickly. They were in good spirits, strong again, and glad to be on land though it was a strange land and likely to comfort them little. There were seven or eight horses, and some men rode on them. The path led them away from the river valley and out on to moorland. When the moon came out they saw the moor stretching far on every side, rising to hills ahead of them and to the north. It was empty

Scabra Head, Rousay

country and they saw no houses. It was rough
marching, they often stumbled, but they had little
difficulty in keeping to the path.

Before the sun rose, but when it was light enough to
see for some distance, they came to a high part of the
road and saw beneath them a valley well cultivated and
in the middle of it a large and strongly built hall with
many outhouses and farm-buildings near it. A stream
ran through the valley and a small wood grew behind
the house.

'Now we have come where our luck has brought us,'
said Skallagrim, and looked long at Ivar's hall of
Eastadale.

Hall the Icelander asked him what his plans were
now.

'I have no plan,' said Skallagrim, 'except this, to ride
to the door of that house and say I have come to see
Ivar the Boneless.'

'There is little wisdom in that,' said Hall. 'It would
be better to hide ourselves here in the moor and wait
till we see folk moving about, that we may know how
many men he has with him.'

'There is no need for that,' said Skallagrim.

Hall said, 'Let us lie hidden in the moor till night
falls. Then we can go down and make a ring round the
house and set fire to it.'

Skallagrim said, 'My meeting with Ivar is overdue
already. I cannot waste another day.'

'There is room in that house for twice as many men
as we have here,' said Hall.

Skallagrim's face grew dark with anger. He said, 'I am
no chapman to count one side against the other, nor am
I in a mood for arguing with any man except Ivar. I am
going now to see what kind of a man he is. Come with
me if you like, or if you choose to play the coward,
stay here. But do not argue with me, for my mind is
made up.'

'I am no coward,' said Hall, 'but I do not much like doing things for which I see no reason. What do you say to all this, Kol?'

Kol said, 'I go with Skallagrim.'

'It seems, then, that I shall do no good by talking any longer,' said Hall. 'And since I have said already that I would humour you in all this, let us go down together.'

Skallagrim bade the men go forward, but there was some muttering among them and a few said there was no sense in going against so great a house when they might find easier enemies elsewhere. Eric Arnison was one who spoke in this way. He said, 'Why should we not go to Ivar in a friendly way, since he is the greatest man of note in this part of Deira? Let us join our company to his, so that we may profit by any fighting we do.'

Skallagrim swung his axe and would have been the death of Eric, but Thorgils stayed him.

He said, 'Do not waste your strength, Skallagrim. You struck me and you struck my brother while we were aboard the Skua, so we owe somebody a blow or two. Let me deal with Eric, whom I do not much like in any case.'

Then Thorgils said to Eric, 'Do you set yourself up to say what shall be done or what shall not be done?'

Eric said, 'I have as good a claim to speak as you have, Thorgils.'

'You are in the right there,' said Thorgils, 'but men who are always in the right should stay at home and talk to their wives.' And he struck swiftly at Eric.

Eric put up his shield, but Thorgils was too quick and the axe went over the rim of the shield and took Eric between shoulder and neck. And he was dead of that stroke immediately.

Thorgrim said, 'One of us two, Thorgils or myself, is usually the first to set things going.'

Skallagrim said, 'There will be time for everyone to play a part in this business.'

Then he rode down the hill, and all followed him. They marched boldly, neither looking for concealment as they went, nor keeping silent. They spoke much, in loud voices, and spread out in a long line. The sun rose and the morning was bright and clear.

When they were still some distance from Ivar's hall they saw men moving about there. One or two came out and looked at them and went quickly indoors again. More came out, and these had weapons, and stood together in front of the house. When Skallagrim and his men drew near there were thirty, standing closely in a line. They were tall and warlike in appearance, well armed. Some carried bows. In the midst of them stood one not less in height or breadth than any there, though he seemed the youngest of them all. He was pale-faced and bore himself nobly, and was well-clad in a kirtle of scarlet and scarlet breeches. There was gold on his helmet, and he carried a shield and a long sword with gold on the hilt.

But Skallagrim and Kol and the other Orkneymen were shabbily dressed, their clothes stained with salt water and weather-bleached, and their beards were ragged and long.

The youth in red raiment said, 'Who are you and where do you come from?'

Skallagrim sat on his horse and looked slowly up and down the line of men.

'What do you seek here?' said the youth.

Skallagrim said, 'Is Ivar the Boneless among you?'

'What news do you bring for Ivar?'

'Bring Ivar to me and I shall tell him,' said Skallagrim.

The youth said, 'I will not do that until I hear who you are and why you seek Ivar. But answer frankly and perhaps I shall help you.'

Skallagrim said, 'You speak boldly. What is your name?'

'Ragnar,' said the youth. 'I am Ivar's son.'

Skallagrim rubbed his chin and answered nothing to that.

Ragnar said, 'Tell your name now.'

Skallagrim said, 'There will be time for that. But is Ivar not within the house? For we have come a long way, and we would not care to go home without having spoken to him.'

'That may be,' said Ragnar, 'yet I told you what questions you must answer before I give you news of Ivar, and you do not seem ready to do that. Moreover you are somewhat mannerless in refusing to tell me your name.'

'We are all hungry and tired,' said Skallagrim. 'We have marched a long way, and before that we were many days at sea. Perhaps our manners would mend if you took us in and gave us meat and drink and a seat by the fire.'

Ragnar spoke to those of his men who were near him. Then he said, 'That does not seem a good plan to me, for you have a large company there, and I scarcely know if you are inclined to be friendly towards us.'

'Set your mind at ease about that,' said Skallagrim. 'I am no friend of Ivar's, nor friendly to any of his people.'

'Then you will eat none of his meat and drink none of his ale,' said Ragnar.

'I am not so sure about that,' said Skallagrim, and took a throwing-spear and threw it hard at a man who stood beside Ragnar and had turned to speak in his ear. He was a great broad-faced man, richly dressed, and seemed to be of note. He saw Skallagrim lift the spear, and stooped to avoid it. But he was too slow and the spear took him in the side of the neck, and cut the large vessels there and sheared through his windpipe, so that he fell at Ragnar's feet and was dead almost at once.

Now Ivar's men gave a great shout of anger, and

those who had bows shot arrows at the Orkneymen, and others threw spears. But the Orkneymen did not stand still, and were not content to fight at a distance, but raised their axes and ran fiercely at Ivar's men and fought with them at close quarters.

Skallagrim got down from his horse and Thorgils and Thorgrim went forward beside him. Skallagrim said to them, 'Do not kill Ragnar nor hurt him much, but take him prisoner and guard him for me.'

'That will not be difficult,' said Thorgils, and ran at Ivar's son, with his shield held high. And Thorgrim went after him.

Ragnar struck downwards at Thorgils and his sword went into Thorgils' shield. Thorgils twisted his shield, throwing his arm stiffly to the left, and wrenched the sword from Ragnar's hand. But now a man called Bard, a great holmgang man, fierce in temper, came in upon Thorgils' other side and hewed at him with an axe. Thorgils let go his shield and threw himself forward, so that Bard over-reached and the haft of his axe fell upon Thorgils' shoulder. Yet the strength of his blow was such that Thorgils' byrnie broke asunder beneath it.

Thorgrim had killed a man on Ragnar's other side. Now he turned and swung a backhand blow at Bard, so that the hammer of his axe took Bard under the ear and cracked his skull and felled him.

'Bare is his back who has no brother,' said Thorgils, and leapt on Ragnar and wrestled with him. Thorgrim struck Ragnar on the head with the flat of his axe, but not hard, so that he was stunned only and lay still.

'He is safe there,' said Thorgrim. 'I was gentle as a girl with him.'

Skallagrim fought with two and had the better of them. Kol slew a man who came at him swinging an axe in both hands. Then Kol fought with a tall man, broad of shoulder and long in the arm, who guarded himself well. They fought a long time till both their shields were cut down to the arm-holds, and they threw them away. Then they rested a little while. Kol heard someone behind him and turned swiftly.

Gauk of Calfskin stood there, holding his sword Leg-biter, and Bran was tied to his belt by a thong. Gauk had struck no blows yet, but the sweat stood on his face as though he had been fighting hard.

He said, 'Do not concern yourself about danger on this side, Kol. We will look to it here. Keep your eyes to the front while Bran and I guard you from behind.'

'A wall might serve better,' said Kol, 'yet do what you can, Gauk.'

Then he fought again, and gave a great shout of laughter as he hewed at Ivar's man. And now he struck him on the sword-arm, a little above the wrist, so that he sheared off the hand. The man gripped the stump with the other hand and fled from the battle. But Gauk ran after him, loosing Bran, and Bran took him by the heels so that he fell. Then Gauk killed him.

Now many of Ivar's men were killed and many wounded, and those who could run took to running, some into the house, some into the wood behind the house, and some down the valley. For the Orkneymen had the greater number, and from being so long at sea they were fierce and reckless, and not to be withstood. Then the Orkneymen scattered and followed those who fled from them.

Skallagrim and Kol went through all the house looking for Ivar, but they could not find him. They came to the women's bower, and there were some women there, but not many. Skallagrim told them to fasten their door and keep behind it. Then he and Kol went to the barn and the outhouses and searched there, but found nothing of Ivar.

A man sat on the ground who had been wounded. He had his back to Kol and Skallagrim, his head was bent down, and he was holding his belly.

Kol said, 'There is a wounded man. Let us ask him if
he knows anything of Ivar.'

But when they came near him they saw that he was
none of Ivar's men, but Deaf Gylfi. He held his hands
pressed against his belly so that his guts should not fall
out, for he had been deeply wounded.

Kol knelt beside him and bade him be of good heart.

'My heart is good enough,' said Gylfi, 'but my guts
are falling out.'

'Lie flat on your back,' said Kol. 'You will be easier
that way.'

'I shall be flat on my back very soon,' said Gylfi.
'But tell me this, Kol, before I die: against whom have I
been fighting and to what purpose? For I am somewhat
deaf, as you know, and men will not trouble themselves
with answering more than two or three times when I
ask a question of them. And sometimes that is not
enough. I asked Hall and some others where we were
marching and against whom we were likely to come to
blows, but they would not answer loud enough for me
to hear. So I do not know who killed me, nor whose
man, a little while before that, I also killed. And it
would interest me to know.'

Kol spoke in Gylfi's ear: 'We came to find Ivar the
Boneless, and the men with whom we fought were
Ivar's men.'

'Speak louder,' said Gylfi.

Kol spoke that sentence again.

Gylfi shook his head. 'It may be I have heard you
rightly, and may be I have not,' he said. 'Did you say
Ivar the Boneless?'

'Yes,' said Kol.

'I am glad it was no lesser man,' said Gylfi. Then he
fell sideways and was dead.

Skallagrim said, 'We must look for Thorgils and
Thorgrim. They will have Ragnar with them.'

There was none but dead men outside the house

now, so they went indoors again, and there was a great stir there. There was all manner of goods and riches, well-woven cloth of many colours, furs, and foreign leather, and large chests with silk cloth in them, and a great store of silver brooches and other ornaments. The men were plundering these and scattering them about. There were fine weapons in the hall, and elsewhere the Orkneymen had found casks of ale and broached them. But Thorgils and Thorgrim were not in the hall.

Then there came a din, louder than the other noise, from that part of the house where the women's bower was. Kol and Skallagrim went there and found that the door had been broken down, and the women stood in a corner screaming. But Thorgils and Thorgrim stood before them and fought with five other Orkneymen.

Kol and Skallagrim thrust them apart and bade them say who first began the brawl.

Thord was one of the men who had been fighting. He said, 'Thorgils began it, for we came here and found him and his brother before us. Then they said that we must wait till they had made their choice among the women, for that was their right since they had been the first to find them. But we said that all had the same right, and we would wait for nobody.'

Skallagrim said, 'The women shall stay here no longer, else you will all be fighting.' and he told the women to take what clothes they wanted, and they should leave the house together.

They asked him where they could go, but he said he cared nothing about that.

Then the men grew angry because the women were to be sent away, but Skallagrim spoke so fiercely to them that none dared object a second time. So the women made themselves ready and came through the hall weeping, and the men there stopped their plundering and stared at them. Many made as though they would take hold of the women, but Skallagrim

forbade them, and again his bearing was so fierce that
no one withstood him. Yet they muttered among
themselves and thought he was too overbearing.

The women went out and came to a bridle-path
leading down the valley, and walked slowly along it.
They carried clothes in bundles and wept loudly as they
went. There were four or five children whom they led
or took in their arms. Skallagrim kept all his men about
him till they were out of sight.

He said, 'You will have enough fighting to do against
others. I will not have you brawling among yourselves.'

Then he asked Thorgils and Thorgrim what they had
done with Ragnar.

Thorgils said, 'He is safe enough,' and pointed
outdoors.

Two or three dead men lay there, and Ragnar was
under one of them. Thorgils pulled him out and
brought him into the hall. He was still stunned, but
after a little while and after they had poured water on
him he came to life again. But he did not seem very
well pleased with the way in which he found things.

Skallagrim said, 'Tell me where is Ivar the Boneless.'

Ragnar looked round about and said, 'Tell me where
are the men who were mine and his.'

'I think they are dead,' said Skallagrim.

'All of them?' Ragnar asked.

Skallagrim spoke to Hall the Icelander: 'Are any of
Ivar's men still living?'

'None except this one here,' said Hall.

Ragnar said slowly, 'You must be men well used to
warfare, and lucky besides, for you have lost few out of
your own company.'

'We are eight less than we were,' said Skallagrim.

'Eight were killed,' said Hall, 'and some are deeply
wounded.'

Ragnar said, 'You have fought well. Will you not tell
me what country you have come out of?'

Skallagrim said, 'Tell me where Ivar is.'

'He has gone to buy horses,' said Ragnar.

'Where?'

Ragnar thought a little while and said slowly, 'To a farm some forty miles away.'

'How long would you take to ride there?'

'The road is bad, but I could reach him a little after midnight.'

Skallagrim said, 'I will let you go free on this condition: when evening comes you will ride straightway to Ivar and tell him that Skallagrim Thorlief's son, Ragnar Hairybreeks' son, and Kol Cock-crow his brother, are come out of Orkney seeking him in the matter of that atonement which he did not pay for Bui of Ness, whom he killed, and also in consideration of certain wrongs he did to Signy my mother, Thorlief's wife and Bui's. Tell him that we shall wait here till he comes, for we have travelled far and do not mean to go bootless home.'

The men murmured when they heard that, and Hall said loudly, 'This is madness, Skallagrim. Will you let Ragnar go free to bring all the strength of the country against us? How many men has Ivar with him? How many neighbours has he over the hill who will find men to help him? Ragnar will say how few we are, and Ivar will bring so many that we shall have no better chance than sheep against him.'

'Are you turning cowardly again, Hall?' said Skallagrim.

'I have said before that I am no coward,' said Hall, 'But neither am I mad, and what you propose now is nothing but madness.'

'Has not my rede been good so far?' said Skallagrim. 'Were we not well-advised to come against Eastadale as we did, and attack it without lying till we were cold to count enemies as a housewife counts her chickens? Have we not done well, doing as I said we should do?'

'Luck has been with you so far to-day,' said Hall, 'but luck will not ride long on the same horse with folly. And I say plainly that to let Ragnar go would be great folly, and I stand against you in such a plan.'

Many of the Orkneymen said that Hall was in the right, and they were on his side in this matter. And there was much talk and argument about it.

Then Skallagrim grew wrathful and said, 'Luck may turn against us indeed, for no man knows more than this, that all men will some day die. But whoever goes against me in this, then luck is against him now. For I am not to be used lightly and thwarted by any man, and if you, Hall, or some other, set yourself up to oppose me, then I will deal with you now, and show that I am not less to be feared than Ivar and all his men. I shall not stir from here till I have seen Ivar, and Ragnar rides to tell him so to-night. That is my plan. Whoever dislikes it can say so now, and I shall answer him.'

Skallagrim stood before with his axe raised.

'That is a good argument you have there,' said Thorgils. 'It will speak sharply.'

'Its lip is too thin for kissing,' said Skallagrim.

Hall spoke to Kol: 'What do you say to this madness that Skallagrim calls a plan?'

'A bold rede is often the best,' said Kol, 'and I stand by him.'

'I do not like it,' said Hall bitterly, 'and I think you two are fey.'

Skallagrim said, 'Do you still speak against me?'

'Put your axe away,' said Hall. 'I see no use in dying under it to-day if I can live beside it till to-morrow. But though I give in to you I do not think any the better of your plan.'

'Think as you like,' said Skallagrim, 'so long as you do what I wish.'

Hall went away grumbling. After he had given in

none of the other men cared to say anything, but they were rather silent for some time.

Ragnar said to Skallagrim, 'It seems, then, that we are kinsmen.'

'There is no love lost in many families that I know of,' said Skallagrim.

'That is so,' said Ragnar. 'And often there are more bold men than wise ones in a house.'

XLI

Skallagrim sat by himself and had his axe on his knees. For a long time he spoke to no one, but fingered the haft and blade of his weapon, and looked so marvellously grim that none cared to come near. Sometimes he would frown and twitch his eyebrows. He took no notice of anyone and seemed not to hear the noise about him.

But Kol was merrier than he had been since Erling drowned, and went among the men and spoke cheerily to them. He said, 'Where is Gauk? For Gauk did me great service to-day, and I have not thanked him for it yet.'

Gauk came. He had been drinking well and was pleased with himself.

He said, 'Are you not glad that I came with you in the Skua, Kol? For I did something to help you this morning, as I promised I would when need arose.'

'You did,' said Kol. 'There was a cold wind blowing, and you stood so close to my back that you kept me warm.'

'Bran also did his share,' said Gauk, 'and Leg-biter was not idle. We three together are worth a lot, I think.'

'You are worth more than a better man,' said Kol.

'That may be true indeed,' said Gauk, 'for these better men are sometimes troublesome to deal with. We grow good things in Calfskin, but not often better things, for they would stir up rivalry.'

'You are far from Calfskin now,' said Hall.

'Not so far but I hope to go back there,' said Gauk.

'You must think well of Skallagrim's plan then,' said Hall.

Gauk said, 'I had no hand in making it, so I cannot be blamed if it turns out badly. Therefore I am easy in my mind about it. As to going back to Calfskin, that has been my intention from the beginning, and I have seen nothing so far to make me change my mind.'

'Here is one who ploughs his furrow straight,' said Kol, 'and does not bother himself with needless fears. It would be better for others if they were like him.'

Hall said, 'Are you pointing at me, Kol?'

'I will quarrel with no man here,' said Kol, 'for you are all my friends, and I will hug you rather than hurt you.'

Thorgils shouted, 'Hug me, Kol, for I am stronger than you and will show you how to hug.' He had drunk much ale and was both restless and merry.

Kol said, 'I will throw you first and throw your brother after.'

Then they stripped off their shirts and wrestled. Thorgils was broad as a door across the back, and very strongly thewed. But Kol was not small, he was more nimble than Thorgils, well-built and hard of flesh. They wrestled for some time, and then Kol twisted Thorgils off his feet and threw him, and fell on top of him.

Thorgils said, 'That was good so far as it went, but you are only half done yet. Thorgrim is waiting for you now.'

Thorgrim was a little bigger than his brother and somewhat fat. He gripped Kol and squeezed him so hard that the breath went out of him. Kol broke that grip and turned round in Thorgrim's arms, so that Thorgrim was behind him. Then he reached up and caught hold of Thorgrim's hair, and stooped suddenly, pulling at his hair, and threw Thorgrim over his head so that he fell flat on his back.

Kol said, 'Are there any more of you brothers? For it is clear that two are not enough for me.'

'We are too many for most men,' said Thorgils.

But Thorgrim said nothing, for he was not able. Kol brought ale to him, and he drank it, and then they sat down and drank together.

Presently Skallagrim got up from his bench and walked to and fro in the hall, looking at the goodly things which the Orkneymen had taken from chests and thrown about or set aside in corners. Skallagrim took the best of them, silk cloth and silver ornaments, brooches, a woman's head-dress sewn with pearls, and two or three swords with gold about the hilts. And he carried them to his own place, and sat there beside them, speaking to no one.

But when it grew to evening time he called to Ragnar and took him outdoors and gave him a horse.

He said, 'If you ride now, when will you reach the farm where Ivar is?'

'Not before morning,' said Ragnar.

'Ride then,' said Skallagrim, 'and tell him what I told you to say, and I shall wait here till he comes.'

Ragnar said, 'Even if he start straightaway he will hardly be here by nightfall tomorrow.'

'That will be time enough,' said Skallagrim.

'You would have done better to stay in Orkney, kinsman,' said Ragnar.

But Skallagrim said, 'Waste no more time, cousin,' and struck the horse a blow so that it set off swiftly, and Ragnar could say nothing more.

Then Skallagrim went back into the hall and said, 'Give me some ale, for I am dry with argument.'

He drank deeply and said, 'Ivar will come tomorrow night.'

'What shall we do till then?' said Hall.

Skallagrim said, 'Is there not ale enough to last the night?' And filled his horn again.

XLII

Presently Gauk came to Kol and drew him apart and spoke to him secretly. Gauk had gone outside some time before, but few had seen him going and no one noticed him coming back.

He said, 'I grew tired of drinking so much, since I cannot hold such a quantity of ale as Thorgils and Thorgrim can. So I went out and took Bran with me. For I remembered that in the morning I had seen one of Ivar's men who was wounded escape from the fight and run northwards up the valley. But he could not run fast, and someone soon caught him and killed him. I would have done so myself had I not been busy elsewhere. And now I thought I would go and see if the path by which he went led anywhere. So I walked carefully, keeping my eyes well open, and after some time I came to a lesser valley, a very small one, that opens off this one. And on the far side of that one are some trees, and among the trees a house, little and mean and not easily discovered. A house nowise so big or fine-looking as Calfskin. And I lay down and watched it, and soon I saw a woman come out, and a girl with her, and they stared for a long time down the valley. And though they were some distance away, my eyes were good enough to see that they were not ill-looking.'

Kol was silent for some while. Then he said, 'I think I also have drunk enough,' and got up and went out with Gauk.

They went northwards up the valley, and Gauk talked a great deal about his skill in finding things that other men were blind to.

Then they reached the little valley that opened westwards, and crossed a narrow stream there, and came to the trees and the house they sheltered. It was very small and there seemed to be no light in it.

The door was barred, but Kol put his shoulder to it and broke it open. There was a turf-fire in the room, and a rush-light burning. Two women stood in a corner by a shut-bed, and cried out when they came in. One was in middle age, and the other was a girl, tall, fair-haired, and comelier than most.

Gauk said, 'There is a cow-shed with clean straw in it. That will do for me, and I shall take the mother.'

He took the elder woman by the arm and pulled her out. She said nothing, but hung her head and wept, and turned again to the girl. But Gauk would not let her go.

Then Kol went to the girl, and spoke to her.

XLIII

When Ragnar, Ivar's son, had ridden some distance he came to the women whom Skallagrim had driven out of Eastadale. They sat by the roadside with their backs to the wind and their heads bent, as though they had lost heart. But Ragnar spoke and cheered them, and said they had only a little way to go before they arrived at that house where Ivar was, and where they would find shelter.

Then he rode on and presently came to a well-built house with a high fence round it, and many farm buildings near by. A man called Asbiorn lived there. He was a man of great wealth and fame, and somewhat evil-hearted. He had often fought beside Halfdan and

Ivar, and now that Halfdan was king in Northumbria
he had taken land there and settled down. He and Ivar
were very friendly, though Ivar was friendly with few
men, and now Ivar was visiting him.

When Ragnar went into the hall he found Asbiorn
and Ivar sitting together in the high seat. Ivar asked
him, 'What do you want here?'

'Nothing, except to tell you news,' said Ragnar.

'Ill news, by the length of your face,' said Asbiorn.

'I have told better,' said Ragnar.

Ivar spoke impatiently: 'Tell, then, and do not bandy
words about it.'

Ragnar said, 'Your household is killed and scattered,
your house is taken by vikings.'

Asbiorn leapt from his seat, bright red in the face,
and shouted loudly, calling for men and arms, but
spoke in such confusion that all was to little purpose.
Ivar sat quietly till Asbiorn had finished, and then said,
'What vikings are these?'

'They come out of Orkney,' said Ragnar, 'and they
are kinsmen of ours. They have done some cousinly
work already, for they have killed all those men whom
you left with me in Eastadale.'

Ivar said, 'Surely it is not my brother Thorlief?'

'Skallagrim, Thorlief's son, and Kol Cock-crow his
brother,' said Ragnar. 'They seek atonement for the
death of Bui of Ness, and have something to say about
a hurt done to Signy, Bui's wife and Thorlief's.
Skallagrim bade me tell you he would wait in Eastadale
till you came, for he had travelled far to see you and
was not minded to go home with nothing done.'

Ivar sat for a long time without speaking. He made
no move, except that his face worked and he seemed to
have meat in his mouth that he could not swallow.
Then he got up from the high seat and walked about in
the hall. Ragnar stood where he was.

Ivar said, 'What manner of men are they?'

'Bold ones,' said Ragnar.

'Bold indeed, to come here where Halfdan is king and sack Ivar's hall,' said Asbiorn.

'And they fight as though fighting were both their trade and their pleasure,' said Ragnar. 'But I do not think they are very wise.'

'How is that?' said Ivar.

Ragnar said, 'They let me go free to bring you this message, and that, to my way of thinking, was folly. Moreover they were easy to deceive, for they readily believed me when I said that it would take me all night to ride here. They do not expect to see you before nightfall tomorrow.'

Ivar grinned and put his hand on Ragnar's shoulder. 'You have more wit than I thought you had. How many men are with them?'

'I think there are thirty or so left,' said Ragnar.

'How many have you, Asbiorn?' said Ivar.

'More than that,' said Asbiorn.

Ivar said, 'And I have twelve with me. Let us ride together and find our kinsmen before they wake.'

He said to Ragnar, 'What were they doing when you left?'

'Drinking deep,' said Ragnar.

Then Ivar grew merry, and was uglier to look at than when he was sober-minded. Asbiorn made a great stir and busied himself to bring in his men and have them armed. Ivar and Asbiorn put on their byrnies and took weapons. In a little while all were ready, and they had sixty men with them. So they set out and rode towards Eastadale.

It was now very dark, but they knew the road well and travelled swiftly. When they were some distance from Eastadale they stopped and got down from their horses. Ten men were left to look after the horses, and the rest went forward. Ivar bade them tread quietly and not talk among themselves.

They came to Eastadale and halted. Ivar and Asbiorn
and two or three more went silently to the house and
looked in. Both the outer and the inner doors were
open, and they could see clearly into the hall.

The Orkneymen had built a great fire far out on to
the floor, so there was light in the hall. Many of the
men lay sleeping. Others sat here and there, two or
three together, and drank, but quietly now. In a corner
by the fire there were six together, and it seemed to
Ivar that they were the chief men among the vikings.

When they had seen all this Ivar and Asbiorn went
back to their company and spoke as to what they
should do.

Asbiorn said, 'Let us set fire to the house and burn
them all within it.'

But Ivar would have nothing to do with that. 'For it
is my house that you would burn,' he said, 'and I can
put it to a better use than that.'

'You cannot make a fire if you grudge the wood,'
said Asbiorn.

'I see no need of a fire,' said Ivar. 'I would rather
catch my kinsmen alive than have them cooked. You
can do more with living men than with cinders, and I
would like to speak with them a while before they die.
We are cousins, Asbiorn, and cousins have much to talk
about. Therefore I counsel this, that we gather quietly
at the outer door, go quickly in, kill those who seem of
little account, and hemming in the others with our
shields, make captives of them. So many lie drunk or
sleeping that it seems to me we shall have little
difficulty in doing this.'

Then Asbiorn agreed to that and told his men
how they should act. So they drew in to the house,
and when they were ready shouted all together, and
ran swiftly in. Some men who lay near the door,
and were dead drunk, they killed at once. But
others woke and took weapons and defended

themselves. Then there was a great stir and turmoil in the hall.

Skallagrim rose from his seat with a loud cry when he saw they were attacked. Ivar was one of the first who came into the hall. Skallagrim looked and saw a man taller than the others, pale-faced and ugly as a troll. He walked swiftly in a loose and shambling way. Skallagrim guessed him to be Ivar, and took his axe and ran towards him. There was a long table between them, with meat still on it. Skallagrim leapt on the table and ran three steps down it. He swung his axe high and jumped far out. striking swiftly at Ivar while he was still in the midst of his jump. But one of Asbiorn's men came between them, pushing Ivar back, and he was a tall strong man. Skallagrim's axe fell on his shoulder, close to the neck, and sank far into his chest. Skallagrim fell to his knees and lost hold of his axe. But the man whom he had killed dropped his sword, being dead on the instant, and Skallagrim took that and thurst fiercely at Ivar. Ivar was somewhat out of reach, yet the sword-point went three fingers' breadth into his thigh, not far from the groin.

Then Skallagrim evaded many blows that were aimed at him, and came back to the table and leapt right across it, and went to the corner by the fire. The men who had been drinking with him there had thrown benches in front of them, and stood behind the benches to guard themselves. They were Hall the Icelander, Thord, Thorgils and Thorgrim, and some others who had joined them.

Skallagrim said, 'Where is Kol?'

But no one had seen Kol for some time.

Then Asbiorn's men and Ivar's came against them, and there was hard fighting, but they were beaten back and three were left dead.

'If Kol were here we might break through them and reach the door,' said Skallagrim.

Now others of the Orkneymen had gathered at the far end of the hall, and fought there. These were men who had wakened and found the enemy round them, and fought singly for a while till they could reach some of their friends. Most of them were already wounded, but when a few came together they fought well and so fiercely that Asbiorn must call off some who were facing Skallagrim in the chimney-corner.

'I wish Kol were here,' said Skallagrim.

'We are enough as we are to break through and join the others,' said Hall.

Skallagrim said, 'I have a plan to do something that will summon Kol to help us if he is anywhere near.'

'I also have a plan,' said Thorgils, 'but it is to help ourselves. I think I am stronger than you, brother.'

'I do not think so,' said Thorgrim.

'Watch this, then, and know,' said Thorgils. Then he gave his axe to Thorgrim and took by the end one of those benches that lay before them. It was long and heavy, long enough for six men to sit upon, and was made stoutly of oak. Thorgils took a step forward and swung it like a club. It took one of Asbiorn's men under the ear and cracked his skull. The others fell back before him and the Orkneymen came out from their corner.

But Skallagrim ran to the fire and kicked the burning coals over the floor.

Now the Orkneymen, with Thorgils swinging his club before them, fought their way to the door. But one of Ivar's men threw a spear at Thorgils and struck him through the belly, so that he fell forward and was out of the fight. Then the Orkneymen gave back a little.

Now matters were in this shape, that in both corners by the end wall, in the middle of which was the door, some of the Orkneymen stood and were hemmed in by Ivar's men and Asbiorn's. And there was fierce fighting.

Byrnies broke asunder, shields were cut to the middle, and many wounds taken.

Skallagrim called to Ivar to come and fight with him, but Ivar stood in the background and held his thigh where it was wounded. Asbiorn said to him, 'This is not so easy as you said it would be.'

'Your men were too slow,' said Ivar.

'No slower than yours in the morning,' said Asbiorn. 'Had you listened to me and set fire to the house all would have been over by now.'

A man called Grani was wounded in the face by Skallagrim and had his left ear cut off. He turned from fighting and ran wildly about the hall, crying he had lost an ear and must find it again. He crawled on the floor and looked under benches, making a great noise all the time. Then he came to the far part of the hall, and saw that the floor there and the end gable were alight and burning fast from the coals that Skallagrim had kicked about. So Grani forgot his ear and shouted loudly to Ivar that his house was on fire.

Ivar turned and saw flames rising to the roof. He said to Asbiorn, 'You have got your wish, it seems.'

'But too late,' said Asbiorn. 'It will rather hinder than help us now.' And he egged on his people, that they might kill or capture the Orkneymen before the fire spread over them all.

Now Skallagrim cried that help was coming, and pointed to the flames. Hall wounded one of Ivar's men. Thorgrim slew another. Thorgrim had slain three since his brother was killed. He said, 'Thorgils did well with his club, but his strength has not lasted as long as mine.'

The Orkneymen on the other side of the door also did well. There was a man called Fridleif there, a bonder's son out of Birsay. While they were in the Skua he had acted quietly and no one had thought much about him. He was young, and this was the first time he had been on warfare. But now he seemed the mightiest of men and none could stand against him. He hewed with his axe and called to those who faced him, 'You keep good ale in England. Who would think I was dead-drunk an hour ago?'

He hewed at a man and missed him.

'That was not so well done,' said the man.

'No tree falls at the first stroke,' said Fridleif, and swung a swift back-handed blow so that his axe came above the man's knee and took off his leg there.

One of the Orkneymen who stood beside him said, 'You have learnt something since you came aboard with us.'

'A man who travels far needs his wits about him,' said Fridleif. 'Anything will pass at home.'

Half the roof of the hall was blazing now, and a cross-beam fell with a great crash. There was a strong breeze blowing, and the fire roared. The air grew hot, so that not only the strength of their blows made men sweat. And Ivar and Asbiorn egged on their men continually, for the fire was coming closer to their backs. But Skallagrim cheered his fellows again and said the flames would help them.

Then the far gable fell and the wind blew through it and swept the fire towards them, and they fought in thick smoke, and sparks flew through the smoke and stung their faces and their arms.

Now those of the Orkneymen who were left alive grew weary. But most of them were dead. On the one side were Skallagrim and Hall the Icelander, Thorgrim, and two more. And on the other side Fridleif still fought and mocked his foes. Olaf, Deaf Gylfi's son was with him, and four others. Their arms were tired, their bodies weak, and they could no longer strike hard or straight. Their blows fell feebly.

Ivar bade his men press upon them with their shields and take them alive, and his men came fiercely in, for the fire was scorching their backs, and the Orkneymen could not stand before them, but fell under their shields.

Then Ivar's men gripped them by neck and arm and drove them through the door. Some had their clothes burning, and some were faint with the smoke that blew upon them.

A little while after they had come outside the other gable took fire, and the flames burnt higher. The roof of the hall fell in and a great cloud of sparks rose.

Ivar's men took thongs and bound the Orkneymen by their hands and feet. Skallagrim said, 'Had Kol been here we might have done better than this.'

XLIV

When Kol and Gauk went into the house where the women were they tied Bran outside. In the middle of the night he took to barking, and Gauk went to see what was amiss. The slope of a hill cut off his view of the larger valley, but over the hill he saw smoke rising, and judged it came from Ivar's hall. So he went quickly in and roused Kol.

Kol came out and they looked towards the smoke. The moon had risen now, it was a day or two past the full, and they saw but little flame. Yet from the quantity of smoke it seemed that the fire was a large one. Kol said they must go at once, and ran in to take his weapons. The women came with them to the edge of the trees in which the house stood.

Then Kol and Gauk ran together, and Bran with them. They ran in the bright moonlight.

But in a little while Kol stopped as though he were short of breath, and looked up at the moon, and then put his hand over his eyes. He began to shake, and his knees weakened so that he could not stand upright. Gauk turned and asked what was wrong with him, but Kol did not answer. He fell forward and hid his face against the ground, and shook with fear. Gauk took him by the shoulder and spoke to him again, but that did not help. Kol's teeth chattered loudly and his water ran out.

Gauk saw that his fit was on him, and the ill-wish that Geira had wished him was working, that the fear he had felt when he killed her and saw the moon shining in her eyes would return and grow stronger, and ill-luck would come on him in that light.

So Gauk sat down beside him and waited awhile. Presently he said, 'When Geira was riding the roof at Calfskin I little thought that this would happen because of her. It is said that a man who travels widely must be prepared for both good and evil, but I think that is harder than it sounds, and what to do in this present case is more than I know.'

Kol rose and tried to go forward again, but the moonlight sickened him and he could not walk. He said, 'Take me back to the women's house, for I have not strength to go farther.'

So Gauk led him back. Kol stumbled as he went. His head was bowed and he hid his eyes.

When they came to the house he lay on the floor like one saved from drowning. The women asked what was wrong with him, and Gauk said, 'He has a fit that comes on him in the moonlight because of a troll-wife he killed, and she ill-wished him. I have seen it before, more than once, but never so bad as this. Yet she said it would grow worse in time and so it seems indeed.'

The woman said, 'There was a king once, and he was well known for his wisdom. But a Finn woman bewitched him.'

The girl sat down by Kol and tried to comfort him.

Gauk said, 'I think he has never had more need of his strength than now when it has deserted him. For if that smoke means anything, our friends are in danger,'

The older woman said, 'Will you sit here and do nothing because he is useless?'

Gauk said, 'I am a brave enough man in the ordinary way, and I have used my sword Leg-biter to some purpose. But I do not care for setting out alone when I know nothing of what is before me. If I wait till Kol is ready to come I shall be worth more with him beside me than by myself.'

So they waited there, and the girl was good to Kol and used him fondly.

XLV

When it began to grow light Kol rose and seemed to have his strength again.

The girl said, 'You are still pale.'

'I have seen a man come out of the arrow-storm,' said Kol, 'and he was pale. Wounds do not make a man fair to look at, and I have suffered worse than wounds.'

Then he bade Gauk make himself ready. So they took their weapons and went out. But before they had gone from under the trees Kol turned and went back, and found the girl standing by herself before the house.

He took a gold ring from his finger, a heavy gold ring from his arm, a silver brooch that pinned his cloak, and gave them to her. He said, 'These ornaments no longer suit me, I think. But they will show well on you.'

The girl took them but paid no attention to them, though they were of great price. She said, 'Stay here and I will look after you and hide you.'

But Kol said that could not be, and left her.

Then he and Gauk walked swiftly, neither speaking. And now Kol seemed marvellously sure of himself, but Gauk looked from side to side and was nowise comfortable. When they came in sight of the hall they saw that it had been burnt to the ground, and some of the outhouses with it. But others still stood, and the fire had not gone into the wood behind the house, for the wind had blown from that quarter. There was no wind now. The day was calm and mist lay on the hills on either side of the valley.

They walked openly to the ruin of the hall and looked about them, and saw no living men. There were weapons lying about here and there. Kol picked up a throwing spear, and saw that it had not been spoiled by the fire.

Then Bran pricked his ears and snarled, looking towards the wood.

'Those who are left will be there,' said Kol, and went into the wood with Gauk behind him. They trod warily and walked without making any noise. The wood was small, and soon they came to where they could see through a fringe of branches what lay beyond, and saw those of the Orkneymen who were still living, and Ivar's men standing about them.

Ivar and Asbiorn had waited till morning and then had taken Skallagrim and his men to the far side of the wood. Ivar would not stay on the other side near the hall because of the smell of burning there. The storehouses had caught fire and still smouldered, and there had been a great quantity of meat in one and of cloth in another.

The Orkneymen had been tied both at wrist and ankle till morning came, but then their ankles were loosed. Ivar made them sit together on the trunk of a tree that had been felled. He and Asbiorn mocked them for a long time, and laughed at them for believing Ragnar when he had said it would take him all night to ride to Ivar.

Ivar said to Skallagrim, 'It seems you are the son of my brother Thorlief and of Signy who was once Bui's wife?'

Skallagrim answered nothing.

'I think it was by Signy's bidding, not Thorlief's, that you came here,' said Ivar.

'Women's counsel is ever cruel,' said Asbiorn.

'They would indeed have fared better had they stayed in Orkney,' said Ivar.

'So also would your house and your men have fared better,' said Skallagrim.

Then Ivar said, 'How much do you seek in atonement for Bui of Ness?' And he jeered at Skallagrim.

Fridleif, the Birsay man, said, 'Why, must we all pay for those whom we have killed? Had I known that I would have spared a stroke or two, sooner than lose all my goods.'

'You will lose nothing but your life,' said Ivar.

'Then my mind is easy,' said Fridleif, 'but I am somewhat grasping where money is concerned.'

By and by Asbiorn said, 'We have talked long enough. Now let us put an end to talking and to these cousins of yours.'

But Ivar said, 'I cannot send my guests away empty,'

and he bade two of his men fetch some ale that had not been spoilt by the fire, for it was kept in an outhouse. Then he gave the Orkneymen horns of ale and bade them be of good cheer and drink a toast before they died. Skallagrim would not drink, but the others took the ale willingly.

Asbiorn said again that they should bring matters to an end, but Ivar said, 'Let us see if my cousins can run fast. They say the Scots of Caithness are swift as deer, but I think an Orkneyman could beat them.'

And he told that man who sat farthest from Skallagrim on the tree trunk to get up and run.

But the man said he was too stiff and too sorely wounded to care about more travelling, and would rather die where he was.

Ivar said he could have things his own way if he liked, and bade one of his men take his axe and strike off the Orkneyman's head there where he was sitting. 'For that is his choice,' he said, 'and I must let my guests order things as they please.'

Then it came to Fridlief. Ivar said, 'You are young and strong. Will you not run?'

But Fridlief said, 'I am at home out in Birsay, and that is too far for me to run to-day.' So he also died without moving from where he sat.

Hall the Icelander was next to him. Hall turned his head and spoke to Skallagrim: 'I have been thinking of our voyage, Skallagrim,' he said. 'The Skua was a good ship, I have sailed in none better. And I think we did well to save it and to save ourselves from the storm. Few would have handled a ship so well when the waves came high in such foaming ridges and the giant waves rose like the cliffs of Hoy above our stern. Often have I sailed in the long-hulled flock of the sea-kings, but never have I known a better ship cleaving the cold sea.'

None of the Orkneymen would run as Ivar bade them, but died where they were. When Kol and Gauk were in the wood, and looked through the branches and saw them, it came to Thorgrim's turn. And he sat next to Skallagrim.

Ivar said, 'You are a mighty man. Surely you will run?'

But Thorgrim said, 'I never go from my bench while there is still ale in my cup.' And he held the ale-horn in his hands.

'Then you will lose your head,' said Ivar.

Skallagrim said, 'Strike off his hands rather than his head, for they will be the greater loss to him.'

Thorgrim said, 'I do not think you are right in that, Skallagrim. For though there is much wisdom in my hands there is more in my head. And now I will prove it. For if my hands are as wise as my head they will still hold this horn when my head falls off. But if they are not so wise they will let it drop.'

Then Thorgrim's head was struck off, and the ale-horn fell out of his hands.

Now Kol looked through the branches and saw a tall man, broad of shoulder and ruddy of face, who seemed by his bearing and his dress to be the leader there. And he said, 'That is not how I thought Ivar would look, but I see no other who seems greater.'

He could not see Ivar, for Ivar sat on the ground because his leg was stiff from the wound he had taken.

Then Kol stepped out of the wood and raised the throwing-spear he had found, and threw it at Asbiorn. And it took Asbiorn in the throat.

Kol walked towards them, and he had no other weapons with him. Bran followed him. But Gauk stayed where he was and hid himself. It seemed to him that Kol was fey and there was no sense in following such a one.

Kol did nothing to guard himself when Ivar's men ran at him and laid hands on him, but let them tie his wrists and put him down on the tree trunk beside

Skallagrim. Yet Bran leapt to bite the man who first touched Kol, and they slew the dog with many sword-strokes.

Skallagrim said, 'I wish you had come earlier, Kol.'

'Luck was against me,' said Kol.

Now Asbiorn lay dead, but Ivar sat on the ground a little way in front of Skallagrim. He was bare-headed and his hair was wolf-grey strawed with white. His face was pale like dead grass, and his teeth jutted out. He looked a mighty man, strong and evil, though he sprawled lazily on the turf. He asked Kol who he was.

Kol told him, and said, 'You, I suppose, are Ivar the Boneless. I thought it was Ivar at whom I threw the spear, but luck has not been with me of late.'

'No', said Ivar, 'for it has been with me.'

'Yet you do not look like a lucky man,' said Kol, 'nor, from all I have heard, have things often gone well with you. It is true that once on a time you managed to steal some fish from Bui of Ness, but that was no more than a dog might have done. And then you killed Bui, when you had men about you and he had none. I do not count that as likely to bring you fame. It was a great deed certainly when you broke into Orka-howe, but it seems a pity you were so frightened of the howe-dwellers thereafter that you locked yourself in a shut-bed and hid your face in my mother's night-gown.

'You speak with a tongue very like Signy's,' said Ivar, 'and now I am willing to believe that you are her son. You are different from your brother here, who has scarcely spoken ten words altogether, but sulks and sits hump-backed on the tree as Thorlief his father used to sit in the chimney-corner. Thorlief Coalbiter was frightened of many things, but of few things so much as the cold. Though he grew a beard I have often wondered if he was really a man.'

'He was man enough to get sons,' said Skallagrim.

Ivar said, 'I do not know about that, for it seems more likely to me that Signy got you on him.'

Ivar grinned at them and picked his teeth.

'Is it horse-flesh you find there?' said Kol. 'Are you still chewing the mare's rump that you offered to King Edmund before you murdered him? Right indeed was Signy my mother when she said that lying with you was like sleeping with a troll, and right indeed have all men been who cursed you for that murder. Troll-like you look and troll-like you are, and though luck seems with you now it will not bide with you long.'

Ivar grew angry and bade him be quiet at that, saying he should die before Skallagrim.

Kol said, 'When do you go into Wessex to fight with King Alfred again? It is true that he has beaten you eight or nine times, but you may do something yet.'

Ivar said he had heard enough now, and called to his man who had the axe.

Skallagrim said, 'We have travelled here to little purpose, Kol, since that which we came to do is still undone. Nor have things come to pass as your dream foretold.'

'What dream was that?' said Ivar.

Kol said, 'We have heard swords scream shrilly, we have felt the wound-hail of arrows and seen the shield-moon turn crimson. That was harder than putting a fair girl to bed. We have seen the white-hooded sea waken in the gale, we have been long thirsty and lacking meat, we have hurt our hands on the oar-loom. That was less pleasant than kissing a young girl in the chimney-seat. We have gathered winter-hail, the coldest of corn, and stood to battle till our byrnies broke asunder, while sluggards stayed warm at home. Yet we have not won that for which we came and that which my dream promised. For I dreamed that after we had fought together there would be some token of friendship between us before we died.'

'That does not seem likely to me,' said Ivar, 'nor have you made it more likely by your jeering speeches.'

'Even a small thing would serve to make my dream true,' said Kol.

'I cannot think of one small enough to suit me,' said Ivar, and made a sign to that man of his who stood ready with the axe. And he took a step nearer to Kol.

But Kol said, 'There was a girl who was kind to me a little while ago, Ivar. My hair was dirty and stiff with sea-salt, but she made a soft lather and washed it, and combed it well, and now, as you can see, it hangs very fairly. I would not like it to be rudely shorn by that axe or soiled with my blood. So do me this courtesy, and let this be the sign of friendship between us, that you hold it out of the way while my head is being cut off.'

Kol's hair had grown long. It was fair in hue and now indeed looked handsome, for as he said the girl in the house under the trees had washed it for him.

Ivar grinned and said that was a courtesy he would grant most willingly, 'For your head will look all the better with such fine long hair still on it.'

Ragnar his son helped him rise, and he came limping behind the tree-trunk, and made a twist of Kol's hair, winding it round his hand, and lifted it up.

Then Kol said he was ready. The man with the axe stood in front of him. He swung his axe and hewed strongly at Kol's neck. But Kol lowered his head and thrust himself forward with a great jerk, and pulled Ivar after him. For Ivar's hand was caught in his hair. And the axe went higher than Kol's head, and fell on Ivar's fore-arm, and cut off his hand.

Kol and Skallagrim turned and threw themselves on Ivar. He had fallen across the tree-trunk. Now many men thrust at them with spears and hewed with swords, but they would not let go. For though their wrists were tied their fingers were loose. They took many wounds before they were dead. And when they were pulled away from Ivar, Ivar lay dead under them.

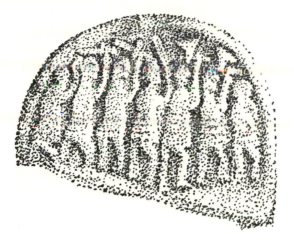

XLVI

Now Gauk of Calfskin still lay in the wood, well hidden, and watched all this, and was very frightened. When he saw Bran killed he made as though to get up and go out of the wood, but he made only a small movement and lay down again. He said, 'It would help Bran nothing though I were killed too. And though I have loved him dearly, and more than a dog is commonly loved, yet only famous men and heroes can afford to throw away their lives to make a show of their love. A hero must protest what he feels and spend all his strength in protesting, though it bring him to his death. But we who are more ordinary men are allowed to save what we have, since that is not much. And perhaps we can find some contentment in being as we are.'

But when Gauk saw Kol's body lifted up, cut deeply with many wounds, and saw that Kol was dead, he wept bitterly and said, 'Now I am not content, and I would that I were great minded as Kol was, for then I would go out and die also. For I see no pleasure in living now, since I am alone in a foreign country and I do not know where to turn. Even Bran did more nobly than I have done, though I have Leg-biter to help me and I was Kol's friend.'

And once more Gauk made as though he would get up, but rose only to his knees and lay down again. When he looked again he saw Ivar's men digging a grave and putting the dead men in it and covering them with stones they took from the stream. But Ivar's body and Asbiorn's they tied on their horses, and presently they rode away. Ragnar, Ivar's son, was their leader now, and they did as he bade them.

Gauk lay for some while till he seemed to be all alone in the valley. Then he went back to the women's house under the trees, and told them what had happened. The girl fingered the ornaments that Kol had given her and said nothing. But the older woman asked Gauk what he meant to do now.

'That I cannot tell,' said Gauk, 'for I have a long way to go to get home, and how I may reach Orkney I do not know. It is certain that I cannot walk there.'

The woman said he could stay that night with her, for no one was likely to come to the house, and they might think of a plan before morning.

Gauk said, 'I must find my way back to the coast and take passage in some ship. But I do not know where ships come in.'

The woman said, 'There is a river called Tees not far to the north of us. You may find a ship there, but I know little of such matters.'

In the morning she gave Gauk food and pointed out his way to him. He took little pleasure in walking and hid himself whenever he saw people moving about. He slept one night in a wood. But when he came to the

river, where the mouth grows broad, he was more
cheerful and behaved in a bolder manner, for he had
discovered what was best to do.

There were some ships lying in the river-mouth, and
Gauk went aboard one and asked if there were any
vessel sailing to Norway on which he might take
passage. But the master said there were only coasting
vessels in the river, and he himself was going north to
the river Tyne on the following day. 'If you come
there,' he said, 'it is likely you will find some ship
sailing east to the Wick or thereabouts.'

Then he asked Gauk who he was, and if he could pay
for his passage.

Gauk said, 'I was sailing in a chapman's ship that was
wrecked not far from here, and I was the only one who
came safe ashore. My home is in a certain town in the
Wick, and I have money enough to pay for my
passage.'

For it seemed to Gauk that he would do better by
taking ship to Norway and finding another ship thence
to Orkney, than by seeking to go north directly. And
he had that half of the gold arm-ring which Kol had
given him in the storm, and that was more than enough
to pay for his passage.

So the next day the master of the coasting-vessel took
Gauk to Tyne-mouth, and after he had stayed there for
some weeks he found a ship sailing east to Norway and
bargained for a passage in it.

They came into the Wick in good time, and Gauk
broke off a piece of the gold ring for payment to the
master. Then he looked for a ship going to Orkney,
and was told there would be no more sailing till next
spring. And Gauk was much cast down by that. But he
found a lodging with a man called Ketil Crook, who
was a friend of Gilli the Chapman, Thorlief's friend,
who lived in Rousay. Gauk stayed with him all winter
and told everybody the tale of his voyage in the Skua,

of the battle at Eastadale, and the death of Kol and
Skallagrim and Ivar the Boneless. And Gauk got no
little fame from his story-telling, for he made out that
his own share in these matters was somewhat greater
than it had really been. He showed a notch in his
sword Leg-biter, and said that came from a blow he had
struck Ivar. But Gauk was not altogether happy, for he
heard that things were not going well in Orkney, and it
was thought there would soon be trouble in the islands.

When spring came he took his leave of Ketil Crook
and found passage in a good ship sailing west over sea.
They had fair weather and came swiftly to Orkney, and
Gauk went ashore at Scapa.

XLVII

By evening of that day Gauk came to Ragnarshall,
and found Ottar there, and told him all that had
happened. Ottar knew that Erling Gleam had been
drowned, and all his people with him, for men on
Stroma had seen the wreck of the Scarf and found
certain bodies, and news of that had gone to Ness. But
he fell into a great sadness when he heard that Kol and
Skallagrim were dead. Yet when Gauk told him that
Ivar the Boneless was dead also, he said, 'My mother
will be glad of that,'

Then Gauk asked him how things had been faring in
Orkney, and Ottar said they had not been going well.

'Earl Guthorm was too weak a man to rule these
islands,' he said, 'and though while he lived there was
peace in name, there was little peace in men's thoughts.
And now he is dead, leaving no son, and there is no
earl in Orkney till Harald sends another, or till Earl
Rognvald of the Mere comes back. Guthorm died in the
last week of winter, and since then there has been

bickering here and there, and before long I think there
will be more. Thorlief has lost his farm at Aikerness.
Two bonders in Birsay made cause together and took it
from him, and we have not strength to win it back.'

'That is not what I looked for when I came home,'
said Gauk. 'I have had enough of warfare, and what I
want now is peace.'

'That is not so easy to find,' said Ottar.

The next morning Ottar gave Gauk a boat and men
to row him round to Ness. Gauk landed there below
the house.

When Gauk went into the hall he saw Hallgerda,
Erling's wife, sitting in the chimney-corner. She was
nursing a child. Signy was also in the hall. She was
scolding two bondwomen, and they were weeping.
Einar sat there. He had grown somewhat taller, but he
was still pale and weak-looking. Gilli the Chapman
talked with him.

Now Signy saw Gauk and went close to him and
took him by the arm. She said, 'Have you come back
then? Where are the others, and why do you come
first?'

Gauk said, 'I am all alone.'

Then Hallgerda came with the child in her arms, and
cried loudly, and said, 'Are Kol and Skallagrim dead
also? Was it not enough that Erling should die, but
must I lose husband and brothers too?"

Signy bade her be quiet and listen to what Gauk said.

Gauk said, 'She is right in that, for both are dead,
and Bran my dog as well. I only am left, and I had no
easy task to save myself.'

'My wealth of sons has been quickly spent,' said
Signy.

Gilli the Chapman said that Thorlief must hear this,
and went to the shut-bed where Thorlief lay. Thorlief
had taken to his bed again and slept much. But he
roused himself when Gilli spoke to him, and came out

and sat by the fire. He wore only his linen shirt and breeches. He was still fat, but shrunken about the legs.

When they told him that Kol and Skallagrim were dead he said, 'Ill luck was ever the end of ill redes. I expected nothing else.'

'It is easy to be wise now,' said Signy. 'Why were you not so wise before?'

'I was,' said Thorlief, 'but none would heed me.'

Then Gauk told his tale again, of the storm and their long while at sea, of the fighting at Eastadale and the burning of Ivar's house, and the death of Kol and Skallagrim.

Signy said, 'And Ivar is dead? You saw him dead?'

'I saw his body taken up and thrown upon a horse,' said Gauk, 'and I do not think that any live man would choose to ride as he did.'

Thorlief said, 'How did it happen that you could watch all this and come off safely?'

'I had my sword Leg-biter,' said Gauk. 'I went out of the wood with Kol, and he let himself be tied and did nothing to defend himself. But I thought otherwise and took to fighting. And when I had fought my way out of the press none cared to follow me, so I stood at some distance and watched all from there.'

Gauk was not much believed when he told that, but he said, 'It is true enough. Bran went with me and fought bravely, but he was killed there and fell beside greater people. And that is how I have come home without him.'

Signy said, 'Was it Kol or Skallagrim who killed Ivar?'

Gauk said he could not answer that, but he thought both had taken a hand in it.

'You have had your way, Signy,' said Thorlief, 'and it was you who brought Kol and Skallagrim to their death.'

'A man will find his own way to death when the

proper time comes,' said Signy. 'And I could not lie quiet while Bui was unatoned.'

'Will you be quiet now?' said Thorlief.

After a little while Signy said, 'Had Ivar any kinsmen with him?'

'He had a son called Ragnar,' said Gauk.

'Is Ragnar living?'

'He lived when I last saw him,' said Gauk.

'Yet it will be long before any here are fit to go out and take a proper vengeance for Kol and Skallagrim,' said Signy. 'Einar is a weakling, and your babe, Hallgerda, will not soon be strong enough to use weapons.'

'Do not talk any more of vengeance,' said Thorlief, 'for you have wrought evil enough already, and we are all like to suffer for it. Had Kol and Skallagrim been here we should not have lost Aikerness. Without Kol and Skallagrim to help us we may lose Ragnarshall and Ness itself. For there will soon be great trouble and stir in Orkney, and I see little hope of that quietness I wish for.'

'There are men enough here to keep us and win back Aikerness too,' said Signy, 'had they someone to lead them.'

But Thorlief would speak no more and went to his bed.

'Trouble or no trouble,' said Gauk, 'I mean to live quietly by myself, so far as a man who has a wife and young bairns can manage that. I have had enough warfare, and now I am going back to Calfskin and nothing will make me budge from it again.'

'Only the nameless man lives out his life,' said Signy.

Gilli the Chapman said, 'Thorlief spoke rightly when he said there would soon be stir and trouble here. You will be lucky, Gauk, if you manage to live at peace while there is fighting all round you.'

But Gauk said, 'It is men who love fighting and men

who wish for great possessions that will do battle. I am neither of the one nor of the other. Men who have a name for being heroes will find it hard to keep out of trouble, and men who own wealth, whether in land or loose goods, will be sought out. But I do not call myself a hero, though I have done something in that way when there was need, nor am I a great man with great riches to make me famous. Calfskin is a little place, and therefore I am rightly to be called a little man. And so if it comes to war, though great men will soon be discovered, I shall not. For little things are always the last to be found.'

XLVIII

Then there was brawling and bickering in Orkney. Vikings came again and harried in the north isles, and Thorlief and all his family had to flee from Ness. They came to Ragnarshall, and Ottar held that stoutly and none troubled them there. But Gilli the Chapman was killed in Rousay.

Earl Rognvald of the Mere sent his son Hallad to take possession of the earldom. But Hallad saw that the islands were all overrun by vikings, and that the bonders themselves were not easy to be ruled. So Hallad went home to Norway and said he would rather be a farmer in the Mere than earl of such a place as Orkney. He got great shame by that, but lived on his farm despite it.

Then Earl Rognvald sent another son, Einar, who was later called Torf-Einar. Torf-Einar was base-born and ugly to look at, he had only one eye, but he was a mighty man and wise, and rid Orkney of vikings and ruled there strongly.

Thorlief died while Torf-Einar was earl, but Signy

lived long after that, and was always shrewish in her temper and ever urging all the men in the house to be outdoors and fighting. But Ottar paid little attention to her. He had much honour from Torf-Einar, and the earl held him in high esteem. Einar, Thorlief's son, never did anything of account, and died young. But the son of Hallgerda and Erling Gleam, whose name was also Kol, grew to be the most hopeful of men, and won fame fighting for Torf-Einar. After that earl died Kol was considered to be the greatest man in all the islands next to the sons of Torf-Einar. When King Eric Bloody-axe and his queen Gunnhilda dwelt some while in Orkney Kol was much with them, and Gunnhilda favoured him greatly. He went into England with King Eric, and fell there in battle beside him.

Gauk lived out his life in Calfskin, and did no more fighting. But he told many stories of what he had seen, and broke several notches in Leg-biter to show how heavy had been his blows. He had a large number of sons whom he named after Kol and Skallagrim and other men who had been in the Skua. His wife grew somewhat hard on him at last, but she always worked well, and Gauk did not grumble much.